LONG TEETH

THE STONE ANGEL SERIES

Stone Angel
Back in the Real World
Get Off at Babylon
Long Teeth
The Last Smile
The Midnight Sister
Bimbo Heaven
The Zig-Zag Man
The Riviera Contract

LONG TEETH

MARVIN H. ALBERT

WILDSIDE PRESS

*This one's for Nora Katherine Demenus, the
all-American international girl.*

CHAPTER 1

What sucked me into the upper-crust witch's brew of Karl Malo's screwed-up family was the kidnapping of his third wife.

The call came while I was balancing precariously atop the big olive tree that shaded the brick patio behind my house. Beyond that the wooded slope began its last steep descent into a small Mediterranean cove. The sea that afternoon was a dark blue flecked with tiny whitecaps under a light, warm wind. I shifted my perch in the tree and went on with what I was doing, letting the answering machine in the house take the phone call.

What I was doing was using a pruning saw to remove dead branches. The thick misshapen trunk looked dead, too. But it wasn't. It had been warped and split and hollowed out by centuries of wear and tear. Killed by lightning and drought and bugs and rare frosts and old age. But new branches kept growing out of the wreckage, sprouting masses of fresh green foliage and healthy fruit. Everyone should have an old olive tree. Wrap your arms around it and experience a nudge of immortality. It inclines you to go along with Einstein's belief that nothing ever really disappears from the universe, including the human soul.

Each time I sent a sawed-off branch crashing to the ground Bill Ruyter carried it over to the woodpile beside my toolshed. He used a hand ax to trim away the smaller branches before coming back for the next big one. Bill and his wife Judith were my nearest neighbors. They lived with their two kids in the next house up our private driveway. The drive ended at my house, and there were no others below that. We usually helped each other with the brute labor maintenance chores, like the retaining wall at the bottom of their lowest garden terrace that we'd had to rebuild the previous month, after it collapsed from the unusually heavy spring rains.

I started sawing the last dead branch, and Bill was waiting for it beneath me when Judith sounded three *bongs* on the Chinese bell in front of their house. Bill couldn't see her from where he was. Too many orange and lemon trees between our two places. But he knew what the signal meant.

He grimaced up at me. "That's the office on the phone. God, I hope it's not another emergency this soon, somewhere the other side of the world."

Bill Ruyter was away a lot. He was a Dutch oil engineer who worked as a troubleshooter for a company headquarters a couple miles away in Monaco. He'd just gotten back that morning from three weeks in the Persian Gulf, which accounted for his taking that afternoon off in the middle of the week.

"If I don't get to spend more time at home soon," he grumbled, "Judith is going to think about having herself a French lover."

"If she does get the urge," I told him, "I hope she'll remember I'm half French. And close by. A practical arrangement."

He scowled at me through the lower branches. "You're supposed to keep an *eye* on her when I'm away. If I find out you've put a hand on her instead, you'll think you've gotten jumped by an angry bear."

I said philosophically, "A fine-looking woman like that's worth fighting for."

"She's worth breaking you in half for, too."

I wasn't sure he could do it, but it was possible. I'm pretty big, but Bill Ruyter is bigger. I looked down at him with a wolfish grin. "Just something for you to think about, nights you get bored playing around with those sexy offshore oil rigs."

"Thank you very much," he said dryly. "It's a comfort having a true friend to buck up my morale." He headed off up the curving driveway with a farewell wave of a hand the size of a sombrero.

I finished sawing off the last dead branch. It hit the ground with a snapping of desiccated twigs. As I climbed down there was a faint shriek of laughter from the cove below.

A teen-age boy and girl were chasing each other in and out of the surf. A few other people were in swimming, and more were sunning themselves on the cliff-flanked beach. Not many. The little cove was never crowded. Most people preferred beaches they could get closer to with their cars.

It was a stiff climb between ours and the nearest public road, the Lower Corniche. Only healthy types cared to expend that much effort. The sunbathers' figures reflected that. The women among them drew most of my interest, naturally. The view from my patio kept me current on changing fashions in beachwear along the Côte d'Azur. There were fewer bikinis this year. The big thing was one-piece bathing suits in bold circus colors, designed to be peeled down to a strip at pubic level.

I do take delight in the beauty of women. It may be a failing. But surely not a major sin.

Shouldering the branch, I carried it to the toolshed and used the ax to trim it. Then I laid it on top of the others Bill Ruyter had neatly stacked. Sometime toward the end of summer I'd get around to sawing the branches into lengths I could use in the living room fireplace on cool winter evenings.

I cleaned and oiled the ax and saw, stowed them in the shed, and went into the house. I was dirty and sweaty and in need of a refreshing drink of cold rose. After which I planned to go down for a long swim in the sea. But when I'd slaked my thirst and rinsed the wine glass I decided to first check on what the answering machine had for me.

The message was from Arlette Alfani. It cancelled my plans for that swim.

Instead I took a fast shower and got dressed up: pale blue sports shirt and jeans, dark blue rope-soled espadrilles. Respectable afternoon wear anywhere along the French Riviera. It was too hot to wear my Levi's jacket, but I took it along. In case the unspecified "urgent problem" Arlette had called me for stretched into the night—or required me to wear a handgun without being conspicuous about it.

I switched on the intruder alarms, locked the house, and drove up the private drive. At the Lower Corniche I turned right and went through the town of Cap d'Ail and on toward Monaco.

* * * *

Normally, the drive from my place into the heart of Monaco took less than ten minutes. But not that afternoon.

The final race of the Grand Prix had been run two days before. The seventy-eight laps of the Monaco Grand Prix use a two-mile circuit of the principality's main streets. During the week afterward traffic through those streets is considerably slowed by work crews dismantling the crash barriers and viewers' stands on both sides. It took me over twenty-five minutes to reach the Loews Monte Carlo Hotel.

A young parking attendant stared askance at my Peugeot 205. The car remained somewhat battered from a skid off a mountain road during the previous year's Monte Carlo Rally. But it ran well, and I kept putting off investing in the costly body work required to make it look presentable.

Nobody would have been disturbed by the Peugeot's disreputable appearance over at the venerable Hotel de Paris. Tradition there stretches back over a century and includes a long roster of noble or merely rich clientele riddled with minor eccentricities, ranging from the baroness with a baboon on a leash to the tycoon who likes to wear old tennis shoes and pajamas.

But Loews, though only a couple blocks from the *belle époque* baroque of the Hotel de Paris, belongs to a different world and looks it. Miami Beach exterior and Las Vegas interior. It was built for people who like both those places and feel uncomfortable surrounded by Old World grandeur. Which means its clientele is mostly American, plus groups of Japanese whose second language is English. Now and then I drop into its bar for an hour or so, just to hear American voices around me. I get homesick for the States after too long a stretch in France. But back in the States I get homesick for France. Makes life a tad complicated.

I over-tipped the attendant, and he tucked my car out of sight behind a couple Mercedes sedans while I went into the lobby.

Beyond the main lobby the hotel's casino reverberated with action. High rollers yelled instructions to the gods of chance around the craps tables. Women pumped away at the slot machines with stony-faced dedication. They'd all come a long way to lose their money in familiar surroundings. Loews's casino was designed by the same people who run Nevada and Atlantic City.

Its entrance yawned invitingly, but I steered away from it. Whenever I get too near any kind of gambling casino I find myself remembering my maternal grandfather. He'd been a prosperous French doctor, but he'd gotten addicted to roulette tables. By the time he'd died he'd lost everything except the family house. An example that inclined me to restrict my own gambling fever to low-stakes poker games.

My other grandfather supplied a different addiction to worry about. He'd drunk himself to death after age forced him to retire from his position as a captain in the Chicago police department. While that didn't keep me from drinking, it did cause me to clamp limits on it.

Nobody can get through life without *some* vices to ease the way. But I didn't need to inherit any. I figured I had enough addictions that were entirely my own.

Sometimes I worried that Arlette Alfani was getting to be one of them.

She was waiting at the bar of the hotel's spacious modern lounge: a vision in white blouse and slacks and raven-black short-cropped hair. She was nursing a Campari and soda and wolfing down the last of a good-sized bowl of cashews. Arlette's appetite was as lusty as her other drives. Her metabolism was such that calories seemed to do nothing but pay homage to that sensational figure and dark-eyed face. Men at nearby tables stared as though hypnotized. Two guys pretending they'd been drawn to the bar by a sudden need for dry martinis were sneaking side glances at her with covert awe.

At twenty-eight Arlette had long since learned to take that kind of attention in stride. Just as she'd learned to anticipate the way most admirers got disconcerted when they came up against her IQ and stubborn professional ambition. As her ex-husband had.

That was one of the things we had in common. Failed marriages. We'd both been losers at the biggest gamble of all. Another thing we shared was time. I'd known Arlette since she was seventeen.

The friendship was an easy one. Our relationship as lovers was more complicated: an on-and-off affair.

We could come up with practical reasons for that. Arlette took her fledgling law career dead-seriously and spent most evenings and weekends hard at work preparing cases for her firm. My own schedule and whereabouts were often unpredictable. But the real reason went deeper. We'd both already failed in all-or-nothing relationships, and were wary of risking what we did have together—a nice blend of companionship and lust—on another try at the real thing.

When she turned from the bar to greet me her admirers regarded me with eyes dipped in poison. You grew accustomed to that around Arlette Alfani. She seized my hand and led me away from that concentration of hate and envy, back through the main lobby.

"Who's the urgent problem?" I asked her as we headed for the elevators.

"Karl Malo." She didn't have to explain who and what he was; not to anyone who read newspapers regularly. The name said it all. "He was having meetings with shipping executives from Japan and California. They booked in here, so he did, too. Most of them have their wives with them. So Malo's wife, Jacqueline, flew in from their home near Arles yesterday to help him host a dinner for the others last night."

We got an elevator to ourselves. As it carried us to the top floor Arlette added quietly, "She went off to do some shopping in Nice early this morning and didn't come back. She's been kidnapped. At this point we don't know where or how it happened. A man phoned Malo shortly after noon, demanding seven million francs if he wants his wife back unharmed."

We got off the elevator. The corridor was empty. Arlette finished quickly: "And the usual warning. No police. Any attempt to trap the kidnappers will result in Jacqueline Malo's death."

The rest of it I got when we were inside Karl Malo's suite, from him and the two senior partners of Arlette's law firm.

CHAPTER 2

Her senior partners were a husband and wife team: Henri and Joelle Bonnet. In my opinion, they were the best attorneys on the Cote d'Azur. Enough other people thought so that they'd been forced to take Arlette into their Nice office as a junior partner to help carry the workload. She was turning out to be better than either of them at pretrial preparations. That freed the Bonnets for what they excelled at: winning cases in the courts.

Arlette's own record in front of judge and jury was uneven—so far. Part of the problem was her looks and youth. People had trouble taking her seriously. There was also her hot Corsican temper, which the opposition sometimes goaded into explosion. She was working on that. But most of her problem was simply lack of experience. Arlette had the ability, but there was no substitute for the years Henri and Joelle Bonnet had spent sharpening their skills.

They were waiting for us in the living room of Karl Malo's suite. Loews's rooms may lack Old World charm but they avoid the tendency of old elegance to deteriorate into ornate clutter. This one had plenty of breathing space and was comfortably furnished with solid taste, if little imagination. It also had what most rooms in the older hotels lacked: plenty of daylight, streaming in through large sliding glass balcony doors that looked across Monaco's crowded little harbor to the ruling palace atop the opposite hill.

Henri Bonnet was at a table helping himself from a room service platter of cookies between sips of tea. He was fifty-six, short, skinny, and balding, with a narrow, sharp-nosed face and equally sharp little eyes that often gleamed with an irrepressible sense of humor. That was one facet of his character he usually took care to conceal from clients.

Joelle Bonnet stood by the glass doors regarding the view—probably to help her resist the temptation to join in her husband's snack. She was the same age as he, taller, with a plump placid face and a figure for which the description "plump" was not quite adequate. Joelle blamed this on the basic imperturbability of her nature. "Nervous people tend to burn off the calories," she'd explained to me once. "Like Henri and Arlette. That's my trouble—I'm crazy but not nervous."

Karl Malo wasn't in evidence when we arrived. Arlette asked about him, and Henri gestured with half a cookie at the closed door to the suite's bedroom. "He's gone to the bathroom. Probably to throw up."

"Poor man."

Joelle's shrug was a touch less than totally sympathetic. "Under the circumstances, it's natural his insides are in knots. But I certainly hope he handles his business crises with more self-control."

"This isn't a business problem," Henri reminded her, and he popped the half cookie into his thin mouth. "It's love."

"But hardly the one grand passion of a lifetime," Joelle said. "The man has a reputation for falling out of love quickly and frequently. Ask the two other wives and countless mistresses he's discarded."

They weren't really arguing. Taking opposite sides in any discussion was habitual with the Bonnets. A way of keeping in practice for trial confrontations.

Henri chewed and swallowed. "Malo's getting older," he pointed out. "That's an influential factor. Another is the heart attack he suffered a few years ago. The combination might cause a man to become overly concerned about his mortality—and his physical frailties. And thus vulnerable to feelings that didn't matter to him before."

"Put more plainly," Joelle said, "you're guessing he began having fears of impotence—and got hooked on a woman capable of reassuring him."

Arlette cut in with a small smile. "You are both trying to explain the unexplainable. Judging by Malo's reactions, his present wife is the passion of his life. In spite of his past record. There needn't be a simple cause-and-effect involved. Even Descartes admitted that logic can't be applied to matters of the heart."

Henri gave her a dubious look. "*Descartes* said that?"

"Absolutely. Look it up."

I said, "If the debating society can take a short rest, what's your connection with Karl Malo?"

It was Joelle Bonnet who explained: "His main law firm is based in Paris, with a branch in Marseilles. But we're under a yearly retainer to represent his interests in any legal matters requiring immediate, short-term attention in this area. We've been on standby, for example, in case he needed anything during his meetings here. He phoned us as soon as he heard from the kidnappers."

"You haven't notified the police," I said.

"No," Henri told me. "Malo was warned not to. And we agreed it's safest to obey that. Until his wife is returned. Or…" He let the other possibility hang there, unstated.

I asked, "What is it you want me to do?"

"Deliver the ransom payment. We advised Malo it would be best to have someone with your experience handle that. It's always possible you'll detect something that will help later in tracking down the kidnappers. He'll meet whatever fee you set. No problem there."

"When do the kidnappers expect the payment?"

"Tonight. They'll phone again sometime this evening. To tell Malo exactly when and where. By then the money will be here. Malo has already arranged for a transfer of funds to the Monaco BNP from his branch in Marseilles." Arlette glanced at her watch. "We've still got that conference in Nice," she reminded the Bonnets. "With Monsieur Joravsky's insurance company. In just under an hour and a half. Nothing there I can't handle alone. But I think they'll feel slighted if at least one senior partner doesn't make an appearance."

"*I'll* sit in on it with you," Joelle said. She looked at Henri with a dour smile. "Our Monsieur Malo will be more comfortable with just you two men anyway. He may love women, but I get the distinct impression he doesn't think they have much to contribute to any *serious* discussion."

Henri nodded, with just a hint of mockery in his sharp little eyes. "He may have a point there."

"Are you looking for a divorce?" Joelle growled.

"You'd never agree to an equal division of property."

"Sure I would." Joelle patted her husband's bald spot as she went past him toward the door. "You get the cats, I get the clients."

* * * *

When Joelle and Arlette had gone Henri asked if I wanted to share his tea and cookies. I shook my head and strolled to a side table set up as a small bar. After looking over the liquor supply I settled for a tall tomato juice. Dropping a couple of ice cubes into it, I took a sip and asked Henri, "What time did Malo's wife leave here this morning?"

"About eight-thirty. She wanted to see what some of the clothing boutiques in Nice are offering."

"How did she travel there? Taxi?"

"No, she rented a car through the hotel."

I held back my next question when the bedroom door opened. Karl Malo came out looking pale and somber but under control.

I'd already known what he looked like from seeing his picture in the papers over the years. There'd been a long period when he'd been in the gossip columns almost as often as the financial pages. He was about sixty now and still extraordinarily handsome.

He was wearing an artfully tailored light brown gabardine suit, with the trousers tucked into comfortably fitting, calf-high suede boots. The boots were his trademark—the badge of his utter self-assurance. He'd been known to show up at society gatherings wearing them with a tuxedo.

There was an ingrained authority about the man that even his present emotional turmoil couldn't erase. Part of it he'd been born to; the rest he'd earned himself. Malo Transport, headquartered west of Marseilles, had already been a prosperous family enterprise when he'd inherited control of it in his mid-twenties. In the decades since, Karl Malo had built it into the biggest trucking and shipping company in the country, bulldozing the competition. *That* showed in his dark brown eyes. They were hard and shrewd, verging on ruthless.

The years had put silver streaks in his thick black hair, weight on his figure, and deep trenches in his patrician face. But those added to the look of authority. Malo was a fighter accustomed to winning, a ruler used to obedience.

Henri made the introductions. Malo didn't offer his hand. The tough brown eyes examined me. His lips thinned, and the short trenches at their corners deepened. It could have been an expression of dislike. But I didn't think it had anything to do with whatever he saw in me. The man was scared and struggling to suppress it.

"I hope Monsieur Bonnet made one point *clear* to you." He spoke with a harsh directness that I guessed was habitual. But his voice strained through a tightened throat. He had to work at bringing it down to its normal pitch. "I'm *not* hiring you to play cowboy. Under no circumstances are you to do anything that might make these kidnappers nervous."

He had to open his mouth a bit to draw a shallow breath. "Naturally, I'd like them caught and punished. I want to *kill* them. With my own hands."

"But first you want your wife back."

"As long as you do understand that. Americans are too fond of cutting the knot rather than taking the time to untie it. The swift and violent solution that courts disaster."

I didn't feel up to trading national failings with him. "I do have some careful French blood in me," I said mildly.

"Make certain *that* part rules your actions in this case." The harshness in his tone was on the increase. "Any notions you might have of earning yourself publicity and a higher payment by capturing these people or staging some reckless rescue attempt—"

"Monsieur Malo," I interrupted, keeping my own tone mild, "you're allowed a certain amount of bad temper because you're in pain. But I run out of that kind of sympathy pretty quickly. Probably my American side.

The Bonnets recommended me to you. If you don't accept their opinion, you can get a list of other available and competent detectives from the *Fédération Professionel des Agents Privés de Recherche*. They have an office in Nice."

Henri Bonnet cleared his throat loudly. Neither of us looked at him. We went on staring at each other.

Finally Malo said, "There's no time... I have to trust you." He sounded like a man who'd been lifting heavy weights and had suddenly lost the strength to go on with it.

He looked at his hands, spreading the fingers. They were trembling just a little. "It's only that...until Jacqueline is safe I don't..." He stopped himself and started again. "If her safety means letting the scum that have her get away with it...if it means they'll never be caught...so be it."

"That's clear," I assured him.

His eyes locked with mine again. "You've had a great deal of experience with criminals, I'm told. In your opinion...*will* they let Jacqueline go after I pay the ransom?"

I gave him the answer he was pleading for. "Probably. It's good advertising for them. They figure it encourages future victims to obey instructions and pay up."

That applied if these kidnappers were professionals. I didn't want to scare him worse with all the things that could go wrong if it was an amateur snatch.

Henri Bonnet got to his feet and told Malo, "I have several calls to make. I'll use the phones downstairs to leave yours free."

Malo's nod was distracted. He turned to the liquor table beside me as Henri left. Twisting the cap off a bottle of scotch, he poured a double into a large glass. He picked up the glass and was reaching toward the ice bucket with his other hand when the glass slipped from his fingers and fell to the floor.

It bounced without breaking and then rolled on its side, spreading a wet stain on the blue wall-to-wall carpet.

Malo stared down at it, momentarily frozen. Then he looked at the hand that had dropped it, his expression faintly puzzled.

I picked up the fallen glass, poured more scotch into it, added ice cubes, and held it out to Malo. He hesitated before taking it. He closed his hand around it carefully, watching himself do it, waiting to see if the hand would betray him again. It didn't. He drank and put the glass down on the table, continuing to hold on to it.

"Thank you," he said softly. "I'm sorry."

I had the feeling he wasn't accustomed to using either of those routine polite expressions.

"I seem to keep losing control," he said in the same soft, slightly angry tone. "That's never happened to me before."

"Then you've never been really frightened before," I told him. "Fear plays havoc with the nervous system."

Malo raised his glass, still careful with it, and took another sip. "You're right, I'm *terrified*. If Jacqueline…if anything happens to her…"

I drank more of my tomato juice, giving him time to find words for emotions that were new to him.

"Are you married?" His eyes and tone were back to tough and direct.

"I was once," I said. "But that was a while ago."

"I suppose you know Jacqueline is my third wife."

"Yes."

"You probably also know there have been a number of other women in my life."

"I read the papers from time to time. You keep the gossip columnists happy."

"I *used* to. Before Jacqueline." Malo finished off his drink and added matter-of-factly, "For a wealthy man, women are always easy to come by."

"Harder to get rid of, I imagine."

"Not really. Perhaps some of them did genuinely care for me. But none of them regarded the attachment as more important than a generous financial settlement."

There was nothing bitter in the way he said it. He was just stating facts, avoiding coming to grips with what did gnaw at him. Malo was obviously not a man given to probing his deeper feelings, let alone revealing them to someone else.

"But with Jacqueline," he said finally, "it is not like that. What we have is…different. I can't do without her. That's something I've never felt toward anyone else. I realize that means I lacked something in the past. Falling in love with Jacqueline made me understand that." He had to force himself to meet my eyes this time. "The thought that they might hurt her or… I can't accept that."

"The man who phoned you," I said, "what did he sound like?"

"You mean his voice? Low, thick… I had the feeling he was disguising it somehow."

"Did he sound like a man with a good education? How was his grammar? Did he use a lot of argot?"

Malo thought about it. "An educated man, I'd say. Though he did speak French with a slight Italian accent. But that could be part of the disguise, couldn't it?"

"It could," I agreed. "What did he say to you? Word for word, as close as you can remember."

"He said, 'We've kidnapped your wife. We'll return her to you, unharmed, for seven million francs. Don't contact the police. If you do that, or fail to obey any of my instructions, we'll kill her. She's been hidden where nobody can possibly find her. She'll die if there is any attempt to trap or follow us.'"

Malo's voice faltered and stopped. He took a few seconds before resuming. "I demanded to speak with Jacqueline, to be sure she was all right. He ignored that at first and went on with what I think was a prepared speech. He told me to get the ransom money in used bills. 'Have it ready by seven this evening,' he said. 'We'll phone you again sometime after that. About how to deliver it to us.'

"I promised to have the money ready, but I told him flatly that they won't get it unless I have proof that Jacqueline is still alive. He finally agreed to let her speak to me when they make the second call this evening. 'But that will be the last time you ever hear her voice,' he warned me, 'if the police or anyone else tries to interfere. If that happens, her death will be *your* fault, Monsieur Malo, not ours.' And then he hung up on me."

I said, "If you've got a picture of your wife, I'd like to see it."

"Just a moment." Malo went into the bedroom and returned with a photograph in a silver frame. "I always carry this with me when I travel."

I took it from him. It was a face shot, in color. She smiled out of it, a smile full of relaxed humor. A woman in her late thirties or early forties. Large green eyes and a small, soft mouth. A wealth of auburn hair coiled around her head with a thick braid.

She was a nice-looking woman. But not in a class with some of the beauties I'd seen pictured with Malo in society columns over the years. Jacqueline Malo had something else, however. Judging anyone by a photograph is tricky. But certain qualities were strongly evident: a warm blend of quiet self-assurance and generosity.

I didn't like Karl Malo too much at that point. Gossip columnists had sometimes spoken of his "charm." So far I hadn't seen evidence of it. Maybe it was something he kept in cold storage, to be extracted only when there was something to be gained from using it.

But it was impossible not to like the face that smiled at me from that photograph. I wondered what she saw in him. I didn't want to think it was his money. I decided he must have qualities I hadn't discovered yet. Arlette and Descartes were right. Love defies logic.

As I returned the picture to him I found myself saying, "We'll get her back."

I had no more reason to be sure of that than I'd had before. But after looking at her smile I wanted it to be true almost as much as Malo did.

CHAPTER 3

The ransom payment arrived shortly after Henri Bonnet returned to Karl Malo's suite. It was brought by two plainclothes guards from the Banque Nationale. Each carried a large, locked canvas sack. Seven million francs came to just over a million dollars at the current rate of exchange, and in any currency it was a lot of cash.

At six-thirty that evening Malo ordered meals sent up to his suite but didn't touch his. He went out onto the balcony and stayed there while Henri and I ate. I ate sparingly. Hotel food is hotel food. I drank sparingly, too. The wine was excellent, but I wanted to keep my head clear. Henri ate and drank with his usual appetite. I'd never known that to balk at even the various French versions of McDonald's fare. I gave him my dessert and went out to join Karl Malo.

He stood gripping the rail and staring down at Monaco's cramped little harbor. The lowering sun tinged all the white yachts with a color somewhere between orange and pink. A yacht that looked like a floating hotel was anchored outside the port because there was no room left inside it for anything that big.

It belonged to Rasul Khdanni, a Middle East wheeler-dealer who'd gotten fat on taking rake-off bites out of sales by European and American companies to Arab potentates. My feelings toward Khdanni were not cordial. I'd learned to dislike him through fending off his efforts to persuade my mother to sell him our house. He'd already bought seven adjacent shorefront properties at double their market value and was engaged in walling them off as his private domain. He was also engaged in a struggle with the Cap d'Ail town hall to keep other people from using *his* beach. French law states that all beaches are open to the public, but that didn't mean he couldn't win. Cash in bulk decides more battles than big battalions.

"When did you decide to have your wife join you here in Monaco?" I asked Karl Malo.

"She phoned yesterday from our home near Arles and said she missed me. I missed her, too. And most of the men I was meeting with had their wives along. So I told her to come and help me host a farewell dinner for them last night."

Malo's harsh voice was once more under control. But he didn't look at me. His gaze remained fixed on the yachts in the harbor. I didn't think he was seeing any of them.

"When did she arrive here yesterday?" I asked.

"Early afternoon. Shortly after two." Malo turned his handsome head to look at me then. "You're thinking that didn't give them much time to prepare the kidnapping."

I nodded. A scant twenty-four hours had passed between the decision that Malo's wife would come to Monaco and the time she'd been snatched.

"Isn't it possible," Malo suggested, "that they had already been keeping track of Jacqueline's movements for some time in our home area? Waiting for their opportunity? They could have followed when she was driven to the airport there. Even boarded the same flight."

"That *is* possible," I granted. But I didn't like it. Professionals plan every detail well ahead of time. The safest place to make the snatch. A place to hide the victim. How to pick up the ransom without being caught or seen. After Jacqueline Malo's sudden decision to join her husband in Monaco they would have had to re-plan each of those details to fit an entirely different area. In less than twenty-four hours.

There was another possibility. The kidnappers might have been hanging around Monte Carlo days or even weeks ahead of time. Looking for a chance to grab *someone*. There was no shortage of wealthy potential victims in this area. Malo's wife might have been only the latest of a number of potentials they'd considered. When she'd driven to Nice they'd followed, seen an opportunity, and seized it.

But I didn't like that either. It would mean they *were* amateurs. Pros don't pull an unprepared spur-of-the-moment snatch.

Either way, it had a puzzling feel. Something didn't fit the way it should.

Malo was back to staring unseeingly at the yachts in the sun-drenched harbor. I didn't ask him any more questions. His answers were the same as mine: guesswork. The first order of business was still to get Jacqueline Malo back.

The call from the kidnappers came at nine o'clock.

* * * *

Malo snatched up the phone. "This is Karl Malo."

I was listening on the extension. The voice that came through was a woman's. She sounded as if she were struggling not to cry. "Karl, I'm so sorry... I..."

"Jacqueline," he blurted, "are you all right? Have they hurt you?"

"No, darling, *please* don't worry too much. I—"

Her voice was cut off abruptly.

Malo shouted into the phone, "*Jacqueline?*"

A man's voice came on: "All right, Malo, I kept my end of it. You heard her. Have you got the money?" It was as Malo had described: a man with a low, thick voice, probably disguised by his having something stuffed in his mouth. And there was the suggestion of an Italian accent Malo had mentioned.

"I have it here," Malo told him. "Let me talk to my wife again."

"No. You wanted proof she's alive. Now you know she is. Whether she stays that way is entirely up to you. Monsieur Malo. Now just listen to me. Carefully. I won't repeat myself. The money is to be delivered by a driver who knows the region well. We don't want him getting lost and driving in circles. If he's late in reaching any of the places he's told to go, you'll have lost your wife."

"I understand," Malo said in a strangled voice. "I've—"

"Just *listen*," the caller growled. "Your driver will take the money into Nice. To the Grimaldi underground parking garage. The sports coupe your wife rented this morning is parked down in the fifth level. An Alfa Romeo 2000, red body with a black top. It's unlocked. The keys are under the left-hand seat. Together with further instructions. Your driver is to transfer to the Alfa, together with the money, and then follow those instructions."

It was a clever choice. A driver and the two sacks of ransom money would take up most of the available space inside a little two-seater Alfa 2000. Not much room for a second man to scrunch down out of sight. It *could* be done, but...

But the man on the phone was already covering that. "There had better not be a second person in that car, Monsieur Malo. And there'd better not be any other car following it. We'll be watching at every stage of the way. Any trick on your part, we'll spot it and pull out. And your wife will be dead."

"You don't have to threaten me!" Malo shouted. "All I want is—"

But the caller had already cut the connection.

* * * *

I didn't have any difficulty finding the sports coupé. It was where it was supposed to be: down in the dimly lit fifth underground level. At that time of night there weren't many other cars left in the Grimaldi parking garage. I stopped my Peugeot beside the little Alfa and found the keys under its driver's seat. Together with a square of paper. My instructions were printed on it with a ballpoint pen:

Drive to Sospel. Be there by eleven. Wait at the phone booth outside the railroad station. We will phone you there with further instructions. Do not use the phone to *make* any calls. You'll be watched.

The quickest way to reach the town of Sospel was to go east to Menton, and then up into the interior via a climbing mountain road. I could make Sospel by eleven, but not with much time to spare.

When I drove the Alfa Romeo out of Nice one of the canvas money sacks was on the seat beside me and the other was on the floor in front of it. I checked on whether any other cars were tailing me. None appeared to be. From time to time I checked again. No tail car.

Maybe they didn't plan to start keeping tabs on me until after I reached Sospel. Maybe the warning I'd be watched at various stages along the way was entirely a bluff. It was probable that they didn't have enough people to do that. But Karl Malo wouldn't risk his wife's life calling that bluff. Neither would I.

I had a handgun with me. A compact Heckler & Koch P7. Before leaving the garage I'd transferred it from its shoulder rig under my Levi's jacket. Now it was tucked in the front of my belt. Where I'd be able to get at it faster, if I had to.

But I hoped like hell I wouldn't have to. All I wanted out of that night drive was for the kidnappers to take their money and let Jacqueline Malo go.

The gun was strictly a last resort.

In case something went very wrong.

CHAPTER 4

Sospel, a half-hour's drive from the Côte d'Azur, straddles a mountain stream called the Bévéra, with an old humped stone bridge connecting the two parts of the town. By the time I got there the only thing open was one bar with a couple of customers left. The rest of the town's fewer-than-three-thousand citizens were inside their houses, watching the last TV programs or already in bed. The little railroad station was locked and dark except for a lamp burning over the outdoor phone booth.

I parked beside it, climbed out, and started waiting.

Sospel was perfect, from the kidnappers' point of view. From that point there were seven different routes on which they could send me through the surrounding mountain terrain. No way to predict which they'd pick.

The waiting stretched. I leaned against the car for a while. Then I paced, though nevermore than fifteen steps from the phone booth, the car, and the cash. Then I sat inside the booth, squinting at the night outside.

By half past eleven I was worried. Nobody else was in sight. If I was under surveillance, I couldn't spot it. I did what I had to: went on waiting. In all the time I waited only three cars went through Sospel. One on its way up the main route to the border crossing into Italy at Tende, the other two coming down from it. No cars at all using any of the smaller routes.

The phone rang at ten minutes before midnight, very loud in that night silence.

I picked it up and said, "Yes."

The voice I'd heard before said, "Who are you from?"

"Karl Malo," I told him.

"Fine. Take Route 204 toward Escarène until you reach St. Laurent-du-Touët. There's a phone booth in the *place* across from the church. Wait there until we call you again. And don't *make* any calls from there. We'll know if you do."

He hung up.

* * * *

The route and timing chosen betrayed a working knowledge of the back country. At midnight there was no other car using that tortuous mountain road.

Between Sospel and Escarène, 204 switchbacks its narrow, potholed way through an agglomeration of rugged hills and tight gorges separating the Bévéra from the Paillon Valley. From one end to the other the road runs only fifteen miles. But that includes thirty-four sharp hairpins that cut back and forth through the rock formations and scrub brush of those steep slopes. They guarantee that you can't drive the fifteen miles in under forty minutes. Certainly not at night.

Back down along the Riviera the coast road would still be carrying traffic between the glittering resort towns. But none of the well-heeled fun-seekers for whom the Côte d'Azur glitters into the wee hours would have any incentive to venture to the road I'd been instructed to take.

It doesn't lead anywhere exciting. The only reason for its existence is to connect several small villages inhabited by farmers and laborers who go to sleep shortly after sunset so they can start their next workday shortly after sunrise. At night there isn't even scenery to lure anyone weary of forking over cash and credit cards for the pleasures dispensed in the fleshpots below.

There are the stars, of course. And that night a lovely sickle moon lying on its back with a bright Venus dangling under it. But I didn't see much of those. Admiring the sky while driving that road at that hour requires suicidal tendencies I lack.

I've never gotten around to visiting the belly of a whale. But it can't be much darker than what I was traveling through. There wasn't a single light showing anywhere other than my headlights. No road lamps, no house lights, no other vehicles.

Any kidnappers stationed along the route would see my headlights long before I reached them. They'd also be able to make sure I didn't have other cars loaded with cops trailing me. Nobody could drive that road at night without lights. At each switchback a bulging cliff on one side nudged you toward a killer drop on the other side. And no safety rails.

It made for scary driving even with my headlights on high. Their beams pushed into the darkness ahead, but the dark pushed back like living matter with a will of its own and no tolerance for intruders. The contest between the night and my lights turned nasty. Jutting rocks and stumpy trees cast shadows that faked bends where none existed and camouflaged those that did.

Slow going. Very.

A couple of electric lights finally appeared ahead when the road approached the village of St. Laurent-du-Touët. None were from the houses; the village was sound asleep. One light illuminated the phone booth across the small square from the church. I stopped beside it, climbed out, and waited again.

Utter silence. Nobody else around. If they *were* watching me, it had to be from a distance, through infrared glasses. I doubted it. I also doubted that they really had a way to know if I made a call on the phone in the booth. But I could be wrong about that. And I wasn't being paid to take that kind of chance with somebody else's life.

This time the wait was less than fifteen minutes. The phone rang. I picked it up and heard the same voice, and we went through the same introductory routine.

"Who are you from?"

"Karl Malo."

"Turn around," he instructed me, "and drive back the way you just came. Along Route 204. Slowly."

Professionals or amateurs, they had given all this considerable intelligent thought. At this point they'd made sure no other car was either trailing or leading me.

"A flashlight will signal you," he continued. "One long flash and two short ones. When you see that, stop and throw out the money. Without opening either of the car doors. Then drive on. Don't stop again until you get back to the railroad station in Sospel. Then wait there for a full hour. Do *not* use the phone there during that time. If you deviate in the slightest from these instructions, Madame Malo will die."

Again he hung up before I could say anything. It was just as well. There was nothing for me to say.

* * * *

The signal came when I was only a few miles from Sospel. It flashed from a slope above the road. One long, two short. I coasted to a stop just below the point from which the flashlight had signaled.

I sneaked a look up the slope while I was dumping the first sack out of the car window. Nothing to see up there. Just shadows and darker shadows. I hauled up the second sack and dropped it out on the roadside. Still nothing moving up there. And there was nothing I could have risked doing about it even if one of the kidnappers had been standing beside the car in plain sight and empty-handed.

What I did do before driving away from the money was check the reading on the dashboard's kilometrage indicator.

I looked at it again when I reached the Sospel railroad station. It was just over twelve kilometers from the spot where I'd dropped off the ransom.

A potentially useful bit of information. Though I doubted it. They hadn't made a mistake so far. But I'd have to check it out. Later.

I looked at my watch and climbed out of the car. There was an hour to wait. I walked away from the station. The bar had closed up while I was gone. I kept walking until I reached the Sospel end of the route I'd just used.

That's where I waited, leaning against a building wall, shrouded in its shadow. But my hour went by, and no car emerged from the road I was watching. They still weren't making any mistakes.

I walked back. Not a creature was stirring. Except some field mice, come to town to reconnoiter open garbage cans.

Dropping a coin in the pay phone outside the dark station, I dialed Loews Hotel in Monte Carlo and asked for Karl Malo's suite.

Henri Bonnet answered. I asked if they'd heard from the kidnappers.

"Less than five minutes ago," Henri told me. "The same man's voice as the two previous times. He said we'll find Madame Malo inside a building in an abandoned quarry. On Route 566, between Sospel and the Col de Castillon. Malo is already on his way. With Arlette driving. She says she knows that quarry."

I did, too. And I was much closer to it. I got back in the car and drove there.

So far I hadn't accomplished much to earn the fee we'd agreed on. Malo could just as well have hired a bellhop from his hotel to do the job. For a lot less. I would send him the bill anyway, of course. He could afford it, and I could use it.

But I'd feel better about it if I was the one who liberated Jacqueline Malo personally.

If she was still alive.

The caller had cut the connection while Malo was asking for reassurance that she was unharmed.

CHAPTER 5

The quarry had been abandoned two years earlier. It was one of the few battles that ecologists of the region had won. Their victory had prevented the total destruction of a large hillside forest of evergreen oaks and Aleppo pines. Nothing could erase the damage already done. By day the scar that had been gouged out of the sloping forest could be seen from a mile away. The night was kinder, shrouding it in black shadow.

The building was deep inside that scar. A squat shed with cinder block walls and corrugated tin roofing. Its single window was boarded up. I shone my flashlight on the door. It had been locked with a heavy-duty safety hasp. The padlock still hung intact in the swivel eye, but the swivel plate had been ripped out of the doorjamb.

The door groaned open on rusting hinges when I pushed with my free hand. I stepped inside. Sand and pieces of cinder crunched underfoot.

A woman's voice, low and shaky: "Who's there?"

I swung the flashlight beam around the interior of the emptied shed. Jacqueline Malo sat on the dirt floor in the far corner. Her left wrist was handcuffed to a sturdy ringbolt screwed into the base of the wall. Her eyes were covered by a thick pad of bandage gauze fastened in place with strips of surgical tape.

"It's all right now, Madame Malo," I said as I moved toward her across the room. "Your husband sent me."

"Thank God…" She still sounded shaky, but there was no hysteria in it. She reached up with her free hand and yanked the blindfold off. One abrupt, determined tug. Wincing as the adhesive detached from her skin.

I'd already turned the flashlight away from her. Even so, she winced again as the light hit her eyes. She squeezed them shut and turned her face to the wall.

She was smaller than I'd expected. Wearing red sandals, white slacks, and a peasant blouse with a Provençal print. A quilted shoulder bag in the same print lay on the ground beside her hip. Her thick auburn hair hung to her shoulders, tangled and dusty. Dirt smeared one side of her face down past the soft, small mouth. Her clothes were wrinkled and soiled. Otherwise she appeared undamaged.

With a sudden angry motion, Jacqueline Malo threw the blindfold away from her. "They warned me not to take that off. They said if I saw any of their faces, they'd be forced to kill me. So I was afraid to…even after they left. In case they came back…"

Her figure was fuller than the women's magazines advised. She would be comfortable to hold. And exciting. I reined in my libido and crouched beside her, putting the flashlight on the ground, and got a flask out of my jacket. She turned her face from the wall and peered at me through slitted eyes, still adjusting to the light.

She looked worn out, emotionally and physically. It didn't detract much from what I'd seen in her photograph. That was still there.

"I've been blindfolded since this morning," she said, her voice rasping a bit under control. "How long ago was that?"

"Yesterday morning. It's after two A.M. now. Next day." I opened the flask and gave it to her. "Brandy."

"I can use it." She took a long swallow and then leaned her head back against the wall, waiting for the liquor to do its work. Her eyes were open normally, examining me. Analytical but not judgmental. "Is Karl all right?"

"Not bad, considering. Under a strain, naturally. But holding up. He'll be along soon."

"Good." She started a weak smile. "You wouldn't happen to have anything to eat, too? They fed me a couple of sandwiches, but…"

"I brought more of those along. Outside in the car." I began examining the handcuff lock.

"There's a key," Jacqueline Malo told me. "She said she'd put it somewhere on the floor before she left."

I picked up the flashlight and went looking for it. "One of them was a woman."

"Yes. And two men."

"You don't know what they look like."

"I saw one of them when they first grabbed me. But not his face. He had a mask. And afterwards… I didn't even *try* to peek. I'm a coward."

"No, you were sensible." I found the key in another corner. Jacqueline Malo was taking another, smaller sip of brandy when I returned with it. I unlocked her handcuffs, and she gave me back the flask. I screwed the top on while she rubbed her wrist.

"You know my name," she said, "but I don't know yours."

"Pierre-Ange Sawyer."

She frowned over it. "Sawyer? That's not French."

"My father was American. Outside France my first name's Peter. And Pete in the States. A kid in a Chicago school can get by fine with a name like Pete. Pierre-Ange would have had me in a fistfight every day."

"Well, Monsieur Sawyer, you have my heartfelt thanks. And now, if you could help me stand up. I've been sitting here so long…"

I put the flask back in my jacket and helped. She rose stiffly and then leaned against me for a few moments. I wasn't the one who broke the body contact. Jacqueline Malo stepped back and looked up at me thoughtfully. Then she smiled again: a better smile this time, with the generous warmth I'd read in her picture. "If you'll take me to the food you mentioned, monsieur—I *am* hungry." I picked up her shoulder bag and led her out of the shed. She hung on to my arm when we made our way through a stretch of rocks and loose stones. She didn't make it an intimate thing. But neither was it like she was holding on to an unresponsive banister.

She was surprised when she recognized the car I'd parked off the roadside. "That's the one I rented this morning…yesterday morning."

"The man who phoned your husband insisted on it. Hard to hide a squad of cops inside there." I opened the Alfa's doors. "But the seats are comfortable. Better than that shed floor."

She shook her head. "I need to stand for a while." She faced the side of the car and leaned her elbows on its roof. Kicked back with one leg and then the other, to restore circulation.

I got the sandwiches from a plastic bag I'd stuck behind the seats and put them on top of the little car. One with a slab of good country pâtè, the other with a thick slice of ham. I opened a bottle of Evian spring water adding, "Unless you'd rather stick with brandy?"

"No, I get tipsy too easily." She gulped down a lot of water and then attacked the sandwiches.

Between bites she told me what had happened to her. From the beginning, the morning before.

CHAPTER 6

"It happened right after I parked in Nice at the Grimaldi garage," Jacqueline Malo told me. "All the way down on the fifth level. The higher levels were already full. For the same reason I went there, I suppose. It's close to the pedestrian shopping street; an easy walk to Cacharel and Anastasia. But I didn't even get as far as the fifth level elevator. This man suddenly appeared in front of me. I don't know where he came from. He could have been in another car, or hiding between a couple of them. The lighting down there was very bad."

"I noticed."

"He was wearing dungarees and a dirty T-shirt," she said. "And he had a ski mask covering his head and face. A big man. As big as you. And almost as strongly built. At the same time that he blocked my way another man seized me from behind. Pinned my arms to my sides."

"Did he wear a mask, too?"

"I don't know. I didn't see him. Not then or after."

"But you're sure it was a man."

"I saw his hands and forearms. Thick, muscular, hairy…definitely a man." Jacqueline Malo paused to eat another healthy bite of pâtè sandwich. Then she said, "Before I could scream the first man—the one in front of me—grabbed my hair and pushed a wet cloth over my mouth and nose. It was soaked with chloroform. I know that smell." She moved her shoulders as though a shudder had gone through her. But her voice stayed level. "It didn't take long. I passed out. When I came to I was in there"—she nodded toward the shed, hidden inside the quarry shadows—"on the floor, handcuffed to the wall. Blindfolded."

"Would you recognize their voices if you heard them again?" I asked her.

"Perhaps…or maybe not… I'm fairly sure they didn't use their normal voices around me. And they didn't speak much. Only to give me orders. 'Don't take off the blindfold.' 'Here's something to eat.' Things like that. When they had something to say to each other they went outside where I couldn't hear them. One of the men had an Italian accent."

"What about the other man, and the woman?"

"No accent. They were French."

"Well educated?"

Jacqueline Malo laughed softly and shook her head. "No. They had a very coarse way of speaking. Unlike the Italian one. He had some culture behind him. But as I said, I didn't hear any of them that much in all the time I was there. There were long stretches of nothing but silence. Sometimes I even fell asleep."

"And once they took you to a phone."

"Yes. The one with the accent told me they were going to let me talk to Karl. They led me out to a car. A large car. Two of them sat in the back seat with me. The other drove. When we stopped they took me out of the car and—"

"How far was that from here?" I asked her.

"I don't know. My sense of time was completely awry by then. It wasn't a long drive."

"Ten minutes? Half an hour?"

"Closer to ten minutes, I'd guess. Perhaps even a bit less. They pushed me into a phone booth and let me say a few words to Karl. They pulled me out before I could say more. Then the one with the Italian accent went into the booth. The other two pulled me away so I couldn't hear what he told Karl."

"Then they drove you back here."

Jacqueline Malo nodded. "They handcuffed me to the wall again. I think the two men went away immediately after that. The only one who spoke to me from then on was the woman. After a while she left, too. Warning me they might return for me. And all I could do then was wait. Getting more and more frightened that they *would* come back, perhaps to kill me—until *you* arrived."

She reached for the water bottle again but changed her mind. "I *could* use a bit more of that brandy now, please."

I gave her the flask. She drank from it sparingly and handed it back. All the while she continued to look at me.

"I don't know anything about you," she said softly. "But I know I'll never forget you."

The feeling was mutual, but I restrained the impulse to tell her about that.

* * * *

I heard the car approaching before I could see it. The first one on this road, in either direction, since I'd been there. It came into view around a bend south of the quarry, coming up from the south. A glossy white Porsche. Arlette Alfani's car. Its powerful engine snarled and the tires squealed as she took the curves in the narrow hillside road with her customary abandon. Arlette grew up with a gangster father who was involved in shooting and bombing wars with his rivals. A childhood that tended to make her as nonchalant about life's dangers as she was about her dynamite sex appeal. A detachment, in both cases, born of long familiarity.

Her Porsche skidded to a stop in front of the Alfa Romeo. Karl Malo jumped out before Arlette turned off the ignition. The next second he and his wife were in each other's arms. I strolled past the back of the Alfa Romeo and looked at the stars.

Arlette came to join me. "Spot anything that might lead the cops to the people who kidnapped her?"

"Not so far. I'd say they got away clean. They planned every move just right. At least one of them has to be a pro. They won't have left any clues behind."

Arlette lit a Gauloise, the pungent smoke drifting my way. "Well, at least Malo got his wife back. And she doesn't seem to have been hurt much."

"She's fine," I said.

Arlette gave me a curious look. "Something bothering you, Pierre-Ange?"

"No. Are the police on their way?"

"They still haven't been notified. Malo wanted to make absolutely certain his wife was safe first. I'll stop in Castillon when I drive the Malos back down and call Henri. Let him know he can contact the cops now." Arlette dropped her cigarette and ground it out with a twist of her foot. "Are you going to hang around until they get here?"

I nodded. "And there's something I want to check on." Not the phone booth in Castillon, though it was close enough to have been used by the kidnappers for at least one of their calls. They could have used the one in Sospel, too. But neither would yield anything useful. Even if they'd left fingerprints. So had too many other people.

There was a sound that made us look toward the Malos.

I didn't identify the sound immediately because it was difficult to believe. Karl Malo was *crying*. His wife was stroking the back of his head with one hand and murmuring something soothing in his ear.

"The man," Arlette said softly, "has hidden depths."

"Apparently."

"Depths that I suspect were hidden even from him," Arlette added. "Until *she* introduced him to them. She must be quite a woman."

"Yes."

Arlette looked at me curiously again. Then she smiled and gave me a hard bump with her hip. "Wake up, Pierre-Ange. The lady is married.

Very married, from the look of it."

"I did notice that," I said.

* * * *

After Arlette left with Karl and Jacqueline Malo I got back into the little Alfa and drove up through Sospel and took Route 204 again. When I was exactly 12.3 kilometers from Sospel I stopped and got out. Using my flashlight, I climbed the slope above the road and looked for the place from which the one who'd picked up the ransom had signaled me. I knew the area well enough not to be surprised at what I found there.

It was a narrow, iron-barred entrance to a military bunker, almost hidden behind a tangle of wild bushes.

The mountain ranges there spread across the nearby frontier into Italy. Between world wars France built a network of underground fortifications, large and small, throughout the region. After World War II they'd all been gradually abandoned and closed up.

The entrance to this one had been secured with a chain. But someone had used bolt cutters on it. The sheared chain dangled, and the iron-barred door was open. I went inside and shone the flashlight around. This bunker was one of the smaller ones. A few connecting rooms. Nothing in any of them but the crumbling concrete of walls, floors, and ceilings. The bunker's interior had been stripped before it was closed up. The kidnappers hadn't left me a forgotten matchbook with the name of their favorite bar on it.

The last room had another barred door, leading out the other side of the hill. The chain lock had been cut on this one, too. I stepped out. An overgrown dirt road curved around that side of the hill. I had passed both ends of that road earlier, while driving Route 204. One end joined it in the direction of Sospel, the other toward St. Laurent-du-Touët.

The brush growing in the dirt road had been crushed by the recent passage of a car. I couldn't judge the direction in which it had come or gone. But no car had come into Sospel from Route 204 during the hour I'd waited there after dropping off the sacks of money. So the one who'd picked it up had carried it through the bunker to the waiting car and driven toward St. Laurent-du-Touët. And not far past that village was the larger town of Escarène.

From there the kidnappers would have had a choice of several major routes to take with Malo's seven million francs. They could have gone west, north, or south. By now they could already be in Italy or anywhere along the Riviera. Or well on their way to Paris, the Atlantic coast, or Switzerland.

Wherever, they were close to being home free. Start to finish, their operation had gone without a hitch.

Planned by someone with considerable experience.

Executed flawlessly.

I wondered if the man who'd made all three phone calls to Karl Malo—the one with the Italian accent, real or faked—was the brains of the operation.

I wondered if there had been others involved in it besides the three Jacqueline Malo had told me about.

I wondered about a number of other things I couldn't quite reconcile in the way it had been prepared and timed. Something about the setup still didn't feel normal. I couldn't come up with anything beyond mutually contradictory guesswork as I returned to the car.

Before getting back in I removed my shoulder harness and holstered gun. A private citizen in France can only carry a handgun around with him if he's first explained the need, via complicated forms, to the authorities—who may then agree to issue a permit for a strictly limited period. The same applies to private eyes. But there hadn't been time to go through that red tape, and Malo hadn't wanted any contact with the cops. I'd counted on his influence to get me out if I got in a jam using the gun.

I stuck it in the plastic bag I'd used for the sandwiches and hid it under the front seat—to be removed surreptitiously later, before the police got around to examining the car. Then I drove back through Sospel to the quarry.

* * * *

Four cops from the gendarmerie in Sospel were there when I arrived. They were having a look around the quarry and shed under a spreading predawn light. But not touching anything. Touching things is reserved for specialists from the various police branches. The first batches of those, from Nice and Menton, got there a couple hours later. More of them, from Paris, began arriving shortly before noon. Karl Malo's name pulled a lot of weight.

I repeated everything I knew to each fresh batch of specialists. They agreed with me that it didn't add up to much.

None of the police branches came up with anything either. Neither in the next few days nor in the next few months.

Detailed examination of the parking garage where they'd snatched Jacqueline Malo, the shed where they'd kept her, and the bunker where they'd waited to pick up the ransom yielded not a single clue. Nobody had really expected to find anything like a clue, though they went through the motions. The French police aren't Sherlock Holmes.

They worked the real investigation their usual way. Probing through the underworld. Pressuring and cajoling and bribing informants. Listening for rumors, searching for criminals who might suddenly have a lot more dough than usual to squander. The police of other countries, alerted by Interpol, worked at the case the same way. All of them gave it their best efforts.

But as time went by their efforts got more and more routine, less and less hopeful.

The snatch had been managed by a pro; everyone agreed on that. But nobody knew who he or his associates were. Which was peculiar. Everyone agreed on that, too.

* * * *

From time to time I checked on how the investigation was going. Most of it I got from two of my best contacts inside the police. One was Inspector Laurent Soumagnac, a friend in the Police Judiciare in Nice. The other was in Paris: Commissaire Jean-Claude Gojon of the Brigade de Recherches et d'Intervention. I was up there for a couple of weeks at one point, helping my Paris partner Fritz Donhoff on a case that needed more legwork than he could handle comfortably at age seventy-four. When the case went comatose on us I treated Gojon to a meal at Balzar and pumped him.

Gojon had access to higher sources than Laurent down in Nice. But not more progress to report.

The cops were continuing to follow up on rumors, but none of them led to anything useful. Underworld informers still scrounged around, and still came up empty. *Milieu* characters sporting new affluence kept getting pulled in and grilled. None of them, and none of their loot, turned out to have any connection with the Jacqueline Malo case.

There wasn't a whisper anywhere that provided a hint of a real lead to the gang that had pulled the kidnap.

Zilch.

Which didn't help me shake the feeling I had gotten while I was doing what Malo had hired me to do. The feeling that something didn't fit the way it should in the way things had gone between the moment she'd been grabbed and the time I'd dropped off the ransom and found her.

But it was no longer any of my business. I'd done what I could for the Malos while I was working for them. I wasn't working for them anymore. Nobody was paying me to dig deeper into the case, perhaps from an entirely different angle. So that was that. Like most folks I know, I work for a living. Scratching an itch of curiosity, just because it won't go away, won't buy you a stick of gum.

So I buckled down to other jobs. Ones I was paid to do.

I still thought about Malo from time to time. More often about his wife. I didn't expect ever to see either of them again.

But I did, two months later.

Blame it on my mother.

CHAPTER 7

"My God," Babette said after she looked up and saw me, "for a moment I thought… You look *so* much like your father. Except much older, of course."

My mother was not normally given to being overly sentimental toward me—except when she saw me again after an absence of some months. Then she'd suddenly remember I was the spitting image of Sergeant James Sawyer. The resemblance had been more striking when I was twenty. Since then the years had gouged lines in my face that my father would never have. By now he was dust.

Twenty was the age he'd reached when he bailed out of a burning American bomber over southern France and been picked up by the Resistance band that Babette belonged to. He'd still been twenty when he'd married her. And when he'd been killed, in the last week of World War II. I'd been born four months later, a week after Babette turned eighteen.

I knew him from old photographs and Babette's romantic memories of their few months together. And from his parents in Chicago, who'd gotten saddled with most of the job of raising me after I'd reached the age of five. From then on Babette had been too occupied in Paris—with her studies at the Sorbonne and subsequently as a professor specializing in the history and psychology of art—to spend more than six weeks each summer with me, at our house overlooking the Mediterranean.

I leaned down and kissed her and sat beside her on the weather-worn stone base between two intricately sculpted medieval columns. "You're looking beautiful, Babette. But then, you always do." That was true enough. Her statuesque figure retained much of its athletic vigor, and she had the type of strong-boned face that ages well.

"I do love male flattery." She gave me a hug and a kiss on the cheek. "How did you find me here?" She laughed at the question. "No, don't bother answering. That *is* your profession, after all. Finding people."

It *had* taken a little professional digging. Nobody had answered my repeated calls to the phone at her Paris apartment. Finally I'd tried the office of Serge, the man she'd married when they were both students at the Sorbonne. But Serge was off in South America, tending to some problems for the company he managed. Nobody in his office knew where

Babette was, except that she wasn't with Serge. So I'd called Fritz Don-hoff. He'd spent half an hour on the phone and had called back with the information I wanted. Babette was down in Arles, working on an article about some aspect of Romanesque symbolism.

If you have a fast car and take the autoroute most of the way, it's less than three hours from my house to Arles. It was mid-afternoon when I got there. I parked on the Place de la République, in front of the church of St. Trophime. Most of the Romanesque imagery to be found in Arles is packed into that one church.

Babette wasn't outside studying the heaven and hell bas-reliefs that decorate its main entrance. So I went through to its lovely little clois-ter. And found her sitting there with a notebook on her knees, making sketches and jotting down thoughts about the carvings on the surround-ing portico columns.

The two we were sitting between were especially thought-provok-ing. The column on our left had scenes from the lives of the saints. The other had a nightmarish demon biting the head off a little man caught in the grip of its claws. Just to remind you of what was waiting for you down below, if your own life failed to be entirely saintly.

"You hunted me down," Babette said, "because it's been too long since we've seen each other and you missed me."

"There is that," I said.

"And because you want something."

"You owe the joy of seeing me to what I *don't* want," I told her. "I don't want you to sell our house to Rasul Khdanni. His real estate pro-curer dropped by again yesterday. He claims you've decided you may sell after all."

"I haven't *decided*. I wouldn't, without discussing it with you first. I'm only *considering* it. Monsieur Khdanni made me a new offer last week. Triple the price anybody else would pay for the property."

"I'd pay you a lot more than that, if I had it."

"But you don't," Babette said. "Monsieur Khdanni does. What he's trying to do isn't new. The Riviera has changed hands many times. It be-longs to whoever has the money to buy it. First the Russian nobility, until the Revolution. Then the English, while they still had their empire. Then all those American millionaires turned on by Scott Fitzgerald's *Tender Is the Night*. Now it's the Arabs."

"A handful. Most never get within sniffing distance of all that oil loot. Khdanni's already bought up seven shore-front properties. Mean-while there are dozens of North African immigrants in our area alone who can hardly afford a single room. Khdanni was asked by a Cap d'Ail committee to contribute a little to help build low-rent apartments for his fellow Arabs. He wasn't interested."

"The rich of any nation have seldom cared what happened to their poor."

I nodded. "The good old Victorian ethic. The rich must be rich because they are especially virtuous and God is rewarding them for it. So people who're broke must get that way because they're lacking in virtues. Which means they deserve their misery."

"Indignation does not become you, Pierre-Ange."

"I know. It pops out from time to time, when I'm not paying attention. About Khdanni..."

"It's his money," Babette said. "To spend as he pleases."

"He spends it the way he gets it. Unpleasantly. Trying to take my house away from me."

"My house," Babette reminded me firmly. "While I'm alive it's mine. By French law. It doesn't belong to you until I die."

"Don't die, Babette. I want you to live forever. Just don't sell the house while you're at it."

"How much time have I spent there over the past twenty years? Not more than a week or two each year. I can't spare time for more."

"But your son *lives* there."

"My son should learn to be more practical about his life. You know I would divide Monsieur Khdanni's payment with you. That would give *me* a nice secure feeling where it counts. In my bank account. And give *you* enough to buy some other place in the area."

I kept a tight grip on my temper. Temper is not a way to win arguments with my mother. She's got a backbone that turns to iron when she's attacked. "I don't want another place," I told her in a reasonable tone. "That one is my *home*, Babette. The only place I feel that way about. It's one of the main reasons I'm here in France instead of back in the States."

The place I'd considered home in America was long gone. The Chicago house where I'd been raised had been torn down three years after my grandmother died.

I decided I'd have to lay it on thick for Babette. This was an emergency. I put a passionate throb in my voice: "It's *your* fault I feel so attached to that house. You're the one who took me there every summer. Taught me to swim there. Told me all those stories of your own childhood there. Made me look on it as a piece of paradise that belonged to me."

Babette sighed. "You are such a sentimentalist, Pierre-Ange. Like your father was." Her eyes got that dreamy look that came whenever she thought about him, forever the young, passionate American stranger in her memories.

I almost had her. "Maybe that's why you fell in love with him, Babette. Because you wanted someone who could balance your logic with emotion. It must get tiresome, being a realist all the time."

She shrugged. "No, I'm a Frenchwoman. We were later than most in getting things like the right to vote or even to have our own bank accounts. We've had to be realistic, especially about men, to get what we needed." She paused, but I didn't say anything because she'd gotten that dreamy look. "But your father," she said softly. "I didn't have to be clever in handling *him*. He was…such a sweet young man, under that tough American facade." She smiled at me. "And you *are* so much like him."

I had her.

"*Don't* sell the house out from under me, Babette. It'll break my sentimental American heart."

"Your heart is only half American," Babette said, and she sighed again. "And you can stop using the cynical French half to manipulate an aging lady's vulnerability. I won't sell the house."

"Thank you, Babette."

"But I'll expect you to repay me in a number of ways over the years to come."

"Ask and you shall receive."

"You can start by taking me to dinner tonight. You know how I loathe dining alone. I'm staying at the Hotel d'Arlatan. Pick me up at nine and take me to one of the more expensive restaurants in town. Now go away and let me get back to work."

* * * *

Dinner with Babette at nine meant having her talk art to me until midnight or one in the morning. Over at least two bottles of wine. I wouldn't feel up to a three-hour drive through the night after that.

The d'Arlatan, a handsome seventeenth-century building that was once the private residence of a large titled family, had one of its pleasantly decorated rooms free. I checked in and left the overnight bag I usually keep stored in my car. Then I went out for a stroll around Arles.

And walked back into the Jacqueline Malo kidnap case.

CHAPTER 8

Arles used to be called the "Little Rome" back when it was the capital of the Roman Empire's colony of Provence. That glory passed away almost two thousand years ago. But the grandiose structures left from that era keep reminding you of it. In spite of their sheer bulk, the strong sunlight of Provence almost manages to blend them in with the surrounding conglomeration of buildings from later centuries. And with the crooked streets and tree-shaded little squares that Van Gogh painted in Arles, before and after cutting off his ear.

All of it is packed into a lively town small enough to walk through without getting sightseer's legs. My hotel was near the Baths of Constantine, close by the bank of the Rhône River. From there I strolled to the Amphitheater, a smaller version of Rome's Coliseum. A real stroll, as opposed to a hike, should include an occasional halt to sit and have a drink while admiring the view. There was a bistro on the corner of a little street across from the Amphitheater.

I took a sidewalk table under a red-and-blue-striped umbrella and ordered a glass of rose from the nearby vineyards of Mas de la Dame, together with some ice cubes. The latter request struck the waiter as peculiar. I had to repeat it. He shrugged, nodded, and went back inside.

I leaned back in my wicker chair and gazed at the looming stone oval of the Amphitheater, imagining what it had been like with the citizens of Roman Arles crowding tier above tier inside it, howling for the deaths of captive Christians—and later non-Christians—by fire or by unequal combat with lions and gladiators. And a thousand years later, when its round walls enclosed the slum and red-light district of medieval Arles, packed with hovels and whores, thieves and stink: a magnet for the plague that drifted up the Rhône Valley like atomic fallout and wiped out almost two thirds of the region's population.

The waiter arrived with my wine and a small bowl of ice. I tasted the rose first. As anticipated, it was too warm for my taste. I dropped in one ice cube and waited for it to do its job.

There was an art gallery on the opposite corner of the little street. Arles has an unusual number of them for a town of that size so far from Paris. Van Gogh's work and dramatic life there lures both painters and art lovers.

A woman appeared from inside the gallery and stood in its open doorway, staring at me.

She was wearing a green silk dress with a pleated skirt. It suited her small, curvy figure. Her hair was coiled around her head, the thick braid catching glints of sunlight.

I stood up and walked across to her. "Bonjour, Madame Malo."

She hesitated. The sight of me worried her. Maybe not a big worry, but it was there. Then she said, "Monsieur...excuse me, it startled me, seeing you here." She smiled and held out her small hand.

I liked the feel of it in mine. I also still liked her smile. But it was concealing the worry. And she wasn't good at concealment.

"Has something happened?" she asked. "Did Karl hire you again?"

I shook my head. "Pure coincidence. I came to Arles to see my mother. And here you are."

"Oh." She looked relieved. But not entirely; maybe she didn't entirely believe me. "Your mother lives here?"

"No, she's down from Paris for a few days, researching an article on Romanesque symbolism. In St. Trophime. She's an art historian."

Jacqueline Malo wore a thoughtful frown. "Has she published before?"

"Quite a bit."

"I try to keep up with the current art literature," she said, "but I don't recall anything by a Madame Sawyer..."

"She uses her maiden name," I told her. "Babette Onimus."

It took Jacqueline Malo less than a second. "The book on primitive and modern art a couple years ago: *The Recurring Dream*."

"That's her." I gestured at the gallery. "Are you buying or just window shopping?"

Her quiet laugh was genuine. The details about my mother had put her at ease. "Neither. I'm *selling*. It's my gallery." Her smile had become easier, too. "You look surprised."

"Not many tycoons' wives are shopkeepers."

"An art gallery isn't quite a *shop*. I had it before Karl and I were married. I see no reason to give it up. He's busy much of the time with his work. This is mine. I have some very good contemporary work here, by local artists. As well as a few paintings of the past, by artists whose work is currently undervalued but sure to become more sought-after in the next few years. And reasonably priced, if *you* are interested in art."

"I'm not up to buying *anything* today," I told her. "I think I just sold a piece of my soul for a place to live." This time her smile was puzzled.

I didn't feel like explaining Babette to her. "I don't see any customers in there at the moment. Can I buy you a drink? You can watch your place from across the street."

"You seem to be offering me a drink every time we meet, Monsieur Sawyer. A choice of brandy or water when you came to my rescue."

"Rescuing you is a nice way to put it. But there weren't any dragons left to fight."

"But I couldn't be sure of that when you arrived. My knight, in shining Levi's jacket and jeans." Her joking tone held a warmth that gently stroked the old male ego. She glanced at her gallery and then nodded. "All right. I would like a coffee."

We crossed to my table. She sat where she could watch her gallery. I sat where I could look at her profile. It was a bewitching profile. The other time I'd seen her it had been night. Daylight didn't dissolve any of her appeal. When she turned her head to look at me fully I experienced a jolt of deep-down pleasure.

When the waiter came out she ordered a *café noir*. I looked at my glass of rosé. The ice cube had completely melted in it by then, which would make it too watery. I ordered another.

"With more ice cubes?" the waiter asked, straight-faced.

"Please."

He went inside, carrying my glass and bowl and his own smug smile.

Jacqueline Malo's skin had turned from pale to bronze since I'd last seen her. It made the big green eyes more startling. The fine sprinkling of almost invisible hairs on her slim forearms looked like spun gold. "You obviously don't spend all your days inside your place over there," I said. "You've gotten a lot of sun the last couple months."

"Not a lot. I tan easily. This is almost entirely from Sundays around our pool, when the gallery is closed."

"Have you had the gallery a long time?" I asked.

"Almost two years. That's where I first met Karl. He came in one day to see what sort of works I had."

"He's a collector?"

"He was only starting to get interested at the time. After his heart attack. That happens more often than you'd think. People discovering that art supplies a feeling of continuity between past and future that they've come to need."

I nodded and thought of my olive tree. And of Henri Bonnet's hunch about Karl Malo's emotional change of life.

"He didn't know much about paintings at that point," Jacqueline Malo said. "But he wanted to learn."

"And you became his teacher."

"Sort of." She smiled to herself, remembering. "We began getting together for long talks. And I gave him books to read on the subject. We went to Paris to tour the museums together—" She interrupted herself, slightly disconcerted at having told me that. But not embarrassed. "Well, he wasn't married. And he *is* the most exciting man I've ever met."

Malo hadn't struck me that way. But then, I hadn't been intimate with him. "Plenty of women seem to have agreed with you."

She nodded, unoffended. "Of course. Women are fascinated by men with an aura of power. Power of any kind."

"And money."

"That matters less to most women than you think. Look how many are drawn to painters and writers and musicians who are impoverished but radiate absolute confidence. It's the sense of *power*. And the kind of secure feeling that gives. Like standing against a solid stone wall when you're tired."

The waiter put our orders on the table. I dropped a fresh ice cube into my new glass of wine. Jacqueline Malo stared. "I've never seen even an *American* do that."

"Americans don't. I do. Waiters in the States get more horrified than the ones here."

She studied me as she stirred sugar into her coffee. "And you don't *care* what people think. Of anything you do."

"That's not quite true."

"I think it is. You're very much your own man. Sufficient unto yourself. That must be a good feeling."

"Sometimes what it feels like is lonely."

Jacqueline Malo regarded me archly. "I doubt it. *You* have that aura I mentioned, too. I don't imagine you lack for friends. Or smitten women."

She did know how to make a man feel good. I grinned at her. She smiled back. I took a sip of my rose. The temperature was just right. I spooned out the ice cube and dropped it back in the bowl with its melting companions. "Were you ever married before?" I asked her.

She held on to the smile, but the wariness was back. "Why do you ask?"

"Bad-mannered curiosity. I've got a professional habit of prying into people's lives. Sometimes when it's not called for. Forget I asked."

The smile was entirely gone. "But you must have had a reason for it."

I put a lot of warmth into the way I was looking at her. It wasn't a chore. "It just strikes me that you're a woman many men would have wanted to marry, before Malo came along."

Her eyes narrowed a bit. "Are you making a pass at me, Monsieur Sawyer?"

"Would it surprise you?"

"Not entirely." She was smiling again. "But I should warn you, I have what some consider an odd attitude about marriage. I prefer being true to my husband. A serious flaw in my character, I've been told."

"By disappointed suitors, no doubt."

"You do tone up a woman's ego, Monsieur Sawyer."

"Pierre-Ange."

"Pierre-Ange." She didn't ask me to use *her* first name. "Will you be staying in Arles long?"

"Only a day or so," I said. "Unfortunately."

By then Jacqueline Malo was relaxed enough to answer my question. "I *was* married before," she said, with no special intonation. "He died before I moved to Arles." She drank from her tiny cup. And changed the subject. "Do you ever hear from the police about…what happened to me?"

"Not much. The little I hear indicates they're not getting anywhere. But you and your husband would be likely to hear more about it than I would. From higher sources than mine." I regarded her questioningly.

She hesitated before responding. "Karl spoke with the Minister of the Interior in Paris last week." The rest she seemed to be reciting by rote: "He was told the police now have very little expectation of finding the three people who did it. Unless one of them gets caught sometime in the future, for some other criminal act, and the truth about this one comes out. Or if some angry lover of one of the gang members goes to the police in an act of vengeance. The Minister didn't hold out much hope of either."

"How do you feel about that?" I asked her.

She was silent for several seconds, looking at her gallery across the street. "The truth, Monsieur Sawyer? Karl and I suffered enough from it. I'd like to be allowed to just forget it ever happened."

"Does your husband feel the same?"

She drained her cup and got to her feet. "I have some paperwork to attend to. If you'll excuse me…"

I stood, and we shook hands again. Her grip was firm but brief. "Thank you for the coffee." She crossed the street, disappearing inside the gallery.

* * * *

I finished my wine and took another stroll through the town. This time to the Alyscamps.

The name has the same Latin derivation as the Champs Elysées in Paris: *Campi Elysii*. The one in Paris became a boulevard of entertainment. This one became an avenue of death.

It was once the holiest ground in Provence. The region's wealthy families would float their dead down the Rhône to be placed in the tombs that line both sides of its long walking path. Legends became attached to it. Even miracles.

One night a fisherman stopped a coffin in the middle of the river and stole jewelry from the body inside. For some days thereafter the corpse stayed where it had been robbed, in midstream, refusing to be budged by the strong Rhône current. Until the thief, crazed with terror, confessed his crime.

A similar miracle in the Malo case was unlikely.

I walked along between the now-empty tombs, having some long thoughts about Karl and Jacqueline Malo. What they led to was no good, because it lacked the essential ingredient. I couldn't come up with a motivation.

It still wasn't my business. Not my onions, in French argot.

I had another drink near the Van Gogh Hospital and strolled back to the hotel.

* * * *

The ringing of my room phone woke me the next morning. I assumed it was Babette, making sure I joined her for a farewell breakfast before she went to work. I was groggy. Dinner the previous night had been what I'd expected. Three hours of art lecture over a bottle apiece. I fumbled for the phone and finally got it.

"I'm on my way," I said with as much heartiness as I could manage. "Just got out of the shower and—"

The voice that interrupted was a man's: "This is Karl Malo, Monsieur Sawyer. I'm sorry if I've disturbed you."

He didn't sound sorry. What he sounded was wide awake and a touch impatient with anyone who wasn't at that hour. But the harshness I remembered was gone.

"What time is it?"

"Eight o'clock. I should have left for the office by now but I've been trying to locate you. This is the fourth hotel I called."

My appointment with Babette was in fifteen minutes. I sat up and swung my legs off the bed. My brain began a hurried job of clearing the cobwebs: "Your wife told you about seeing me in Arles."

"Last evening. She wondered if you were back working for me."

She still hadn't quite believed me. It had made her nervous enough to double-check. But if she truly wanted the case forgotten that had been a mistake.

"It started me thinking," Malo told me. "This morning I decided. I *would* like to hire you again, Monsieur Sawyer."

CHAPTER 9

"Are you free to meet me this morning?" Malo's tone anticipated an affirmative answer. Though the aggressive manner that had gotten my back up the last time was missing, the authority was not. The man was troubled, but not uncertain of what to do about it.

"When and where?" I asked him.

"My local headquarters are down in the Fos industrial complex," Malo said. "Behind Dock Three in the Gloria Basin. You'll see the company sign. From Arles you can drive there in less than three quarters of an hour. I'll expect you at nine-thirty."

"I can't make it that early," I told him. "I've got a breakfast date."

"Can't you break it? You'll be well compensated for any inconvenience. This is important."

Not as important as making sure Babette didn't lose that rare feeling of motherly sentiment I'd generated. "I can be there at eleven," I said.

"I have other pressing business to attend to by then." Malo wasn't accustomed to argument from hired hands. But if he felt anger, he didn't allow it to surface. Something stronger than habit was working on him. The man did have unexpected depths. Like the incredible one I'd witnessed when he'd gotten his wife back. Love, thy spell weaves designs too magical for the mortal eye.

"We can meet later in the day," I told him. "You name it."

There was a short silence. "No," Malo said, "I want to get this settled. I'll rearrange my schedule—and expect you at eleven."

* * * *

The region of Provence around Arles contains some of the most pleasant scenery in France.

It also contains the ugliest: the Grande Crau, south of Arles between the east bank of the Rhône and Marseilles. The highway I took, the N568, cuts down through the middle of it.

On either side of my car the Crau's sullen plain spread as far as I could see. A barren stone-and-gravel wasteland, gray and almost treeless, depressingly flat. There was nothing to prevent the N568 from running dead straight all the way. Not a hill, not a village. Seldom even a lone sad house. Only dire necessity would induce anyone to live in the middle of the Crau's desolate landscape.

When I neared the southern end of N568, approaching Fos, the scene got even uglier. Manmade ugliness. Some scattered industrial structures appeared—and then a great many of them, separated by stretches of shingle desert bisected by polluted drainage canals. Factories and huge sheds, steel-and-plastic office buildings, sprawling oil refineries, and chemical plants belching noxious smoke.

The Fos industrial zone had been created by a steady increase in commercial shipping over the past three decades. It became too much for the port of Marseilles to handle. More docks kept being added westward along the coast until they reached Fos, at the bottom of the Crau.

Industry moves where there are shipping facilities and cheap land. The Grande Crau was the cheapest available anywhere along the south coast of France. Nobody else wanted it.

It was still growing, helter-skelter: miles of shattered jigsaw puzzle. I got lost trying to find my way through it. A couple wrong turns got me to a water's edge dead end, behind a mineral terminal between docks 1 and 2.

A patient terminal guard showed me a detailed map of the complex and gave me directions. I drove back through a forest of giant gas storage tanks, made a long left swing around a tangle of pipelines, and maneuvered between a power station and a steel plant. That brought me into a bumpy road full of TIR trailer-trucks going to and from Dock 3. The sign I was looking for finally appeared:

MALO TRANSPORT

It was above the drive-in gate of a chain link fence enclosing a truck parking area, three big warehouses, and a boxy modern office building. The guard at the gate had been briefed. I showed my I.D., and he waved me through. The walls of the four-story office building were painted in an abstract blue-and-white pattern. But the original color was almost hidden under the layer of dust glued to it by the fumes of Fos.

There was no dust or chemical stink inside the building. The interior was isolated from the outer world by sealed windows and air conditioning. The receptionist pointed to a small elevator that took me to the top floor and let me out in an office with three secretaries. One was working at a word processor and another at a computer console. The third told me sternly that I was almost ten minutes late before using her phone to inform Malo that I was finally there. Then she indicated a leather-padded bench where I could wait.

It wasn't a long wait. A tall, lean man came out of Karl Malo's office.

He was carrying some bulky folders under one arm and a small cassette recorder in his other hand. His impeccable silk business suit was dark blue with just a hint of a paler stripe in it. The necktie was black. A serious outfit, to go with his expression.

He was about thirty-five. His craggy, intelligent face was already marred by executive damage. Too many make-or-break decisions, too little sleep, too much single-minded ambition. In France they say men that dedicated to climbing the ladder have *les dents longues*: long teeth.

He looked at me with meditative eyes. Then he gave me a nod and a polite smile. "You can go in now."

The smile transformed him, offering a glimpse of a younger, lighter man. Without it his wide, thin-lipped mouth was grim.

He went past me to the elevator. I got up and went through the door he'd left open.

* * * *

"The man who just left is my son-in-law," Malo told me. "Jean-Noel Triolet. I'll introduce you to him later. After I've explained why I called you. It's best you know before you meet any of my family. It's…a delicate problem."

"Which you consider me delicate enough to handle."

The dark brown eyes were as hard and shrewd as I'd remembered. They regarded me steadily. "If I didn't, you wouldn't be here."

We sat facing each other across his desk. Through the window behind him I could see a line of container ships waiting their turn at the docks in the oily waters of the Gloria Basin.

The office was large but fairly Spartan, with only a few personal frills. Two of them were on one wall: water-colors that looked like Turners. I wondered if Jacqueline Malo had chosen them for him. The framed picture of her that he'd shown me in Monaco stood at one end of his desk. Behind it were three smaller ones. A handsome boy in his late teens. A sulky-looking woman in her mid-twenties. A baby about half a year old.

"There is no shortage of other private investigators I could hire," Malo resumed quietly. "But I've used you before. On a matter as delicate and even more important to me. I know you can be depended upon to do as you're told."

He quickly raised a hand to stop me from reacting. "No, let me re-phrase that. I know you'll do what *you* say you will—and not deviate from it. You have a code of honor. Or call it a strong sense of respect for yourself. When you give a client your assurance on any point you stick to it."

"You're good," I said. "Shifty. If somebody won't adapt to you, you adapt to them. Push or pull, kick or cajole. Either way you get what you want."

We smiled at each other. It surprised us both and didn't last long.

"What matters is the end result," Malo said blandly. "One works with the tool best suited to the job. You can't handle a drill the same way you would a hammer."

The secretary who'd disapproved of my lateness slipped in and out silently, leaving behind a tray with coffee service for two. We poured from an antique silver pot into Spode cups. The coffee tasted like what you get out of a cafeteria dispenser in plastic containers. I drank it anyway. It was still caffeine. I wanted to stay alert with someone like Malo.

* * * *

"I spoke with the Interior Minister last week," Malo told me. "According to him, the police have given up hope of finding the kidnappers via their usual methods. They think that if it was done by professional criminals, *something* would have surfaced about it in the underworld by now. Do you agree?"

"They have a point," I said. "But it wasn't planned by an amateur."

Malo nodded. "Whoever he is, the police think he must have used nonprofessional assistants. They also believe he must have gotten his information about Jacqueline's movements from someone close to home. *My* home. Nobody outside it could have known she intended to come to Monaco—in time to arrange to seize her there."

Even then the planning time would have been *very* tight. But I didn't say that. I said, "I imagine you have a number of servants in your house."

Malo nodded. "But each of them has been minutely checked by the police. Their movements before, during, and after the kidnapping. Their backgrounds, friends, relatives, contacts of any kind—even people they'd known only briefly and superficially. The police are now quite certain none of the servants was involved."

He fell silent. The next logical step was harder for him. So I said it: "That leaves any of your family that was around your home at the right time."

"Yes." Malo took another moment, but he didn't look away from me. "The Minister hinted—with extreme embarrassment—that the police have come to the point of considering that possibility. But they would not dare to actually investigate my family without my permission. I believe I can count on that."

"Sure you can. No cop wants to ruin his career by tangling with somebody like you. Especially when there's no real pressure from anybody else to solve the case."

"Why should there be? Nobody suffered from it except Jacqueline and myself."

"And you want me to do what you won't let the cops do."

"Yes—I want to *know*."

"Just between you and me," I said.

"Yes."

"Because you can control what I do about whatever I find."

The hard eyes remained fixed on me. The voice stayed reasonable. "Because *you* can control it. *I'll* decide what to do about anything you learn. And I'll want your promise that none of it will go beyond the two of us without my…agreement."

The word he'd started to use was "permission." Malo did adapt himself to the tool he had to use.

"That's standard procedure," I told him. "I work for the client. If I decide I don't want to go further unless the cops are brought in—and the client won't agree—I drop the job and walk."

"And keep silent."

"Yes." That wasn't always true. But I wanted this case. And lying is part of my trade.

CHAPTER 10

Malo indicated the framed photographs on his desk. "As you can see, my family is not a large one. That narrows the possibilities for you from the start. Other than Jacqueline there are only my son and daughter. That picture of Alexandre is more than a year old. He's twenty now. Claudette is six years older. She's from my first marriage. Alexandre is from my second."

"You don't have any brothers or sisters?"

"No. But I do have a grandson now." He looked at the baby's picture with a rare sort of smile. Rare for him. "Michel—Claudette and Jean-Noel's child. He's named for my father."

Malo lost his smile when his eyes switched from the baby to me. "*If* someone in my family was involved, it would have to be Alexandre or Claudette. My hope is that you will find it was neither."

"You're forgetting your son-in-law," I said.

He shook his head. "Jean-Noel wasn't around at the time of the kidnapping. He was off in New York. Occupied every day with conferences for the company. Jean-Noel handles the more strenuous business trips for me these days."

"Since your heart attack."

"Yes. The doctors warned me I had to cut down the work pressure if I don't want to be dead soon. They ordered me to relax and indulge in more leisure time." His laugh was rueful. "That is difficult for me. My entire life has been devoted to working very intensely."

"Judging by reputation," I said, "you managed to squeeze in some fun."

"If you mean the parties and social functions, I only attended those important for my business and government contacts."

"Keeping in touch with other members of the winners' circle."

"Exactly. And if you were referring to the women in my life—I'm afraid none of them got much of me. That accounts for their numbers, I suppose. I always preferred my pleasures in strong but brief doses. A minimum interruption of my busy schedule."

"You make it sound like taking medicine," I said "Necessary, but not to be savored at length."

"True. Until Jacqueline." Malo displayed another of those rare smiles. "It was with her I first began to learn how to relax like any normal person. She's still teaching me. I'm not an easy pupil."

"What's your son-in-law's position in your company?" I asked him.

"Assistant director. Second in command, after me. He's been with the firm almost ten years, in lesser positions, learning it inside out. When Hubert Loy, my former assistant director, died I gave the job to Jean-Noel."

"Was that before or after he married your daughter?"

"After. Five months ago. Pure nepotism, I know. But he's done an excellent job for me. A hard worker. Jean-Noel and I are surprisingly alike."

I thought of the grim-mouthed man I'd seen leaving Karl Malo's office. "How long did he stay in New York?"

"He was there for almost a week before the kidnapping," Malo said. "And didn't get back until three days afterwards. So you see—"

"But your son and daughter *were* around at the time."

"Yes. At our chateau. Claudette still lives there. With my grandson and Jean-Noel. They have one wing to themselves. Alexandre has his rooms in another wing, though usually he's away in Paris now. He's a second-year student at *Sciences Po*."

Sciences Po is the nickname for *L'institut d'études politiques de Paris*—a ranking member of the top trio of universities for future leaders of French business and government. Three of the last four presidents of France had graduated from *Sciences Po*. Thousands of young candidates compete in its annual entrance tests. Out of the small number of those who get accepted as first-year students, a large percentage is dropped before the second year. "Your son must be a bright student," I said.

"He's more than bright. Alexandre is brilliant. I bought him his Paris apartment as a present when he passed the first-year finals near the top of his class."

"But sometimes he comes back to your chateau."

"He's there now," Malo told me, "spending the summer. And he was there for the school Easter vacation. When Jacqueline came to join me in Monaco."

"Is there anything," I asked, "that makes you suspect your son or daughter of having a hand in what happened?"

"Neither would have any *reason* to. I give them both generous allowances and seldom say no when they need more. Each will inherit a third of the company, like Jacqueline. *Almost* a third—Jean-Noel gets five percent. Alexandre and Claudette don't lack for money, for God's sake."

I said, "That isn't an answer to my question."

"I *know*," Malo acknowledged. "You mean something in their characters or past actions. The truth is that neither of them has ever been easy for me to control." He swung around in his chair and gazed broodingly at the photographs on his desk. "Another truth is that I didn't really *try*. I didn't pay that much attention to them when they were growing up. Like with the ladies in my life. I never let them interfere with my work."

Malo was silent for a few moments, continuing to look at their pictures. "The heart trouble started me rethinking my life. Too late, of course, where my son and daughter are concerned. I know they don't care a great deal for me. I don't expect them to. But they *are* my immortality—the only kind I can believe in. A thought that would no doubt annoy them."

He swung back to face me. "So…I finally did begin to really observe them. And I don't like what I see. They have unpleasant resentments… angers. They hate each other, for example. A result of the nasty rivalry, in the past, between their mothers."

"How do they feel about your present wife?"

Malo looked uncomfortable. "They do resent Jacqueline. In spite of her best efforts… I imagine most children resent it when their father takes a new wife."

"Enough to have a hand in kidnapping her and gouging you for that ransom?"

"I don't *know*…"

* * * *

I questioned him further about his son and daughter. Malo gave me something about his daughter first:

"Claudette was rather wild when she was younger. She had an attraction to much older men. Some even *my* age. It made me furious. I assume that's why she did it. To get back at me for my own life-style."

I didn't want psychoanalysis at that point. "Her husband isn't that much older than she is."

"No. And she settled down after she married him and had the baby. Stopped making a fool of herself. And of me. To tell the truth, I was surprised she was attracted to Jean-Noel. But obviously she was. Their baby was born six months after the marriage."

"Does she still find her husband attractive?"

"I've no reason to think otherwise." Malo frowned over that one. "It's hard to tell. Jean-Noel *is* like me. He's busy elsewhere much of the time. But Claudette has shown no signs of being upset by that so far."

I said, "It sounds like she's gotten to be a fairly well-adjusted grown-up."

"I think so."

"That leaves your son."

Malo hesitated. "I told you Alexandre is brilliant," he said finally. "Perhaps *too* brilliant. He doesn't have to grind away at his studies, like most of his fellow students. That leaves him with too much free time on his hands."

"What does he do with it?"

"I know Alexandre has at times frequented some of the illegal gambling clubs in Paris," Malo said. "Twice he's had to come to me to pay off his losses. They give him credit, of course. They know there's wealth behind him."

"Anything else?"

"He seems to delight in associating with the worst elements of the lower classes. Riffraff. Last year a couple of young hoodlums talked Alexandre into helping them loot and vandalize a Paris apartment. He took part purely for the perverted amusement of it. Something new and daring. They were caught. My attorneys up there had considerable trouble getting the owner and the authorities to drop the charges against him. Which meant letting the other two go as well. Though they have records as petty criminals. Both are in prison now, for other crimes."

"But your son could have met other criminals through them," I said. "Or through the gambling clubs."

Malo made some unnecessary rearrangements on his desk. He moved the phone, the intercom, a teak tray of papers awaiting his signature, shifting the position of each no more than an inch. "I have considered that," he said.

"And you figure your son is a fast learner. As well as being smart enough to be the one who *planned* the kidnap."

Malo used both hands to shift the intercom back to its original position. "I fervently pray that I'm wrong."

His intercom buzzed softly. Malo stabbed the button and growled, "Denise, I told you to hold all calls."

"I'm sorry, Monsieur Malo," his secretary quavered, "but it's Monsieur Triolet, and he wants—"

Malo interrupted her curtly: "All right, put him on." His son-in-law's apology over the intercom was more a matter of politeness than worry. "Sorry to break in on you, Karl, but I can't attend that lunch meeting with you. Some problems have come up in Marseilles. Nothing major, but I should get over there soon and take care of them. May I bring the notes I made for the meeting up to you now?"

"Give me another five minutes, Jean-Noel. I don't think Monsieur

Sawyer will take much longer."

I didn't. I asked him a few more questions. Some concerned his wife.

"Where did she live before she moved to Arles?"

"Paris. That's where she was born. She's lived there most of her life."

"Including during her previous marriage?"

Malo scowled at me. "Yes. Why?"

"The more I know about you and your family, the more I have to work with."

"It's not my wife's past we're concerned with here," he pointed out with an edge of his former harshness. "I'm hiring you to find out whether my son or daughter had any connection with what was done to her. Stick to that."

I managed to wangle his wife's maiden name out of him and then let that line of inquiry drop. The rest I could get without pushing against his resistance. In France marriages and divorces are appended to one's birth certificate. Jacqueline Malo's birth would be registered in Paris, along with her previous husband's name, date and place of birth, and his address at the time they were wed. In this case it would be his death, rather than their divorce, that would be included.

Malo and I settled on my per diem fees and expenses. The latter was to include keeping my Arles hotel room as a base. He would also have a guest room kept ready at his chateau for any time I wanted to work from there. He took a folder from his tray and began studying its contents. I was dismissed.

Jean-Noel Triolet was waiting in Malo's outer office. We exchanged polite nods. He only had one folder with him this time, and no cassette recorder.

* * * *

There was a PTT on the edge of the Fos industrial zone at a junction of three main roads. I went in and gave a postal clerk Fritz Donhoff's phone number in Paris. Then I entered the numbered phone booth assigned to me and waited until we were connected. I was in luck. It wasn't Fritz's answering machine that picked up the call. The heavy, charm-laden voice that came through was Fritz in person.

"How are you, my boy?"

The voice was one of his major assets. It evoked a feeling of trust from other men. Women of all ages still tended to get turned on by it. His accumulated decades hadn't changed that.

I gave him everything Karl Malo had told me—and some things he hadn't. It wasn't necessary to explain what I wanted. Fritz had been an investigator since well before I was born. First as a police detective in Munich. And then, after he'd fled the Nazi takeover in 1938, as a private operator in Paris. Except for some years underground, during the occupation of France by Hitler's forces. Fritz was reputed to have murdered more Nazis than any other member of the Paris Resistance. Something that was difficult to reconcile with his placid amiable manner.

"It seems," he said, "that the first order of business up here would be a thorough check into Alexandre Malo's criminal and quasi-criminal contacts. As well as an investigation of Jacqueline Malo's past life in Paris. Which would include anything interesting I can dig up on her late husband."

"I'd appreciate your getting on it as soon as possible, Fritz."

"Naturally. I'm always pleased to be of help to you, my boy."

I paid the postal clerk for the call and left the PTT building. Next to it was a roadside bar. I took a table under its shade awning. I wanted something to wash the taste of Karl Malo's lousy coffee out of my mouth.

But before anyone came out of the bar to serve me a new Citroën BX station wagon emerged from the industrial complex. When it stopped for the road junction traffic light I saw that the man in it was Malo's son-in-law, Jean-Noel Triolet.

The light changed. Triolet made a left turn and drove west.

If he had a pressing problem in Marseilles, he should have taken the road to the right, going east. No way he could reach Marseilles on the road he *had* taken.

I got back into my car and began following him.

Just a little itch of curiosity about why he was going in the opposite direction from what he'd told Malo.

And at that point in the case I didn't have anything better to follow.

CHAPTER 11

Triolet's route led to the east bank of the Rhône, to the landing for the Barcarin vehicle ferry. His Citroën was one of the first aboard the open, single-deck ferryboat. I squeezed my Peugeot on last. That put several trucks between our cars, blocking our view of each other. There was little danger of Triolet strolling back and seeing me. The crossing takes only six or seven minutes. People are supposed to stay in their vehicles so there'll be no delay in driving off on the other side.

Beyond the west bank of the river the landscape underwent an abrupt, dramatic change. I tailed Malo's son-in-law into the eerie beauty of the Camargue: more than two hundred square miles of salt marshes spreading across the delta of the Bouches-du-Rhône. It resembles parts of the Florida Everglades and Louisiana bayous. There's nothing else like it in western Europe.

Seawater dominates the region. Dry land is at a premium, much of it the work of man; the rest is the result of sand banks built up where the multiple mouths of the river flow into the Mediterranean.

I followed Triolet north from the Barcarin ferry. Then he switched to a road leading west. And finally to another going back south toward the sea. There aren't many roads through the Camargue. The paved ones have to avoid fifty square miles of restricted area: a nature reserve for migratory birds. Triolet's route circled it.

I stayed well behind his Citroën all the way, keeping other vehicles between us where I could. The first leg of his route took us past extensive salt pans and rice paddies, alternating with wild seas of tall marsh grass surrounding networks of little lakes. Going west we had the vast Vaccarès Lagoon on our left. To the right were stretches of terrain drained of water and salt for the cultivation of my favorite wine, *rosé des sables*—so called because it comes out of sandy soil.

Flights of pink flamingos and white egrets passed overhead as I turned south after Triolet. I caught glimpses of the black bulls and white horses raised in the Camargue, wading knee-deep through the marshes. One bull had wandered close to the roadside. While he munched at a clump of Saladelle grass a heron perched on him, eating the flies off his back. A mutually satisfactory partnership if ever I saw one.

But it reminded me that I still hadn't had my own lunch. My stomach began complaining about it—still polite at that stage, but persistent.

The road ended at the small seaside town of Saintes-Maries-de-la-Mer. Triolet parked behind the fortified twelfth-century church whose massive stone tower dominates the town. I watched him leave his Citroën and hurry away, turning into Rue Victor Hugo. Getting out of my own car, I walked after him down the cobbled pedestrian street leading toward the beach.

A lot of the pedestrians were Gypsies. Legend has it that the remains of their patron saint, Sara of Egypt, lie inside the church. The Gypsies of Europe have been making annual pilgrimages to the town to do her honor since the century America was discovered. Many wind up living there.

Triolet crossed the coast road and halted outside the modest local bullring. The cheering inside it could be heard a block away. They were staging a Provençal version of bullfighting that day, with amateur bullfighters and free admission.

I waited on the other side of the road, close to a bakery. Tempting odors rose from its outdoor vending counter. My mouth watered as I watched Triolet stand there irresolutely, looking around at latecomers hurrying past into the bullring.

The two-way traffic between us made it unlikely that he'd spot me when he turned to look back across the street. But I made extra certain by half turning away and bending to purchase a fist-sized *feuilleté à la viande*. I kept my head lowered, watching him out of the corner of my eye, while I took a healthy bite. The fresh-baked croissant dough was nice and crispy, its stuffing of veal, pork, and herbs delicious. My stomach seized on it gratefully.

I lost sight of Triolet when he abruptly turned and entered the bullring. Chewing a second bite of my portable lunch, I dodged the traffic, got to the other side of the road, and went in after him.

* * * *

I entered through a short, shadowy tunnel and re-emerged into the sunlight of the ring's interior oval. Triolet wasn't in sight anywhere close by. I climbed to the top row of the spectator stands for a better view.

It didn't take long. He was standing halfway down, surveying the cheering audience in either direction. He didn't look up toward where I stood. Triolet was concentrating on the ringside area. I finished eating while I kept him under surveillance.

He couldn't seem to find whomever he was looking for. Finally he sat down and watched what was happening on the sandy floor of the bullfight arena.

Traditional Provençal bullfighting doesn't involve murdering bulls. It's a sporting game. The game can get dangerous, but not for the bulls—for the bullfighters, volunteers referred to as *razetteurs*.

There were half a dozen of them down inside the battle zone, chasing and being chased by a fast Camargue bull. In contrast with its shiny blackness, each *razetteur* was dressed entirely in white: sweatshirt, slacks, socks, sneakers. And each was very young. The game requires the agility of youth, as well as its reckless daring.

There was a garland of flowers between the bull's long, curved horns. And an acorn stuck on one of the sharp points. Somebody had already managed to grab the one off the other point. That's the object of the game: to sprint close enough to a charging bull to snatch an acorn while dodging the thrust of its deadly horns.

Malo's son-in-law seemed particularly interested in what was happening. So I watched, too.

Two of the young *razetteurs* were fleeing across the ring with the bull pounding close behind them. Though the bulls aren't trained and tortured into being killers, pure excitement can make them gore or trample a *razetteur* who doesn't move fast enough. Over the years several young men have been killed as a result of being clumsy in the ring.

Suddenly a third *razetteur* executed a risky dash between the fleeing two and the bull pursuing them, shouting and clapping his hands to draw its attention.

He looked somehow familiar.

The bull skidded to a halt, turned, and charged after him. The boy in white made a swift about-face and leapt to one side, ready to grab the acorn from the horn when the bull went past. But this bull was quicker. It turned on a dime, its horns just missing the boy, who jumped backward against the red-hung ring barrier. The bull lowered its head and drove straight at him.

With the barrier against his back, the boy had no space or time to dodge. He did the only thing left: vaulted over the barrier into the safety corridor that was behind it.

Sometimes bulls get so worked up by the chase that *they* leap the barrier, too, and go charging around the circle of the safety corridor. When they do everybody in it has to jump the barrier into the ring to get away. But this one contented itself with butting against the barrier twice. Then it turned around, swinging its head back and forth while it decided which of the taunting *razetteurs* it was going to chase next.

Triolet was no longer watching the action inside the ring. His gaze followed the boy who'd leapt the barrier. The boy was striding around the safety corridor, getting closer to my vantage point. Then he hauled himself up to the lowest row of spectator benches, where a young man and two teen-age girls hugged and kissed him.

I moved halfway down through the stands and squinted, focusing on the boy's face. I'd seen that face before, in a frame on Karl Malo's desk.

Malo's son, Alexandre.

In person he looked like a much younger edition of his father. And from what Malo had told me, they shared much else besides that handsome face. They'd been born into the winners' circle with the same lucky combination: looks, wealth, and brains. Enough to make other men hate them on sight.

Alexandre Malo plopped down on the bench, grinning and panting. I watched him reach behind the bench and bring up a plastic water bottle. He drank thirstily before putting the bottle back down where he'd gotten it. Then he slipped his arm around the waist of one of the two girls. She was worth squeezing: pretty and scrumptious in cut-off jeans and a skimpy halter. But Alexandre was concentrating more on what was going on in the ring.

The black bull still had the acorn on its horn. The boys in white were dancing around while it did some broken-field runs between them.

I looked back to where I'd last seen Jean-Noel Triolet. He was no longer there. I glanced around quickly but couldn't find him in the crowd. Working my way down to where he'd been sitting, I tried again. I still couldn't locate him.

I was doing a slow, methodical scan of the circle of lower benches when the sight of somebody else stopped me.

It was a sturdy man of medium height, wearing a flamboyant shirt of fire-engine red. He was making his way through the stands in my general direction. But he didn't appear to have seen me yet.

It had been a long time since I'd last seen him. But he wasn't someone I'd ever be likely to forget.

Johnny Duncan.

He went all the way back to my youth in Chicago. We had shared a good chunk of the years between then and now. In ways that bind people as surely as blood ties.

My instant impulse was to cut over to where I could intercept Johnny. But first I had to relocate Triolet. I resumed my detailed scan—and spotted him.

Triolet was about two hundred feet away, partially screened by a cluster of spectators, staring my way. I saw the grim mouth open slightly in shock as he recognized me.

In the same moment Johnny Duncan appeared in front of me, slapping my arm with a hard muscular hand, his tough face lit by the same old devil-may-care grin:

"Christ sake, Pete! What're you doing here? Last I heard you were living all the way over near Monaco."

"Still do," I told him. "But I'm on a job."

Triolet had stopped looking my way. He sat down and gave his attention to the bullfight.

Alexandre Malo had jumped back into the arena and was racing over to make the bull come at him.

Johnny was still grinning with delight. "I can't get over this. You look great, Pete. Same as ever."

"You, too, Johnny."

"Nah, I'm getting old."

He'd be fifty-two now, but if age was catching up with him, I couldn't see it. I said, "How's life been treating you?"

"Better than I treat it, I guess." Johnny shrugged. "Not too bad, all things considered."

"What're you doing here?" I asked him.

"I live nearby, lately. In Aigues-Mortes. Come over here sometimes to watch their bullfights. Not as much of a turn-on as the Spanish ones, but—"

He was cut off in midsentence by an alarmed roar from the crowd.

* * * *

Young Alexandre Malo had fallen in the sand near us with the bull charging him. None of the other *razetteurs* was close enough to divert it. Alexandre rolled just in time. The hooves pounded past him, churning sand from the spot where he'd fallen.

He rolled again and came up on one knee, rubbing a hand across his forehead. The bull skidded to a halt and swung back toward him. Alexandre lurched to his feet and ran toward the barrier below us. But he was very slow, and his movements seemed badly coordinated.

He tripped over his feet and fell again.

The bull was almost on top of him when it stopped and hesitated. What it would do next hung on the extent and temper of its excitement. The black head lowered, those long, sharp horns aiming at the kid.

Johnny had already dropped into the safety corridor behind the barrier. His reactions had always been just a notch quicker than mine. The next instant he was over the barrier and inside the ring, waving his arms and stamping his feet, snarling insults at the bull.

It raised its head and looked at him, still hesitating. Maybe it was the outrageous red of Johnny's shirt that tipped the scales. The bull turned from the boy and went for Johnny. He ran away across the ring as fast as he could, which was still pretty fast. His survival drive was on a par with his reaction time.

A couple of people jumped the barrier to help Alexandre Malo out of the ring. Three young *razetteurs* raced toward Johnny and diverted the bull away from him.

By then I'd switched my attention to the bench where Alexandre had rested briefly with his friends. They were climbing down to him, still looking scared. He leaned against the base of the stands for support, shaking his head groggily. Then he slid down to sit on the ground, his friends bending over him anxiously.

A stocky, swarthy man with a short mustache had been seated directly behind them. Now he was making his way to the exit tunnel. He carried what looked like the water bottle Alexandre had drunk from.

I shoved through the crowd after him. He vanished inside the tunnel. All the other people were pushing toward ringside for a better look at what was happening there. I got past the last of them and hurried into the tunnel. The guy I was after was already going out the other end, turning into the street outside.

As I went after him there was a sound behind me. But I was too intent on catching the swarthy man with the bottle to spare a look behind.

Something slammed across the back of my skull.

It was lucky the tunnel was carpeted with sand, because I landed hard, face down.

CHAPTER 12

My brain went numb for a while. But the blow hadn't connected solidly enough to send me all the way out. Probably because I'd been moving, and so had whoever slugged me. My assailant jumped over me and sprinted away. I caught a blurred glimpse of black sneakers and the bottoms of a pair of dungarees just before they vanished beyond the street end of the tunnel. That's all I got to see of the slugger. I was too engrossed in lifting a heavy, throbbing head and wiping sand from my eyes.

In time I got my hands and knees under me and crawled to one side of the tunnel. Sitting there, leaning against the wall, I gave my scrambled brain a chance to sort itself out.

The throbbing got more painful, but localized itself around the spot where I'd been hit. My vision cleared.

An elderly couple coming out through the tunnel—farmers, judging by their clothing—stopped to ask if I was all right.

I said I thought I would be.

The man advised me it wasn't good to drink too much out in the midday sun.

I agreed with him.

The woman asked if I wanted some help getting up.

I said, "Not yet, thank you."

Before leaving, they advised me to get some sleep.

It sounded like a swell idea, but I resisted it. More time went by. Finally I summoned the initiative to try standing up. It wasn't as bad as I'd expected. I had a headache, but I didn't shake or sway.

I walked back through the tunnel slowly, like an old man who needed a cane but had forgotten to bring one.

* * * *

The midday sun the farmer had warned me about made me narrow my eyes to slits. I stopped on the steps between the stands. A different bull was out in the ring now, bigger but less enthusiastic. The boys in white were having difficulty making it break into a real charge. It preferred fending the *razetteurs* off with minimal efforts, snorting and kicking up sand, then making quick surprise turns with threatening feints of the horns that prevented them from getting close enough to snatch an acorn.

Alexandre Malo and his three young friends weren't anywhere in sight.

Karl Malo's son-in-law, Jean-Noel Triolet, was gone, too.

I sat down on a step and thought about what had happened to me. And why it had happened.

Somebody hadn't wanted me to catch the guy with the water bottle. That much was clear. What wasn't clear was how that somebody had known I was a threat.

The one who'd slugged me in the tunnel had not gotten the information from Triolet. I was certain Triolet hadn't been aware I was following him until he registered shock at seeing me in the stands. After that I'd had him under surveillance. He hadn't pointed me out to anyone. There'd been no one close to him who wore that combination of dungarees and black sneakers.

He'd been watching Johnny Duncan lure the bull away from Alexandre when I'd headed for the tunnel after the guy with the bottle. Even if Triolet had immediately gone and found the slugger and sent him after me, it would have been too late by then. The slugger wouldn't have had a chance of catching up with me.

I hadn't been slugged just because I happened to be going out through the tunnel behind the guy with the water bottle. I could have been anybody leaving the bullring to tend to other business.

Unless someone had known, well beforehand, that I was a potential source of trouble. Someone who'd kept me under close watch, ready to deal with it if I did become an active threat.

The headache didn't help my problem-solving prowess, and it wasn't getting better. I thought about getting myself out of that hot sun and into a cool, dim bar.

Johnny Duncan came through the stands toward me. "Where the hell'd you get to? I've been searching..." Then he was close enough to see the sand still clinging to my face and clothes. "What happened to you?"

"I got clobbered." I touched the back of my head and winced. I winced more when Johnny moved behind me and probed the sore point with his blunt fingers.

"No blood," he told me. "Skin's not even broke. Just a big bump, and you'll have a bad bruise. You're not at death's door." Johnny sat down beside me. "Who did it?"

"Didn't see him."

"Something to do with the job you're on?"

"Probably," I said. "What happened to Alexandre Malo?"

"Who?"

"The kid who fell in the ring. The one you jumped in and played hero for."

"Oh. His friends took him away." Johnny waved a hand toward one of the other exit tunnels. "Said they'd drive him home."

"Did a doctor get a look at him first?"

"Yeah, but the kid wouldn't let him do any real examination. Said there was nothing wrong with him. He just got dizzy out there all of a sudden. Said it must have been the sun and something he ate."

"Or drank," I said. "He was drugged."

Johnny nodded. "He sure acted like it. That'd be why he wouldn't let the doc examine him. The kid probably took too many uppers or downers to set his nerves right for tackling the bulls. Maybe a combo of the two."

"No," I said, "he didn't know he was taking it. Somebody slipped the dope into his water bottle."

Johnny looked interested. "*That* got something to do with the job you're on?"

"Tell you about it over some medication." I got to my feet. Carefully. "Strong coffee with a lot of brandy in it. And some aspirin. Codeine would be better, if you know where to get it in this town."

"Uh-uh," Johnny said firmly as he stood up beside me. "Not around me you don't. *You* know better than to mix drugs and liquor."

"Sometimes it does the job quicker."

"It'll put you in your grave quicker, is what it'll do. You get one or the other. The dope or the liquor. Not both."

There weren't many people Johnny really gave much of a damn about. Like a lot of men who've spent years as cops, he'd built up too thick an armor against becoming suicidally disgusted with humanity. But he'd gotten into the habit of acting as my mentor long before. It had started when I was a rookie and Johnny was already a detective first grade. After he'd switched to being a federal narc he'd talked the brass there into taking me, too. He'd been my boss, and a good one, when we'd begun operating for them overseas in France.

Johnny's concern for me was as genuine as it was rare for him. It was his way of returning the favor he felt he owed my family. My grandfather had been his rabbi in the Chicago police force, the one he could always turn to when he needed help.

"Let's find us a bar first," I told him. "The nearer the better. Then I'll decide."

Whoever had clobbered me in that tunnel had to be long gone by then. It still felt safer, going through it again in my present condition, having Johnny Duncan along with me.

    Only I didn't want to believe one of the reasons it felt safer.

    So I forced the thought out of my aching head.

    But it didn't go far.

CHAPTER 13

"Remember the first time we met?" Johnny Duncan had an uncharacteristic tinge of nostalgia in his tone. He was working on his third brandy, which may have had something to do with it, but the Johnny Duncan I remembered could hold his liquor better than that.

"I can still smell it," I said. "Hair tonic and talc."

"Yeah. The Drake barbershop, in the arcade on East Walton. You were there with your granddaddy. You must've been, what—about fifteen?"

"Sixteen, I think."

"And already taller than me. I didn't like that much. Always *was* sore about not growing up to be Gary Cooper. But I forgave you—on account of your granddaddy. He was one wonderful guy."

"A good man," I agreed.

"He's why I was there that day," Johnny said. "There was this shitheel lieutenant giving me a hard time about how I'd handled an armed robbery suspect. Going to louse up my promotion over it. It was a Saturday, and I knew your granddaddy always went to the Drake every Saturday noon for a trim. From old Angie Sorello—he was still head barber in those days. And you were getting your hair cut in the next chair. And your granddaddy introduced us to each other, real formal-like."

"And he got the lieutenant off your back."

"Yeah. Your granddaddy—I really loved that man. Shame he had to die like that, only three years into retirement."

"He didn't *have to*," I said. "He committed suicide."

"I wouldn't exactly call it suicide, Pete. He was always a pretty heavy drinker."

"Not like after he retired from the department. He got to be a genuine alcoholic, Johnny. And he wouldn't take the pledge, even after his insides got shot to hell."

Johnny's grimace of regret momentarily softened the tough, square face. "Well, here's to him." Johnny raised his brandy glass in a toast to my grandfather's memory. "He was the best, in his time."

I nodded. I could do that by then without my head exploding. Four aspirins, a strong *café noir*, and the soothing cool of the air conditioning were bringing the ache under control.

Johnny had driven me a short way out of Saintes-Maries-de-la-Mer, to one of the coastal defense installations left over from the war. It had been part of an artillery block, most of which had been blown apart long before.

What remained included a raised observation and gun cupola. Its reinforced concrete hulk rose out of the beach, dividing a long stretch used by normal sunbathers from a section assigned to nudists. An enterprising couple had bought it from the government, cut some windows through its thick walls, and converted it into a bar. They'd had a hyperrealist artist cover it with a giant-sized painting of the head of a girl sticking her tongue out. Her face was taller than me, and the tongue was as wide as my chest. Cute. Trendy.

The big attraction inside the girl's head, other than the drinks, was the air conditioning. People who'd had enough of broiling their bodies under the summer sun kept wandering in to cool off. Which required buying at least one drink apiece. The bar wasn't going broke.

At the next table a couple of women were taking their time over some kind of tall pinkish cocktails. They'd come in off the nudist beach, wrapping themselves in towels that hung from under their armpits to a few decorous inches below their hips. One towel was white and the other green. I kept getting distracted by the green towel. Which proved Johnny had been right: I wasn't at death's door.

"So tell me," Johnny said, "what's this job that got you the bump on the head?"

I returned my attention to Johnny. In addition to the fire-engine-red shirt he was wearing a suede sports jacket, black leather trousers, and high-heeled Mexican style cowboy boots. The flamboyance was normal for him. So was wearing more than anybody else could tolerate in the summer heat. Johnny didn't sweat. Not emotionally, either. Any inner turmoil stayed inside. Outside, all he ever showed the world was a hard stare. Except when he flashed that rakish grin—and that didn't always mean he was full of joy.

I told him about the Malo case in detail, including its background. While I talked I let my gaze drift back to the woman in the green towel. She was looking my way. She smiled at me. I smiled back.

And then, in midsentence, I suddenly switched my attention back to Johnny's face.

But all I saw in it was a normal amount of interest in what I was telling him.

I did my best to shove that ugly notion out of my head again.

* * * *

When I got to the part of my story where I'd been instructed to drop off the ransom, Johnny interrupted me: "Hey, that's close to where we spotted Theo Moreale. Remember?"

"I remember," I said. It wasn't the first time that memory had surfaced since my running into Johnny at the bullring.

It had been in my early months as a federal narc in France. Johnny had gotten me assigned to his undercover operation along the south coast. One reason he'd wanted me was that I could pass as a French criminal, blend into the underworld *milieu,* and pick up rumors. Johnny's French had been excellent by then, but he never did lose his American accent.

But it had been Johnny who'd turned up the tip about a smuggler named Theo Moreale. Most of the unprocessed heroin that passed through labs around Marseilles before being sent to the States came in by ship. But Moreale was said to be bringing regular loads of the raw *blanche* across from Italy into France via some trail through the mountains behind the Riviera. I spent almost three weeks in those mountains with Johnny before we got lucky one night, a few miles above Sospel, and spotted Moreale coming through with a couple of helpers.

Since we didn't have the right to arrest anyone in France, we passed the information about the trail Moreale was using to the *stups*—French narcotics agents. They laid traps along that trail for almost a month. But Moreale didn't use it again in all that time.

"Some cop," Johnny growled over a sip of his brandy, "got himself a nice bundle of cash for tipping off Moreale. All that work for nothing."

I smiled at him and said carelessly, "Except we got to know that part of those mountains real well."

"That we surely did," Johnny agreed, just as carelessly, and he took another sip of brandy.

* * * *

I continued my account of the case I was on, bringing him up to date. When I described the man I'd seen carrying away Alexandre Malo's water bottle, Johnny said reflectively, "Short and swarthy—could be a Gypsy."

"Or any of a dozen other dark Mediterranean races," I pointed out.

"Sure, but there does happen to be a big concentration of Gypsies in this area. Most of them okay, but some are professional thieves."

"He wasn't *stealing* the kid's bottle, for Crissake. He was removing it—because somebody knew that I'd guess it was used to dope Malo's son and that I'd want to have it analyzed. So somebody there knew *me*—who I am and what I do. And that I'd worked for Malo before and might again."

"There's Malo's son-in-law. This Triolet."

"It wasn't him," I said. "He didn't have the opportunity, after he spotted me there, to sic somebody on me."

Johnny gave it some thought. "You've dealt with a hell of a lot of French criminals in your time, Pete. One of them *could* be involved somehow with this case you're working. Been there at the bullring and recognized you."

"That is one possibility," I admitted.

Johnny called for a refill. I ordered another *café noir* and a glass of cold milk.

He gave all I'd told him some thought until our orders arrived. "Figure there's a connection between the kidnap and what just almost happened to the kid?"

"Beats me," I said. "Except one happened to Malo's wife and the other to his son."

Johnny nodded. "Sure sounds like they could be connected. Then again, they might not be. You don't know enough yet to tell one way or the other."

"I'm just getting started. Give me time."

"Wild thought," Johnny said, "in case you need help with your investigation. You *could* hire *me*." He was half kidding, but only half. "Put me on your expense account. For a guy like Karl Malo that'd be small change. He wouldn't even notice. And I've been kinda at loose ends lately."

"I'll keep it in mind," I said. I drank some cold milk, watching him over the rim of the glass. I didn't let my attention stray back to the temptress in the green towel. "What *are* you up to these days?" I asked it casually. That wasn't easy with Johnny Duncan; he didn't miss nuances.

But neither did I, and we were equally experienced at concealment. You don't survive years as an undercover narc without being a competent role player. It requires looking the enemy in the eye without letting him see you're his enemy, sometimes over months of close contact, before you finally drop the boom on him.

Just then Johnny and I were a couple old friends naturally interested in each other's doings. The fact that we could play those roles didn't necessarily mean they were false.

"I guess," Johnny said, "you know all about my getting fired."

Not all, but a little had come my way. Johnny had dropped his job as a narc when the CIA had dangled a better offer for his accumulated know-how and undercover contacts. That was some years before I'd made my own shift to being European investigator for the Senate Foreign Relations Committee. A long period had followed during which I hadn't seen or heard much about him. Then, a bit less than two years back, rumors had started circulating that Johnny was using his CIA leverage to earn private income on the side.

I said, "I heard you quit."

"Sure—like you *quit* being a Senate investigator. I hear they found out you destroyed evidence against a gangster brokering illegal deals between U.S. and French companies."

"It was an old debt," I said. The gangster was Arlette's father. I'd still been living the carefree life inside my mother's womb when he'd saved Babette from the Gestapo in the last weeks of her war. "Like most old debts, when it finally fell due it had to be paid off the hard way."

"To Marcel Alfani."

"You've still got long ears."

"I keep some of the old connections here and there. They say you only managed to stay out of the slam for that one by blackmailing a senator on the committee." That was one of the reasons I was working in Europe instead of in the States. There were too many government characters back there eager to nail me the next time I made a misstep.

I drank the rest of my milk. "It wasn't exactly blackmail. I only asked the senator if he was in love with the hooker he kept sneaking off to Baltimore to spend his weekends with."

Johnny laughed. "I guess I'm the one who taught you how to play that dirty."

"I sure didn't learn it from my grandfather."

"No," Johnny said seriously, "he was a straight arrow his whole life. I admired that, but…"

I nodded. "A hard act to follow."

Johnny picked up his glass, swirling the brandy remaining in it. "Well, I didn't *exactly* blackmail the CIA either. I didn't want to go to jail, and they didn't want me spilling my guts in court about some of their nastier covert operations. So we just parted by mutual agreement. Mutual, but not too friendly."

"And since then?"

Johnny shrugged. "This and that. Whatever I can pick up. Some of it's even legal. And the rest's not *too* illegal. But none of it's making me rich." He leaned back in his chair, looking just a bit weary. "I've got a girlfriend over in Aigues-Mortes. Runs a little restaurant she got from her parents. When I'm around I get free meals and bed. I don't know what she gets out of it. She's only twenty-six. And me—I'm not that great a lover anymore."

"You never were that crazy about women," I reminded him.

"Sure. Get my rocks off and get out and forget 'em. That was me.

But…maybe it's age. I really *like* this girl, Pete. Name's Suzanne." His smile was small but genuine. "Sweet girl. More'n I deserve."

What he was saying, along with the tone and smile, reminded me strongly of Karl Malo talking about his present wife. The similarity was startling in men so different in every other way.

Johnny finished his drink and got a thought: "Hey, come on over to Aigues-Mortes with me and meet her. You can have dinner with us. Suzanne's a real good cook."

"I'd like to, Johnny, but there's too much I've got to start checking into around Arles right now. Can I take a rain check?"

"Okay, but I'm not always around. Sometimes I've got to go off one place or another to earn a buck."

"I'll phone and make sure you're there when I can make it," I promised. I took out my notebook, and he gave me the number to call.

When I paid our bill he started to protest: "I'm the one invited you here."

"But I'm the one with the fat expense account."

"True." He draped an arm across my shoulders as we left the bar. "And don't forget, I *am* available, if those expenses can handle a well-paid assistant sleuth."

His car was a ten-year-old Volkswagen. He drove me to the *place* where I'd left my Peugeot. Triolet's Citroën was gone.

Johnny flashed his grin before we parted. "Be *sure* you call us, Pete. I'll see to it Suzanne whomps up one of her really special dinners when you come. Don't make it a long wait."

"You'll hear from me," I assured him.

* * * *

All the way up through the Camargue to Arles the ugly notion kept nagging at me.

Johnny Duncan had spent several long periods in Italy, both as a narc and as a CIA agent. He *could* have used an Italian accent to cover his American one when speaking French.

I reminded myself that Johnny wasn't tall enough to have been the kidnapper with the Italian accent. Jacqueline Malo had described him as being as big as me.

I also told myself that what Johnny had said was valid: it could have been *anyone* from my past who'd recognized me at the bullring. That wouldn't be any more of a coincidence than Johnny's being there.

And no connection between him and Jean-Noel Triolet would fit the quirky timing of the kidnap. Triolet had been far away in New York when it happened.

That added up to several solid reasons for not allowing the suspicion about Johnny to exacerbate my headache. Plus, I didn't want to believe it.

One additional factor in his favor: Suppose there *was* some connection between the kidnap and Malo's son being doped a couple months later in an attempt to get him killed in the bullring. *If* Johnny had something to do with the latter, why had he jumped in to help the boy?

Unfortunately, I could come up with an obvious answer to that one, if I really wanted to. I didn't. But it *would* fit with the way I'd been put out of action—for just long enough, and with the very minimum of violence necessary. It also fitted one of two opposite reasons for feeling safer when I'd had Johnny escorting me.

Suspect a friend and you wind up judging yourself. I was probably wrong, as well as unjust.

Right or wrong, he was no longer with me. That thought made me pull over onto a muddy shoulder between road and marsh. I took the H & K P7 out of its hiding place and strapped it on. That meant having to put on my lightweight denim jacket to conceal the gun, in spite of the swampy Camargue heat.

I drove the rest of the way feeling both worse and better: less comfortable but more secure.

CHAPTER 14

"Monsieur Sawyer, this is Jean-Noel Triolet. I need to meet with you in private. To discuss something extremely personal. Are you free now?"

I seemed destined to be wakened out of a sound sleep by phone calls from members of the Malo family. To be fair, they did call when they assumed a normal person would be awake. Daylight still filtered through the louvers of my hotel room's window shutters, though not as strongly as when I'd stretched out for a short nap. I squinted at my watch beside the bed. The nap had stretched. It was a few minutes past eight P.M.

Time to pull myself together anyway. I had another dinner date with Babette. And another breakfast date in the morning before driving her to the train for Paris. By which point, hopefully, she would feel I had carried out my filial duties so charmingly that she wouldn't have the heart to sell the house out from under me.

"Where are you calling from?" I asked Triolet.

"I'm down in the lobby."

"I can join you there in about twenty minutes."

"I would prefer to meet in your room," Triolet said. "For the privacy. Is it possible?"

"Give me the twenty minutes," I told him. "Then come up." I disconnected, called room service, and ordered a pot of strong coffee before climbing off the bed and heading for the shower.

* * * *

I had intended to go on to the Malo chateau when I drove north out of the Camargue. But the aspirin had stopped helping before I reached Arles. So I stopped off at a pharmacy and bought the strongest painkiller they could give me without a prescription. I downed two of the pills with a tall glass of Vittel in a bistro near the pharmacy and then sat there waiting to see if they worked. They did. But they also had a more powerful sedative effect than I'd expected. The pain went, and heavy lethargy settled in its place.

It was only a few miles further to the chateau, but there was no point in driving there half-asleep. I wouldn't accomplish much until my brain came out of its stupor. So I trudged two blocks to my hotel instead.

I managed to assert myself against the sedative long enough to make just one phone call from my room. It was to the Malo chateau. I got the butler. His name was Claude Girard. Karl Malo had already briefed him about me by phone.

Girard told me Alexandre had returned home some time earlier and gone to his suite for a nap, leaving instructions that he wasn't to be disturbed. He was still sleeping. If what had been slipped in his bottle was as powerful as the pills I'd taken, I could well understand that.

I told Girard to warn the boy, when he did wake up, that somebody might have been trying to get him killed in that bullring. I didn't know why. Nor was I sure there'd be another attempt—at least as long as I was around. Whoever had been involved in that day's attempt knew I had been alerted. That would make it difficult to pass off another try as an accident.

But just in case, I told Girard, "Try to see to it that Alexandre stays put at the chateau until I get there and have a talk with him. Have his father lean on him, if that's what it takes."

"We'll try," Girard said. He didn't sound too confident of success. "When should we expect you?"

I said I'd probably be there shortly before noon the next day. Between my nap and Babette and some necessary morning chores, I wasn't likely to get myself loose any earlier.

After hanging up the phone I'd stretched out for that nap—and it had developed into the deep sleep I'd finally been jarred out of by Triolet's call.

* * * *

My head no longer hurt except when I touched the tender swelling at the back of my skull. I couldn't think of any reason other than masochism to try that more than once. Inside the skull all departments seemed back to functional. A cold shower cleared the last of the fog out. Coffee arrived while I was getting dressed. It continued the good work. I was on my second cup when Triolet knocked at my door.

It was a big room, and my dining table was a long way from the door. I had to shout my invitation to come in. I'd taken the precaution of stuffing my gun down between the two cushions of the small sofa on which I sat. But Triolet didn't have anybody else with him, and there was no hint of threat in his manner. He just looked worried and embarrassed.

The floorboards creaked under his feet as he came across the room. They were beautifully polished but warped by age. I gestured to a chair, and Triolet sat in it, facing me, holding himself stiffly.

"I've come here to ask you to do me a favor," he said uncomfortably, and then he paused to consider how to phrase what he wanted to say next.

"How did you know where to find me?" I asked.

"Karl—my father-in-law told me you were staying here."

"When he told you what I was doing for him."

"Yes."

"When was that?"

"Less than an hour ago. At the chateau." Triolet tried to work off some of his nervousness by making a slight and unnecessary adjustment to his perfectly positioned necktie. This one was maroon. The suit he wore with it was brown, and as sincere as his blue one. His basic expression was as grim as the one he had worn when I'd first seen him.

"My father-in-law," he said, "was a bit surprised not to find *you* at the chateau—already starting your, ah…investigation."

"I had some investigating to do here first," I told him.

The fact the Malo hadn't told him about me until that recently didn't mean Triolet couldn't have worked it out for himself well before. He'd been in Malo's office when Malo had mentioned my name over his intercom. He would have known that name belonged to the private eye Malo had hired in Monaco two months before. It didn't take all the intelligence Triolet obviously possessed to figure out I must be working for Malo again.

And that, if my hunch was correct, was what had sent Triolet scurrying to Saintes-Maries-de-la-Mer after telling Malo he was going to Marseilles. Hunches can be false. This one felt solid enough to lean on, unless and until something came along to disprove it.

Triolet bent toward me with his elbows braced on the arms of his chair and his lean hands locked together. "I've come here to ask you *please* not to mention my being in Saintes-Maries-de-la-Mer today. To my father-in-law—or anyone else. That would force me to make up explanations that…"

He let it hang there, his eyes probing mine, seeking a willingness to share and keep his secret.

I stared back and waited.

"You see," Triolet resumed finally, with increasing embarrassment, "the fact is, I went there to meet a woman. A friend. A—I'm sure you understand."

I said, "You're not worried I'll tell *that* to your father-in-law. Or your wife."

"Why *should* you? It has nothing to do with what you are investigating. It's purely a personal matter. An indiscretion, perhaps. But—between men, you can surely understand how these things arise, in any marriage."

My nod wasn't committal enough for him. He added after a moment, in a tightened tone, "I'll *pay* you—if that is what you want to keep what I've just revealed between the two of us."

I said, "You didn't know your brother-in-law was going to be in that bullring today?"

The change of subject didn't knock him off stride for more than a second. "No, but it didn't surprise me." Triolet shrugged. "Alex often acts like a fool, well below his intelligence level. Always testing his courage in ways that have nothing to do with real courage. Bullfighting is one of his less dangerous stupidities."

"It got dangerous for him today," I said.

"Yes. It was lucky for him that man jumped in to distract the bull on time."

"You don't know that man?"

That seemed to startle him. "No, I can't recall ever seeing him before. Why?"

"Just a stray thought." I took a sip of coffee and put the cup down without taking my eyes off him.

He smiled uneasily. "I must say, I was quite surprised to see *you* there."

"You looked it."

"I assume you followed me there from Fos."

"Why would I do that?"

"I imagine you consider all of us as suspects, Monsieur Sawyer. Isn't that how people in your line of work go about it? Checking on everyone in hopes of discovering something that will narrow it down for you?"

"I went to that bullring for the same reason you did," I said. "To meet a friend."

"Oh." Triolet managed to keep disbelief out of his tone. Polite of him.

"My friend's an American," I said. "John Duncan. He's the man you saw jump into the ring to save your young brother-in-law."

"Really. That's interesting. Your friend is a brave man." If Triolet knew Johnny, I couldn't detect a hint of it in his reactions. But Triolet had to be practiced at stonewalling his way through company negotiations. He had to be *very* good at it to remain Malo's second-in-command. Being a son-in-law isn't enough to carry you far through the unforgiving machinations of the big business inferno.

I asked him, "What do you think happened to your brother-in-law in that ring today? The way he was suddenly fumbling and falling?"

"I imagine Alex took too many pills to work up his courage."

"That's what my friend John Duncan said," I told him. "Almost the exact words."

"It would seem to be the obvious explanation, wouldn't it?" Triolet dropped that subject and returned to his reason for coming to see me. "Monsieur Sawyer—*will* you keep my being there today to yourself?"

"Probably."

"Thank you," he said, with considerable relief. "If you do want payment for doing so, my offer *was* a sincere one."

"I'm sure it was." I drank the rest of my coffee.

Triolet studied me. "But you don't want money."

"Not that kind."

"Then I must thank you again. With more feeling. You have my gratitude. Perhaps I can repay you in other ways in the future." He got up, ready to leave.

I said, "I'd like to know what you think about what Karl Malo has hired me to do."

He hesitated slightly and then said it: "I think Karl is wasting his money and your time. But if it reassures him…"

"You believe whatever I learn *will* reassure him."

"Certainly. Claudette—my wife—would have had absolutely no reason to be involved in what happened to Jacqueline. And Alex—he can be a headstrong fool at times, but he's not insane. And since I know *I* had nothing to do with it…" He ended with a humorless smile.

"You've no thoughts at all on who *might* have done it."

A small, cynical grimace thinned Triolet's mouth. Grimacing came more easily to that mouth than smiling. "Obviously it was someone who had done that sort of thing before, made a small fortune out of doing it this time, and got away with it. Beyond that, I've no idea at all."

He thanked me a third time before leaving. When he was gone I put through a call to Paris. This time I got Fritz's answering machine. I left a message for him to add Jean-Noel Triolet and Johnny Duncan to his list of names to be investigated. I was especially interested in finding out if their paths had ever crossed before.

CHAPTER 15

I saw Babette off on the train to Paris the next morning at ten-thirty. Then I bought myself a new suitcase and filled it with new clothes and a spare toilet kit. The best of everything. The cost was going on the Malo expense account. Some of the new clothing I left at the hotel. The rest I took along when I drove the few miles from Arles to the chateau.

The Malo estate spread over a low hill. Every truly old habitation in the area is on a hill, including Arles. Back in the Middle Ages the region was as waterlogged as the Camargue. The inhabited hills were islands in those days, and travel between them required a boat.

Parts of the Malo chateau were very old, though there were additions that didn't date back further than a century or so. All of it was in excellent condition, which was not that common among the chateaux of France. Most of the old families no longer have the Malo kind of loot to invest in extensive repairs and constant maintenance.

The main building had angled wings, one ending at a square tower that looked fifteenth-century. The bottom of the tower had been converted into a four-car garage. I reached it via a winding graveled drive shaded by enormous plane trees. There was a Bentley outside the garage.

It was being polished by a chauffeur in his sixties. I parked beside it, got out with my new suitcase, and explained who I was. The chauffeur promised to give my Peugeot a wash as soon as he finished with the Bentley.

I told him not to bother. He replied with a severe brand of dignity, "It is my pleasure as well as my job, monsieur. An idle old man is a dead man."

He used a phone inside the garage. I was met at the main building's entrance by a man in his late fifties wearing a light tan jacket and dark trousers. Claude Girard, the Malo butler.

He had a round, entirely bald head set on heavy shoulders with not much neck between. His thick body was encased in the kind of hard fat that usually means harder muscle underneath. Like a walrus. He carried himself with military erectness, and there was an old soldier's patience in the cool gray of his deep-set eyes.

Girard took my suitcase and led me up a wide, curved staircase and along a corridor to the guest room assigned to me. It was a good size, with its own bathroom and furnishings that were comfortable but not ostentatious. The windows overlooked the extensive gardens out front. Girard put my suitcase down on a mahogany luggage stand and informed me that Karl Malo and Jean-Noel Triolet had long since left for the company headquarters in Fos.

I asked if Alexandre Malo was around.

"He drove off half an hour ago," Girard said regretfully. He didn't know where the boy had gone or when he would be back. "He said," Girard added, "that your notion that somebody tried to kill him was... mistaken."

I knew the boy had used stronger words than that. I'd already heard about his reaction the previous night—from his father. There'd been a message to call Malo waiting for me at the hotel when I'd returned from dinner with Babette. It had been late, but Malo was waiting for my call. He'd wanted to know exactly why I thought someone was trying to murder his son.

I hadn't given him all the details, but there was enough in what I did tell to make Malo ask if it wouldn't be a good idea for him to hire a full-time bodyguard for his son. I'd said it might be helpful as a short-term precaution.

In the long run, the only way to stop a determined, patient assassin is to catch him before the attempt.

I asked Girard, "Has the boy got somebody with him?"

"I'm afraid not, monsieur. Alexandre rejected his father's suggestion of a bodyguard. Quite forcibly."

I'd already noted the butler's familiar use of the boy's first name. He didn't do that when speaking of other family members.

"Your Alexandre," I said, "isn't much for taking advice, is he?"

"Not even from me," Girard acknowledged. "And we have always been very close."

"At least *you* take my warning seriously," I said. "What kind of gun is that you're wearing?"

Girard patted a slight bulge in his jacket at the small of his back. "You're the first to notice. It's a compact Smith & Wesson .38. Old but still dependable. We've been together a long time."

I didn't ask how experienced he was with it. Everything about Girard answered that. He would be as dependable as the weapon. I asked if it was part of his normal attire or only since my warning the night before.

"I've been keeping it handy since what happened to Madame Malo," Girard told me. "Monsieur Malo is particularly concerned that the same thing should not happen to his grandson."

I asked if Malo's daughter, Claudette, was at home.

Girard nodded. "Madame Triolet is out at the pool."

"With her child?"

"No, the baby is usually with Agnes, his nurse. The nursery and Agnes's quarters have a floor to themselves in the east wing. Above the suite of Monsieur and Madame Triolet."

Girard took me back downstairs to show me the way to the pool. We went toward the rear of the chateau through a long, wide hallway. Marble flooring with old Persian carpets. Darkly glossy oak-paneled walls with ornately framed ancestral portraits. Regency side tables with collections of pre-Columbian pottery and Byzantine silver. We passed several closed doors and an archway to a library where a couple of maids were busy dusting and vacuuming.

At the end of the hallway tall louvered doors opened onto a large courtyard flanked by a square stone tower like the one out front. The courtyard in turn opened on a vista of landscaped grounds. They contained a red clay tennis court and a swimming pool surrounded by a blue-tiled patio, with a white-painted changing cabin between them. The rear gardens spread past those to a large greenhouse. Behind it three gardeners were at work along a terrace of fruit trees and stone fountains. Beyond that the land dropped out of sight. The next things in view were Montmajour Abbey atop one distant hill and the orange-tiled roofs of the village of Fontvielle on another.

Malo's daughter, Claudette Triolet, appeared as I followed a flagstone path leading to the pool. She was climbing onto the diving board at the far end. Her wet helmet of curly blond hair was bleached pale by the sun. She wore a black bikini-style bottom. Every inch of skin not covered by it was tanned the same dark brown. Her figure was a slim contrast to the round face. The combination gave her the look of being only a year or so past adolescence.

She bounced off the board, executed a neat jackknife, and disappeared underwater with scarcely a ripple.

* * * *

I could see her again when I reached the near end of the pool. She was still under water, swimming breaststroke the length of the pool. She didn't surface until she reached my end. Opening her mouth for a drag of air, she braced her elbows on the edge of the patio and blinked up at me.

I started to explain my presence but didn't get far before she interrupted: "Oh, the *detective*... Father told us about you last evening." Her small voice had a slight squeak to it. Not unappealing. "I must say, you're more interesting than I expected. Come in and join me?"

"I appreciate the offer, Madame Triolet, but—"

"I'd rather you called me Claudette. And there are all sizes of swimming trunks in the cabin, if you're shy."

I sat down in one of the white poolside chairs and smiled at her. "The thing is, your father's paying me to ask people questions. Easier to do if you join me up here."

"And easier for you to watch my expression when I answer them."

"That, too."

She hauled herself out of the water in one smooth move and stood before me dripping on the blue tiles. "All right. Ask away. I've nothing to hide." She grinned and looked down at herself. "As you can plainly see."

"Plainly," I agreed amiably.

She sauntered past me to pick a T-shirt off the raised back of a patio lounge chair. She had a pert little bottom. What she wore didn't cover much of it. The way she moved it was a premeditated challenge.

Two choices. Either I was so devastating that any woman would turn on instantly at the sight of me—or it was an act Claudette Triolet fell into automatically around any reasonably presentable male. I preferred the first explanation but guessed the latter.

She tugged on the T-shirt and sprawled on the lounge chair. I turned my chair to face her. The T-shirt was already soaked through, clinging to her slim torso, indenting at the navel. Her sharp nipples poked the wet material. The total effect was more provocative than nudity.

She gave me another grin and linked her hands behind her damp blond curls. "Are you going to ask those questions—or just go on looking at me like that?"

It was said with humor, but not her stepmother's kind. Claudette Triolet's had a hard, nervous edge to it. I was reminded of her father's manner when he was holding back the habitual harshness. She didn't look like him, the way her kid brother did. But Karl Malo's genes weren't entirely missing from her makeup.

CHAPTER 16

My questions worked their way around to the day Jacqueline Malo had flown off to join her husband in Monaco. Malo's daughter didn't mind acknowledging that she'd known where her stepmother was going.

"Jacqueline announced it after her phone call to my father that morning. Everyone in the chateau that day must have known."

"Including your brother."

"I guess so. Alex *was* around that day. He couldn't have missed knowing." Claudette Triolet got a spark of new interest in her eyes. "Do you think *Alex* had something to do with the kidnapping?" she asked me eagerly.

"To be honest with you, Claudette, I haven't the faintest idea about any of it so far. My job is to do whatever I'm paid to do. Right now I'm mostly just stumbling around in the dark."

Claudette Triolet laughed. "Doesn't sound like very demanding work."

I eyed her wet T-shirt. "At this moment it's rather pleasant work."

She accepted that with a smug little smile.

I asked if her stepmother had told anyone of her intentions before that phone call to Monaco.

"Not as far as I know," Claudette said, uncaringly. Stretching like a kitten, she rested one bent leg on the raised knee of the other and peeked at me through five spread toes.

But she began forgetting to act cute as we got deeper into discussing Jacqueline Malo. A nasty anger came through. I encouraged it with sympathetic nods and sounds. My expression assured her that I found her thoughts as fascinating as her person. The smiler with the hook. Fishing for whatever might come swimming up out of her disturbed depths.

"If you think *I* had something to do with snatching that bitch," she told me after a while, "I only wish I *had*. She wouldn't have come back alive."

"You don't like her much," I said understandingly.

Claudette's giggle was jarring. "That's some understatement, Monsieur Detective. I loathe her."

I dredged up another sympathetic nod. My emergency supply of those seemed fully stocked, but hauling them out in the open was getting to be brute labor. I said, "She's hurt you in some way."

"Isn't that obvious? My father's an old man with a bad heart. Jacqueline comes along and grabs him. Figures she can screw him to death in a few years—and inherit all that money, along with part of the company. That's not bad pay, is it, for a few years' hard work? A third of everything. Exactly what I'm cut down to, since *she* married him."

"Not quite a third," I reminded her. "Your husband gets a little, too."

"So? That doesn't change the fact that she's going to inherit as much as I will. And that's just not *fair*. I've had to live my *whole life* around my father. All she's got to do is put in a short stint at the end."

"You think it's the inheritance she married him for."

"Why else would she?"

I made a face she could interpret as agreement and tempted her to get more of the bile out of her system. "Does your brother feel the same way about her?"

Claudette's smile was closer to a sneer. "I guess Alex would like to get into her panties. But outside of that, his feeling about Jacqueline's homing in on our inheritance is probably the only thing the little pest and I see eye to eye on."

Alexandre might be a pest, but he'd become a good deal bigger than his sister. The lack of endearment in her tone went a long way back, but the passage of time hadn't drained one drop of the old venom out of it. I leaned on it.

"I imagine you know about your brother's getting himself into serious trouble up in Paris."

"Sure." Claudette liked this subject. "The trouble *should* have been worse. Father bailed him out. Claimed it was the fault of the brat getting mixed up with bad company. My opinion, *he* was the bad company. Got *them* in trouble."

"Your father gave me the idea that the others had been in trouble before. Hoodlums, according to him."

"Naturally he'd think that," Claudette said disgustedly. "His lawyers didn't do anybody a favor when they got Alex out of that one. Should have let him go to prison. Maybe teach him not to be so fucking full of himself."

"Does he associate with hoodlums around here, too?" I asked, ingratiatingly attentive to her every word.

"I'd *bet* on it."

"It would help me do some digging into what he might be up to," I told her, "if you could tell me who some of them are."

Claudette gave it some frowning thought. She didn't mind the notion of helping me find out something bad about her kid brother. But finally she shook her head. "I just don't know who any of them are. Alex and I are not on confiding terms, as you must have guessed by now."

"You might have heard him or somebody else mention a name or two among his local friends."

She shook her head again. "There's a local girl he's been messing around with lately. Micheline Simeoni. She's the only one I know about." Claudette added scathingly, "Daughter of a town *baker*, tells you something about Alex's taste."

I thought of the attractive teenager Alexandre had hugged at the bullring. "What's she look like?"

"Search me. All I know is her name."

"Where'd you hear it?"

She grinned. "My father got a call from *her* father. Complaining that Alex is keeping his snotty little girl out too late, all night sometimes, and she's too young for that. He doesn't think Alex's intentions are *honorable*. Do you believe that? A lousy little baker, trying to louse up his kid's chance to get herself pregnant and *maybe* get herself a catch like Karl Malo's rotten son."

"How'd your father react to the baker's complaint?"

"Pointed out to him that his daughter's *not* underage and has a right to her own life. You see," Claudette added bitterly, "my father thinks men are entitled to have their fun. Girls and women, too—as long as they're not *his*. His women are supposed to be as pure as spring water. If he thinks they're not, he gets furious. Have you ever seen my father in a fury?"

"No."

"You don't want to, believe me. It's scary."

I continued to probe along those lines for a while, but all she did was embellish what she'd already said. At last I swung over to another track.

"What does your husband think of your stepmother?"

"*My husband*," Claudette Triolet said scornfully, "makes a profession out of liking anybody who might be of use to him, now or in the future. That's his major quality."

"He does seem an odd type for somebody like you," I said carefully. "I couldn't help wondering why you'd ever marry a man like that."

Either my charm had suddenly evaporated or I'd hit a nerve. Her eyes narrowed. I watched something shut inside her. She took several moments before speaking again.

"Please forget what I just said about Jean-Noel. Married people say things about each other sometimes that they don't really mean. Just the normal irritations of married life, I guess. Jean-Noel does have his good points."

"For instance?"

She shrugged. "You'd have to know him much better to understand."

After that I ran into a blank wall no matter which way I tried to probe further into the relationships between Claudette Triolet and her husband, brother, and stepmother. She'd become cautious, thinking out each answer before voicing it. I switched back to the kidnapping for a while, asking if she had any thoughts at all about it that might be of use to me.

"I've only got *one* thought on that subject," she told me in a rigidly restrained tone. "My father should never have paid that ransom. As far as I'm concerned, that's just more money gone from my inheritance."

"I get the feeling he would have been willing to pay a good deal more than he did to get her back."

"I know. He must be getting senile. He could have bought a bunch of the most expensive call girls in the world to keep him happy until he dies—for a fraction of those seven million francs."

Claudette drew a deep breath and sat up straight, hugging her knees. "I suppose what I've been saying about Jacqueline makes me seem a not-very-nice person to you. But at least it's honest. I *won't* lie and pretend I feel anything else."

I assured her I appreciated and admired her honesty. But my subsequent attempts to nudge her into other intra-family revelations continued to be wasted efforts. She managed to field all the questions without giving me anything of interest. Her coquettishness was gone without a trace. Wariness had taken its place.

Finally she seized my wrist and looked at my watch. "My God—I have a date in town. I'll be late if I don't hurry." She rushed off without a single flirt of that snug little bottom and vanished inside the chateau.

After she was gone I strolled back inside, too, and went up to my room. Its windows gave me a view of the garage in the front tower. My Peugeot was alone outside it now, shiny clean. I stood at the windows and watched until Claudette Triolet drove out.

She was driving a blue Mercedes 500 SL convertible with the top opened. Her six-month-old child was in a portable bassinet strapped to the front seat beside her.

I made it down to my own car fast. Claudette Triolet's convertible was at the end of the drive, turning into the road to Arles. I started the Peugeot and went after her.

Why not? Tailing her husband had turned out interesting. It had led to Johnny Duncan and a sore head. Maybe Claudette Triolet would lead to something less painful and puzzling.

CHAPTER 17

The five-story house on Rue De Grand Prieuré was like several connected to it and like many others in the heart of Arles. Solid stone walls dating back to the seventeenth or eighteenth century with traces of earlier sculptured decorations around the door and windows. All of it renovated sometime in the past twenty years, making it once more what it had been originally: a desirable, expensive address.

The narrow, crooked street had no room left for parking. Claudette Triolet had left her convertible a short half block away, outside the ruins of the Baths of Constantine. I parked at the other end of the ruins and watched her carry her baby along the narrow street to the five-story building. From that distance I couldn't see which button she pressed beside the doorway. When she went inside I got out of my Peugeot and walked to the building.

There were five large brass plaques fastened to the front wall next to the entrance door, inscribed with doctors' names, specialties, and visiting hours. All of the house's interior had been converted into medical offices.

One of the doctors—André-Maurice Brun—was a pediatrician. That would explain Claudette Triolet's bringing her son with her: an appointment with the child's doctor. In which case I'd followed her there for nothing.

Or so it seemed at the time.

However, there was always a chance she'd go someplace interesting after leaving the pediatrician's office. There was an old, small hotel almost directly across the street, with a gift shop window beside its entrance. I went inside. Across the little lobby, behind the gift shop, was a bar. I bought a glass of rose and a sandwich made of crispy baguette with thick slices of good country pâtè. The bartender dropped an ice cube in my wine without looking either surprised or offended.

Carrying the glass in one hand and the sandwich in the other, I walked to the open end of the gift shop and pretended interest in its racks of postcards while I watched the doctors' building through the window. I was obviously doomed to stand-up lunches on this job.

It wouldn't be the first time. I'd chosen myself a profession that proved often intriguing and occasionally lucrative. It could also be hard on the feet and digestion.

I was finishing my lunch when Claudette Triolet reappeared with her child. The appointment had been shorter than I'd expected. Probably nothing wrong with the kid, just a superficial checkup.

She disappeared down the street in the direction of her car. I waited a few seconds longer before leaving the hotel. She was getting into her convertible, strapping her baby into his bassinet. I approached the ruins of the Constantine Baths at a slow stroll until she drove off. Then I sprinted the rest of the way to my Peugeot and began following her again.

She drove out of Arles and back to the chateau. No interesting stops along the way. Which seemed to confirm that I'd spent the last couple of hours accomplishing nothing at all.

After she'd gone up into the east wing to return the baby to his nurse I went in and checked with Girard the butler. Alexandre Malo wasn't back.

Going down to the garage I found the elderly chauffeur tinkering with the Bentley's engine. I asked him a question that had been on my mind for some time: "What kind of car does Jacqueline Malo drive?"

He told me she had two. A Volvo four-door, plus a Fiat station wagon she kept in Arles most of the time and used to deliver or pick up artworks.

Staid, practical vehicles without a trace of anything flashy to them. I thought about that while I drove back to Arles to see if I could locate Alexandre or find out something useful about him via his girlfriend, Micheline Simeoni.

* * * *

There was only one baker named Simeoni in the Arles phone book. Felix Simeoni. There were two listings: business and home. I called the home number first, on the off chance that Micheline Simeoni would be there, perhaps with Alexandre Malo. No answer. I left my car beside the Roman Theater and walked six short blocks to the bakery.

It was in a little street just off the Place du Forum, a medium-sized square crowded with bistro tables, plane trees, and weather-worn Corinthian columns. One end is dominated by the big statue of Mistral— the Nobel Prize poet of Provence who got his name from the wind that sometimes roars down the Rhône Valley, plastering birds against buildings and rubbing people's nerves raw. The Simeoni bakery was behind it.

Felix Simeoni wasn't there. His thin, middle-aged wife was and would continue to be, selling her husband's wares to afternoon and evening customers until eight that night. Like all bakers, Felix Simeoni had to start work hours before dawn. He'd just left for the day, Madame

Simeoni informed me, to go to a bistro on the *place* and drink enough to be able to sleep through the sunlit hours. Bakers and their wives don't get to spend much waking leisure time together.

There were no customers at the moment, and Madame Simeoni answered most of my questions easily. Her daughter had gone off with Alexandre Malo at noon in his beautiful automobile. She didn't know where they'd gone or when they would be back, but that didn't trouble her. Unlike her husband, she believed it possible the girl just might wind up snaring the most eligible boy in the area. Why not? He had to marry somebody eventually. And Micheline was extremely pretty.

Madame Simeoni described her daughter. She did sound like the girl with Alexandre at the bullring. Madame Simeoni had nothing bad to say about Malo's son. She admitted he was headstrong, adding, "But that's only natural, a boy his age, and so rich."

She didn't know anything about his associating with local hoodlums. It appeared she didn't know any of his friends, in fact, nor those of her daughter. The girl was a normal, active teenager with plenty of free time. Her parents put in long, hard days that left them too weary for anything but sleep. They hadn't seen much of Micheline the last few years.

I mentioned that her husband wasn't as accepting of the relationship between Micheline and Alexandre.

Madame Simeoni shrugged. "Felix has no faith in happy endings."

A customer came in. Madame Simeoni went to take care of business after telling me I would probably find her husband in the Mistral Café.

The bartender pointed him out to me: a pale fat man slumped at a rear table finishing a drink. There were two other glasses in front of him, emptied. He looked sullen, but that was fatigue. He had no objection to my buying him a fourth glass of the local *marc* he was drinking. One more should do it, he said: stun him into sleep in spite of the sunshine and crowd noises that filtered through his bedroom shutters.

I ordered him another and one for myself. He invited me to sit down. I did. Simeoni relaxed completely when I explained that Karl Malo wanted me to check into whether Alexandre might be getting himself into any kind of trouble. He was pleased to learn that Malo was finally wise to that damned son of his.

But it developed that Simeoni didn't know any more about Alexandre, or his daughter, or their friends, than his wife did. The only difference was that he didn't believe Alexandre would ever marry his daughter even if she got herself pregnant by him.

His wife was right. No faith.

The *marc* provided the only satisfying aspect of my brief stay at the Mistral Café. A bit on the rough side, but an honest, fruity taste and strong enough to soothe my growing impatience with the way the day was going.

I left the Place du Forum hoping the rest of that day wasn't going to be more of the same. So far, I thought, it had failed to provide me with anything of any significance at all.

I was wrong.

But I didn't find that out until late that night.

CHAPTER 18

"Alexandre Malo is a little too smart and sure of himself for his own good," Lieutenant Laffite told me. "It gets him into trouble sometimes. But nothing more than nonsense trouble. Nothing drastic enough to require our interference."

Laffite was one of several contacts I'd acquired during a previous case that had taken me to Arles. The window of his office in the Arles Gendarmerie looked out across the boulevard des Lices to the Jardin d'Eté sloping up to the Roman Theatre. He was a large slab of a man in a handsome uniform, with graying wavy hair and a bullet scar in each cheek. One where the bullet had gone in and the other where it had come out. Half of his teeth were artificial replacements for the ones the bullet had destroyed.

He'd gotten shot while preventing a bus driver from committing suicide with a small revolver. Laffite had squashed the charges, claiming it had been an accident. The bus driver forgot about killing himself, and visited Laffite every day in the hospital, and they were now close friends, godfathers to each other's kids.

"Alexandre got himself in real trouble up in Paris," I told Laffite. "He's been associating with shady characters. Just small-fry hoods, as far as I know at this point. But they might have introduced him to some that're bigger."

"He doesn't hang out with anyone like that around here," Laffite said. "Not that I know of."

"You'd know."

"Probably. This isn't that large a town. We do have our petty criminals—and keep close track of them. Once in a while we get a bigger one in town. But foreign. From Toulon or Marseilles, mostly. Passing through. If they stay more than a couple days, we notice."

"And roust them."

Laffite's scars distorted his cheeks when he smiled. "We advise them to move on."

"Which they do."

"Invariably." Laffite cracked his large, flattened knuckles.

He was fairly sure Claudette Triolet didn't have any shady acquaintances either—around this area, at least. Laffite gave me the local gossip on her. She'd been wilder than her kid brother since adolescence, devoting herself primarily to the seduction of other women's husbands. Some people had suspected she wasn't right in the head, and others thought Malo's daughter just got a kick out of breaking up marriages. But that had stopped after her own marriage, a bit more than a year ago.

A lot of people had known that Triolet had been courting Claudette determinedly for some years. Once in a while she'd gone out with him. But people who saw them together said she treated him with an amused contempt that would have turned off any man of normal sensitivity. Nobody was surprised that it didn't turn Triolet off. He was already solidly entrenched in the Malo business and stood to rise much higher if he could overcome Claudette's resistance and become Karl Malo's son-in-law. Everybody was surprised when he actually did it.

"Persistence," Lieutenant Laffite said. "I guess he finally wore her down. Or she got addicted to having him panting after her that resolutely."

"Could be," I said.

Most locals, he told me, were not overly fond of the Malo clan. But that was probably nothing but sheer envy. The only member of the family none of that applied to was Malo's present wife. Jacqueline Malo was universally liked. People admired her as a down-to-earth, intelligent shopkeeper of the type the French are fond of considering to be the backbone of their nation. They also respected the way she'd gone on being that, putting on no airs, after marrying Karl Malo.

"That was only three weeks after Malo's daughter married Triolet," Laffite said, "so some people joked that it was the daughter's marriage that inspired Malo to do it, too. But me, I think that woman he's married to now is inspiration enough. She's a lovely person."

"Yes," I agreed.

The joints of Laffite's chair creaked in protest when he leaned his bulk backward and eyed me with a half smile. "I get the feeling I haven't told you much you didn't already know."

"Not much."

"Perhaps I could give you more, if *you* gave me some notion of what it is you're trying to find out."

"Partly I don't really know," I said. "And partly it's confidential. Malo hired me to look into a private family problem, as I told you. At this point I can't tell you more than that."

Laffite opened a side drawer of his desk and brought out a blue file folder. "According to this, you're operating as a bodyguard for the Malo family, to prevent another kidnapping."

"There's some truth in that." I nodded at the folder. "If that's my permit to carry a gun in the performance of my duties for Malo, it's fast work. It's only yesterday I asked him to see if he could push one through for me."

"He pushed," Laffite said dryly.

"Last time I applied for one it took eleven days."

Laffite's smile was sardonic. "I imagine you didn't have a high enough official endorsement of your application."

"Who endorsed this one?"

"The Minister of Defense."

"I should work for people like Karl Malo more often."

Laffite opened the folder and pushed it across the desk to me. "Sign all six copies. The bottom one is for you." I signed them and folded the last one in my wallet next to my I.D. Laffite said, "If what you're doing ever gets less confidential, come and see me again."

I said I would and went off to talk to my other Arles contacts.

* * * *

None of them were able to give me any more than Lieutenant Laffite had. It was a few minutes before eight that evening when I walked to the Hotel d'Arlatan to check for messages and passed Jacqueline Malo's gallery. It was closed for the day.

I had passed it earlier, while it was still open, and had been tempted to go in and talk with her. But I hadn't given in to that temptation. I had a very strong feeling that she was under some kind of pressure, and that my being around was making it worse. I wanted to wait and see if I was right.

If I was right—and the pressure got strong enough—she would come to me.

CHAPTER 19

There was a message to call Fritz Donhoff waiting for me at the desk in the hotel. I made the call from my room. As soon as he came on I asked, "What have you got for me?"

"There *are* certain amenities adhered to by well-bred people, Pierre-Ange," Fritz chided. "You and I are not merely business associates, after all. Even among those there are usually polite exchanges before one leaps directly into—"

I interrupted his lecture on manners: "Good evening, Fritz. How are you? How's the weather up there? What have you got for me?"

"I'm feeling rather fit, thank you. Paris has been quite hot, but it seems to be cooling off this evening. I don't have much that will be of use to you so far. I've only started, you realize, and there *are* four different people whose backgrounds you've asked me to check. Five, if we include Jacqueline Malo's late previous husband. I just wanted to assure you that I'm into the preliminaries on all of them."

"All right," I said. "I don't mean to push you, Fritz. Just tell me whatever you've learned so far."

The truth was that Fritz was an incredibly fast gatherer of information. In spite of his age—and also because of it. His treasure house of sources was vast and varied. Some went all the way back to his early days as a police detective. More had been acquired during decades as a private eye. And a good number were from his time between, in the Resistance—surviving members still forming the best old-boy network in Europe.

"First," he began, "there is Jean-Noel Triolet. Middle-class background, but he did well enough in lower schools to get into ENA." That was the *Ecole Rationale d'Administration*, a prestige university for future managers of big business.

"Triolet," Fritz went on, "graduated from ENA near the top of his class. Not a brilliant intellect, according to my source at the school, but Triolet compensated for that lack by intense dedication to his studies. Sheer unremitting hard work. I get the same on him from the first company he joined after graduation, Niarchos Shipping. He was an extremely determined young executive, grinding away at any project until he accomplished what needed doing. They were sorry to lose him. And angry at the way Malo Transport lured him away."

"Who lured him?"

"Malo's previous second-in-command, Hubert Loy. You might try asking him—"

"I'd have a tough time getting an answer," I interrupted. "Loy's dead."

"Oh. What did he die of?"

That gave me a pause. "That *might* be worth checking into."

"Yes, it might," Fritz said, pleased to have been one step ahead of me on that one. "Now, as to what I've been able to detect so far, Triolet's record is entirely clean. No shady moves or acquaintances. And no connection with your old friend John Duncan."

"That you've detected so far."

"Correct. Let's take Alexandre Malo next. He seems to have dissociated himself from the young hoodlum crowd since his father's attorneys got him out of that spot of trouble. And he stopped gambling. The worst thing that can be said of him since is that he likes to drive too fast and pursue women. Fancies himself a young Lothario, apparently. Not a terrible flaw in a boy his age."

"Nor in a man of yours," I said.

Fritz chuckled.

"What about Johnny Duncan?" I asked him.

"Nothing. Zero. I had a couple of decent connections in the American Embassy here, but they've been transferred. One to Washington. I put through a call to him, but it seems John Duncan is not a name anyone in your government feels able to discuss freely. It occurred to me that you might be able to find a way around that reluctance with the help of your friend Captain Gallion, in the DGSE."

The DGSE is France's equivalent of the CIA. Thierry Gallion had been a desk officer there since a sub he'd commanded had sunk, doing damage to his hearing and heart that rendered him unfit to continue his navy career at sea. We'd known each other since we were kids, through a friendship between my mother and his father, a retired admiral.

"Good thought," I told Fritz. "I'll give him a try."

"That brings us to Madame Jacqueline Malo," Fritz said, "about whom I have virtually nothing useful to report. Solid middle-class family, excellent education. A woman many people like and no one seems to dislike. Quite popular; all of her friends entirely respectable. She had an antique shop in Paris for some years but became more interested in art and wanted to open her own gallery. She decided there was too much competition in Paris, so she explored other possibilities after selling her antique shop at a good profit. And, as you know, she moved to Arles after her husband's death two years ago."

"Which brings us to that previous husband."

"Yes. His name was Emil Fassler. A German. He owned a small import-export firm in Hamburg and traveled frequently on business. To Paris, among other places. There he met Jacqueline. They married after knowing each other only two months. According to friends, they were much in love—though often separated for long periods because of his business travels. The friends say she took Fassler's death very hard."

"How did he die?" I asked.

"He was down in Marseilles on business," Fritz told me. "One night he didn't return to his hotel. His body was found the next day in an alley. Fassler had been stabbed to death. Also severely beaten. His money, watch, ring, and gold cufflinks were gone, so the police assume he was the victim of a mugging. Though they did wonder why the thieves beat him up first. Perhaps he put up a fight."

I said slowly, "That's the first potentially interesting item you've come up with."

"It might be," Fritz acknowledged. "My police contact in Marseilles will see if he can turn up something further on the circumstances around Fassler's death for us."

"I've got some good connections of my own there," I reminded him.

"True. The *milieu* friends and enemies of Arlette Alfani's father. Let's see first if my cop can give us some kind of lead. Then you can try following up on it among those underworld contacts."

"Have you checked Fassler out with anyone in Hamburg?"

"Not as yet. You have to remember, I've only had a limited amount of time to work on all this."

"Get on it, Fritz," I said impatiently.

His pride was hurt. "I think," he said with a touch of stiffness, "that I have accomplished quite a bit already, considering."

"You have," I admitted. "And I do appreciate that. I know nobody else could have gotten that much information this fast. But make Emil Fassler's background your priority at this point. Please. Something's worrying Jacqueline Malo. A lot. I want to find out what it is."

There was a moment's silence at Fritz's end. Then he said gently, "Do I detect more than professional interest, my boy?"

"I *like* her," I said, with a tone more prickly than I'd intended. "She's a nice woman. Don't go building it into a love story in that feverish brain of yours. The lady is not only married, she's also entirely devoted to her husband."

"And therefore unavailable," Fritz said in his most understanding tone. Which can sometimes be irritating. "Loves impossible to consummate have always been the most potent. That explains the enduring appeal of the Tristan and Isolde romance. Forbidden and doomed from the start."

"Spare me your ancient wisdom right now, Fritz. What I *could* use is some help down here. My local sources aren't coming through with anything I can use as a handle on this investigation. Have you got anybody in Arles?" He did, of course.

"Arles was a hotbed of Resistance activity," Fritz said. "But the Nazis got most of them before the war ended."

"I know. Including the mayor and chief of police."

"I got to know some of those who survived, but most of them have died by now of natural causes. There is one left, however. Alain Rodi. He was only a boy during the war and is still a young man. Only sixty-five."

For Fritz, that was young.

"He's a coiffeur," Fritz told me. "Actually a barber, too. His salon de coiffure has two sections, for men and women."

I liked that. "Hairdressers usually pick up more of what goes on in their areas than the cops."

"In addition to which Rodi moves in a special circle whose members tend to be more observant than most. And inclined to spread the latest gossip among themselves. The homosexual crowd."

"Your Alain Rodi is gay."

"I've never been able to understand why Americans apply that term," Fritz said. "Nor the way French argot has picked it up. Few of the homosexuals I know seem overly cheerful. Alain Rodi is certainly not *gay*. He's an introverted man with a strong tendency toward masochism. Actually, that's what enabled Rodi to survive under Gestapo torture—without giving them the name of a single member of his cell."

"Christ, how'd he manage that?"

"He kept telling himself that what was being done to him was something he *wanted*. A perverted form of sexual pleasure."

"That's some trick, if you can pull it off."

"Alain Rodi did. A brave man."

I said, "Bravery's seldom enough, under those circumstances."

"True. But he also has an unusually strong mind. And the willpower to make it rule his body. When he wishes. Wait a second, I'll get my address book."

I took out my notebook and pen. When Fritz came back on the phone I copied Alain Rodi's address and two phone numbers. "The first is his salon," Fritz told me. "But it is probably closed by now. The second is his apartment, above the salon. His widowed sister lives there with him now."

* * * *

It was the sister who answered my call. She told me her brother had gone fishing. "This is his day off," she said. "Fishing is his way to get some time alone and think. He won't be back before late tonight."

I gave her my phone number at the hotel and asked her to give her brother a message to call me when he returned. "Tell him I'm a friend of Fritz Donhoff." I had to spell out the German name for her.

My next call was to Lieutenant Laffite's home number. I asked him if he knew the circumstances of the death of Malo's former assistant director, Hubert Loy.

"Of course," Laffite told me. "Loy's position made him one of the most important men in this region."

"How'd he go? Natural death?"

"No, automobile accident. His home was between here and the Baux-de-Provence, in the foothills of the Alpilles. Loy was driving home at night and apparently lost control of his car. It was late; he may have fallen asleep at the wheel. At any rate, the car went off a cliff. His skull was broken by the impact. Died instantly."

"Any chance it wasn't an accident?"

"You mean did someone hit him on the head and push his car off that cliff. There was no reason to think so, at the time."

"When did it happen?"

"Five months ago," Laffite said. "Have you come across something to indicate it might have been murder?" He wasn't asking for vague suspicions, so I told him no, I was just filling in background.

My last call was to Thierry Gallion's apartment in Paris. I got his wife, Anne, first. Remembering Fritz's lecture on civilized amenities, I asked her about their kids and the weather.

"The children are fine," Anne said, "but it's been terribly hot up here. Thierry suffers from it. Tonight seems a bit cooler, but most nights it's not. Bad for his heart."

"Maybe you should air condition your apartment," I said.

"We thought about that, but Thierry's doctor doesn't approve of the idea. He thinks going in and out of the air conditioning would be harder on Thierry's heart than the heat is."

That didn't surprise me. Most of the French continue to believe air conditioning in the home is a health hazard.

I said, "Why don't you come down to my place on the coast for a week when Thierry has his vacation in August? The days are hot there, too, but most nights are cool enough to sleep under a blanket—as you'll remember from your last time there. It was good for him."

"That's kind of you, Pierre-Ange, but we don't want to impose. You must have every Parisian you know asking for invitations to come there in the summers."

"With most of them I come up with excuses. You and Thierry are among the exceptions to that."

"Well—we just may take you up on that offer."

"Do it," I said firmly.

Thierry took the phone. "You seem to be making a date with my beautiful wife."

"You were eavesdropping again."

"That's my profession. The DGSE expects me to keep in practice."

"You can come along with her," I said, "if you insist."

"I do. And thanks. I could use a change of scene, as well as air." Thierry paused and then resumed in a quieter tone. "But I don't imagine that's what you phoned about."

"Not originally, though I *would* like to have you and Anne spend that week with me. Does the name John Duncan mean anything to you?"

He thought about it. But not for long. Thierry's memory was one part of him not injured when his submarine sank. "John Duncan was in France as an American narcotics agent for a time," he said. "I believe you worked for him."

"That's right."

"Then he was with the CIA—and left it under some kind of cloud."

"I want to find out details about that cloud," I said.

"I don't believe I ever heard any details," Thierry told me. "I can see tomorrow if we've got a dossier on it." Anything the DGSE might have on Johnny was unlikely to be enough for my purposes.

"I need more than that," I said. "I want to talk to whoever's your Paris liaison with the CIA."

"He might not want to discuss it," Thierry said. "Especially not with *you*, if he knows your background. And if he doesn't, I'm sure he'll make a point of finding out."

"I was hoping he might owe you a favor."

"More than one." Thierry gave the matter a little consideration. "And, of course, my superiors would be pleased with any inside information I might pick up from this. The CIA hasn't been too open with us lately."

"So twist his arm."

"The hell with that." Thierry kept his voice low. "I'll twist his balls." Anne must have left the room. He was careful with his language when his wife was within hearing. "I'll call him at home," he told me. "Call you back after I talk to him. Give me an hour or so."

I gave him my number. Then I went out to have dinner.

There was a former stable behind the Van Gogh Hospital that three women had converted into a superior restaurant. I stuffed myself on their fabulous bouillabaisse. With a *demi* of Châteauneuf-du-Pape white—a treat almost impossible to find outside the immediate area. Nutritious and delicious.

It was dark when I walked back to the hotel. There were two messages waiting: one from Thierry Gallion and one from Alain Rodi.

* * * *

I called Thierry first.

"The man you want to talk to," he told me, still avoiding using the name of his CIA contact over a public phone, "will meet us in the American Embassy tomorrow at two P.M. Can you get here by then?"

"Yes. He knows what it's about?"

"He does. The subject does not thrill him. Neither do *you*. He knows about your little problem with that Senate committee. But he is prepared to talk to us."

"You're going in there with me."

"To protect you. And pick up whatever I can from your conversation."

"He knows *you'll* be there."

"He insisted on it," Thierry told me flatly.

Interesting.

I phoned Marignane Airport outside Marseilles. As usual in the summer, most flights to Paris were already booked full. The only seat they could offer me was on a plane leaving earlier than I'd wanted: nine A.M. I took it. Then I called Alain Rodi.

CHAPTER 20

"That's wrong," Alain Rodi told me. "What everyone's told you about Malo's daughter stopping her screwing around after she married Triolet."

"I know she still flirts," I said. "But I got the feeling that's just habit, mixed with checking to make sure her sex appeal's still operational. A game where she controls the cutoff point. My impression was that she wouldn't deliver what she was advertising."

"She doesn't," Rodi said with conviction. "Where you're wrong is about *when* she stopped."

We were sitting in adjacent barber chairs in the men's section of his salon, looking at each other in the mirror wall in front of us. He'd had me meet him there to be certain his sister couldn't eavesdrop. Since I came from Fritz, he'd figured what I wanted was confidential.

Rodi was a sinewy, grizzled man with resolute eyes and a firm mouth. His voice and manner had an otherworldly gentleness you find in some priests, though not many. I avoided looking at his hands, which rested on the leather-cushioned arms of his barber chair. There was scar tissue where most of his fingernails had been. Only four of them had grown back. I didn't want to think about what else the Gestapo might have done to him and the way he'd held out against it.

When we'd settled into the barber chairs I'd decided against wasting time repeating the same old questions. Instead I'd begun a summation of all I'd learned till then about the Malo family, asking Rodi to stop me whenever he had something to add or correct. He'd stopped me when I got to Claudette Triolet.

"She stopped fucking everything in pants well *before* she married Triolet," he said. The discrepancy between the harshly graphic words and his compassionate tone was disconcerting. "That happened when she fell in love with a man almost as old as her father."

"There were a number of those in her life, from what I've heard."

"Not like this one. The difference may be in Claudette's having known him since she was a child. Or her being intrigued by realizing from the start that she couldn't have him. I mean, she could get him into bed with her, but she knew he wouldn't marry her. He's a staunch Catholic, for one thing. And his wife is a very ill woman, bedridden the past five years. For both reasons he would never divorce her."

I said, "Claudette couldn't have wanted to marry every man she went to bed with."

"No, but she liked dangling the *possibility*. Here there was none. Whatever the reason, there's no question Claudette did finally decide she was in love this time. Her first time."

"How long was this before her marriage to Triolet?"

"It may have been going on sporadically for a long time," Rodi said. "But she quit going to bed with anyone else about two years before she married. It was some months later that her father learned of the affair. He became extremely angry. Had a confrontation with her lover in a *café* where I know the owner. Malo threatened that if he didn't stop seeing Claudette, he, Malo, would create a scandal that would ruin his practice."

"His *practice*?"

"He's a doctor," Rodi told me.

I felt a tingle. It didn't go away as he continued speaking.

"A general practitioner. He was the Malos' family doctor until that scene in the *café*. Which became violent. Malo slapped him, and he threatened Malo with a steak knife. After that Malo warned his daughter he'd have her confined to a sanitarium if she didn't end the affair. Legal or not, Karl Malo does have the power to carry out that sort of threat."

"I know he does," I said, thinking of how fast he'd gotten me the gun permit, with one direct call to the Minister of Defense. "Tell me, what's this doctor's name?"

"Hugues Bardin."

I cursed myself.

* * * *

It's always easy to jump to the wrong conclusions. But in my line of work you're supposed to double-check even what seems obvious.

Claudette Triolet had taken her baby with her into that doctors' building on Rue de Grand Prieuré. So it was natural to assume she'd gone to see the pediatrician there.

But one of the other doctors listed outside the building was Hugues Bardin.

"I have a feeling," I told Alain Rodi, "that Malo's threat didn't succeed in ending the affair."

"I believe Hugues Bardin did want to stop it at that point," Rodi said. "But Claudette didn't. And despite his probable reluctance she's managed to keep it going. Though much more discreetly, so no one would know."

"*You* know."

Rodi nodded. "Dr. Bardin's receptionist-nurse is an old friend of mine. And Claudette's get-togethers with Bardin seem to take place fairly often in his office, outside his visiting hours. Twice when my friend returned from the two-hour lunch siesta she spotted Claudette leaving."

The visiting hours listed on the doctors' plaques outside the building all had a break between 12:30 P.M. and 2:30 P.M. It had been shortly after one P.M. when I'd seen Claudette go in there. I'd assumed she'd phoned the pediatrician from the chateau to say she'd be late for her appointment, and he'd agreed to wait for her. Wrong obvious conclusion again.

But if she'd gone there to make love to Dr. Bardin, why would she have taken her child along?

I said, "You think the affair's still active."

"Oh, yes."

"And she hasn't had other affairs in the meantime?"

"I don't believe so," Rodi said judiciously.

"But she married Jean-Noel Triolet. And conceived their child before the marriage."

"It *is* strange," Rodi conceded.

"Unless the baby's not Triolet's."

"Yes." It was not the first time that thought had occurred to Alain Rodi.

* * * *

This time I did double-check what seemed obvious. I phoned the Malo chateau from my hotel room and got Girard the butler. I asked him the name of the pediatrician who took care of Claudette Triolet's child. He gave it to me. It wasn't the one in the doctors' building she had visited that afternoon.

That made it almost certain. She'd gone there for a rendezvous with Dr. Hugues Bardin. With the baby.

I asked if Claudette Triolet was still at home. Girard said she'd driven off after dinner. Without mentioning where she was going.

While I had Girard on the phone I asked about Alexandre. The boy had been home and gone out again.

"None of the family is here at the moment," Girard informed me. "Monsieur Malo is being driven to Marignane Airport to catch the last flight to Geneva. Some company matters came up that require his presence there for the rest of the week. Madame Malo went along in the car to see him off."

"When do you expect Triolet to come home tonight?" I asked.

"He won't be home tonight," Girard said. "Monsieur Triolet had to go to Marseilles late this afternoon. The company keeps a suite of offices there, with an apartment. He left word that any calls for him were to be relayed there for the next few days."

I hung up and looked for Dr. Hugues Bardin in the phone book on my room desk. Since it was long past his visiting hours I called his home number. A woman answered. She had a weak, trembly voice, draggy with fatigue, though she didn't sound sleepy. She identified herself as Dr. Bardin's wife and said he wasn't home.

"He has some patients to see in their homes this evening," she told me.

Unlike most advanced nations, France still has doctors who consider it a natural part of their profession to make house calls. So that wasn't unusual. But Dr. Bardin wasn't at home, and neither was Claudette Triolet, and his office was only a few short blocks from my hotel. I walked them.

The narrower streets in that part of Arles were deserted at that time of night. And fairly dark, except for the patches of light under infrequent street lamps. But it wasn't difficult to recognize Claudette's Mercedes convertible. There weren't many cars that expensive around town.

It was parked where she'd left it the last time. Beside the dark maze of the Constantine Baths. The top was up, but nobody was in it.

I walked to Dr. Bardin's building. His brass plaque told me his offices took up the top floor. I crossed the street and looked up. No lights showed in the top floor windows. Maybe the curtains were closed inside. Maybe nobody was up there. Maybe they were there with the lights off. I crossed back to the building entrance. There was no buzzer button that would let me into the building. You had to press an individual doctor's button and identify yourself over the intercom beside the door in order to be buzzed in.

I walked past the front of that building and the next ones and found an alley that curved behind them. When I was at the rear of Dr. Bardin's building I looked up again.

Still no lights in the windows up there. I studied the back door. Most rear door locks are easier to pick than the ones installed in front doors. This one looked like it would be a cinch. But I'd left my little burglar kit in my car.

Leaving the alley, I went into the small hotel on the other side of the street. Using the phone at one end of the bar, I dialed Dr. Bardin's office number. There was no answer. After ten rings I hung up, waited five seconds, dialed the number again, let it ring exactly ten more times.

I did that a third time. If they were up there, it would make them nervous.

Hanging up and tipping the barman, I went outside and stood in the darkness of a recessed doorway, waiting to see if anything happened.

After five minutes something did. The entrance of the building across the street opened. Claudette Triolet stepped out with a man. I got a few seconds' look at him in the light of the entry foyer before he closed the door behind them. He was a burly man in a nicely tailored suit, with white hair and a seamed, careworn, blunt-featured face.

Dr. Hugues Bardin, I presumed. Subject to further investigation.

They looked furtively up and down the narrow street. Seeing no one, they became less furtive. Claudette took his hand as he walked her past my hiding place and toward her car.

I took my time about strolling after them. It seemed at that point that I might be able to dig out more if I braced him when he was alone.

When they reached the convertible Claudette turned and kissed him. I stopped where I was and observed them. After a second he put his arms around her, but his embrace seemed less fervent than hers.

A gunshot cracked from inside the ruins of the Baths.

The bullet smacked off a brick wall just above their heads, showering them with dust. The shock of it made them spring apart.

I was sprinting toward them, yanking out my gun and thumbing off the safety.

"Get *down!*" I yelled.

But they were still standing there, frozen, when the second shot came.

CHAPTER 21

The second bullet cut between Claudette and Bardin, chest-high. It thudded into the wall, spattering them with more brick dust.

I reached them a split second later, crouching and snarling at them again to drop down. They cringed away from me and my gun, dazed with fright. Then Claudette recognized me. Her eyes went wide as I darted past them.

I got a section of ancient wall between me and the position the shots had come from and went up and over the chain link fence surrounding the ruins. Landing behind the cover of the inner wall section, I spared a swift glance behind me.

Claudette and Dr. Bardin hadn't dropped to the ground. They were running away, back through Rue de Grand Prieuré toward his building. Nobody fired at them again. The shooter inside the ruins with me would be concentrating on coping with my approach.

I concentrated on what the shooter was most likely to do next. There was no reason for him to hang around. Him or her. Could be either. But when an assailant's gender is unknown it automatically gets marked down as masculine. Maybe because we're still not at ease with the thought of a woman trying to murder people, in spite of all reforms and past proofs of equal capability at homicidal arts and crafts. Victorian prejudice hangs in there.

Man or woman, his targets were gone, I was in there with a gun, and people in nearby apartments would have heard the shots and called the police by then. It was time for the shooter to get out of there.

The deeply shadowed spread of the ruins was three hundred feet long and a hundred and fifty feet wide. I was at one end. He'd head for the other—or for either of the long sides.

I angled off to my right and worked my way in deeper, keeping low and leading the way with the P7, my finger tensed across its trigger. There was no shortage of cover—for me *and* the shooter. It was fifteen hundred years since the place had been Roman public baths. After that it had been a fortress and palace for waves of conquering invaders: Goths, Moslems, Vandals, Franks. Each had smashed it getting in and rebuilt parts before getting booted out by the next wave.

What was left was a haphazard labyrinth of wall sections of varied heights—some brick, some stone, some a mélange. The darkness inside that jumble was varied, too. It required close attention to determine which patch was shadow and which was solid. I'd had experience at this kind of night stalk, from the back alleys of Chicago to Nam to the nasty corners of Europe. I hoped my adversary didn't have that much practice.

I'd threaded my way about twenty yards when another gunshot came from ahead of me and off to the left. I went flat to the ground. But the bullet didn't come close. Its ricochet off the top of a marble column stump was six yards away. The shooter hadn't seen me; just detected movement and fired in my general direction. The shot's only purpose was to slow my approach.

It did. I shifted direction, crawling behind a mosaic terrace webbed with wide cracks and then snaking through a trench that had been part of the Roman underfloor heating system. That took me to the support wall of the ancient furnace house. I went around it and on toward the other end of the ruins, moving through a stretch of heavy shadow behind a long section of wall that was a couple feet higher than my head.

When I reached the wall's end I stopped, held my breath, and listened. If anyone was stalking or retreating in my immediate vicinity, it was being accomplished soundlessly. I hauled myself on top of the wall and stretched flat with the gun ready in my fist. Below me was an open space surrounding an ancient bathing pool filled with rubble. Beyond that was another confused clutter of wall stumps and broken shadows. Nothing in movement.

A street lamp outside that end of the ruins revealed a large hole cut through the fence there.

From a distance came the distinctive bleating of an approaching police car. I kept watching the area between me and the hole in the fence. The shooter would have to get out now, if he hadn't already.

The police klaxon came rapidly closer. Still no movement inside the ruins below me. The shooter was gone. I dropped from the wall and headed for the hole in the fence as the cop car squealed to a halt at the other end. I was out of sight and into a side street before the cops were out of their car. But I didn't put the gun away until I was almost to my hotel.

* * * *

I used my room phone to call the number in Aigues-Mortes that Johnny Duncan had given me. The woman who answered sounded young. I asked if her name was Suzanne.

"Yes," she said, "Suzanne Proslier. Who is this?"

I told her my name and that I was an old friend of John Duncan.

"Oh yes, John said you might call." She pronounced his name the French way: *Jean*. "But I'm so sorry, he isn't here now."

"Know where I can get in touch with him?"

"I'm afraid not. He drove off about four hours ago but didn't tell me where he was going. He seldom does." Her laugh held no trace of reproach or hurt; she accepted Johnny. "That's the way he is. He comes and goes, with no announcements. So I don't know when he'll be back, either. Would you like to give me a message for him?"

"Just tell him I called," I said, and I thanked her and hung up.

I'd hoped that I would find Johnny down there in Aigues-Mortes. That would have eliminated my latest ugly suspicion.

I told myself I was being viciously unjust again. The fact that he wasn't in Aigues-Mortes was no reason to suspect he'd been in Arles, shooting at Claudette and/or Dr. Bardin. The shooter could have been anybody. There was even less justification for thinking it might have been him than there'd been for wondering if he'd had some hand in what happened to Alexandre at the bullring.

There wasn't even any circumstantial evidence this time. Only opportunity.

I also reminded myself that Johnny was a damn good shot. If he'd fired at either of them at that range, he would have hit them.

That is, *if* the shooter had intended to hit them.

I could think of a couple reasons why someone might have wanted to shoot and miss.

I went out to my Peugeot, got what I needed from behind the rear seat, and put it in my pocket. Then I drove back to the Baths of Constantine.

There was a second police car parked at the end with the hole in the fence. Three gendarmes were prowling inside the ruins with flashlights and submachine guns. A fourth was coming back from a fruitless prowl of Rue de Grand Prieuré.

Claudette's convertible was still parked at that end of the Baths. She wasn't going to remerge from Dr. Bardin's place until the cops went away. Her car didn't draw any special attention in the meantime. No reason it should, among all the other cars using that space for overnight parking.

Two gendarmes stood on the corner asking questions of neighborhood people who'd come out of their apartments. I stopped beside them and poked my head out the car window long enough to hear that the witnesses had heard the shooting but had not seen anything. One of the gendarmes gave me an irritated stare.

"What's going on here?" I asked him.

He didn't answer, just motioned impatiently for me to move on and let him do his work. I did.

Driving to the other end of the Rue de Grand Prieuré, I turned the corner, continued for half a block, and parked. I got out of the car and went into the alley. I'd been right about the back door of the doctors' building. A few minutes' work with my lock pick and I had it open.

There was an open-cage elevator inside. I took it to the top floor. There were two doors. One bore the same brass plaque Dr. Bardin had outside the building. The other, unmarked, would be for the doctor to slip in and out by, when he didn't want to be seized upon by waiting patients. I knocked on that one.

No response. I banged on the door with the flat of my hand and called my name through it. "Tell him to open up, Claudette! Unless you'd rather I go down and bring up the cops."

They opened the door and let me in.

CHAPTER 22

Dr. Bardin couldn't come up with anyone he could believe might have tried to kill either of them. "Not us specifically," he added. "It must have been some insane person—one of those who kill for the thrill of it—who went out tonight to shoot at *somebody*—anybody."

"That happened around here before?" I asked him.

"Not here. But one reads of it elsewhere. In Europe, America. So why not here? Lacking any reason to think otherwise, I have to assume that's exactly what did happen."

It was possible—though easier to believe in if it hadn't been for the attempt against Alexandre and the kidnapping of Jacqueline Malo.

For Claudette, however, there was a different possibility that had more appeal: "With me dead, Alex and Jacqueline would each inherit *half* of everything. Papa's money and the company."

"Not quite half." I reminded her again. "Your father's will leaves five percent to your husband."

"That's only two and a half percent off what each of them would get with me gone. They'd share the rest fifty-fifty. That's a big jump from a third each."

"Either of them used to handling guns?"

"I don't know. Maybe one of them has been practicing. Or either of them could have *hired* somebody to kill me." Another thought appealed to her: "Maybe Alex and Jacqueline even got together on this."

But it seemed to me she found her theory more intriguing than likely.

It was pleasantly cool in Bardin's rear office, though the windows and heavy curtains were closed. He was one French doctor who didn't believe air conditioning to be a health hazard. The room was cozy: dark-paneled walls, a large oak desk, a built-in stereo and shelves full of medical tomes, records, and cassettes, a couple of heavy armchairs, and a wide studio couch covered by a colorful Moroccan rug.

They sat together on the couch. I sat on the edge of his desk, looking down at them. That's supposed to give a psychological advantage. Sometimes it does—if the people you're looking down at are unsure of their situation anyway.

Dr. Bardin was. Claudette was holding one of his hands in both of hers. She wore bright orange long johns and a V-neck pullover the same color made of a soft, thin cotton by one of the top fashion houses. Blue ballet shoes and big dangling earrings, also blue, supplemented her outfit. Standard leisure gear for the elegant young set along the Med.

Beside her Bardin looked drab; and decades past a nodding acquaintance with any young set. But close up there was a vigor in the seamed face and a kindly strength in the eyes. And some of the lines around his eyes and mouth had been dug there as much by humor as by anxiety.

There was no humor in him now. He was scared—by something more than having been shot at.

"Are you going to tell Malo?" he demanded, trying to armor an untenable position with dignity. The dignity was genuine, but the armor had gaping holes in it. "About Claudette visiting me tonight?"

"It's not a one-night affair," I said. "It's been going on for years, in spite of Malo's warning."

"Please—*don't* provoke a scandal. My wife has suffered years of sickness that have left her very little resistance. Please don't make her last few years even more miserable."

"She doesn't know about you and Claudette."

"No."

Claudette tightened her grip on Bardin's hand, fiercely protective. I found myself liking her more than I had during our meeting by the pool. "I'll make it worth your while," she told me with a hard defiance. She wasn't as frightened as he was; just worried. "Name your price. I'll give it to you."

"For keeping quiet about you and Dr. Bardin."

"Yes."

"Blackmail isn't one of my sidelines. I'm working for your father."

"There's no conflict," she said. "What exists between Hugues and me doesn't have the slightest connection with what you were hired to do. So my offer doesn't violate whatever *scruples* you might actually possess."

Bardin hadn't paid much attention to what she'd said. He'd been studying me; trying to estimate my character. He voiced his decision with more hope than certainty: "You are going to keep what you've learned about us to yourself, aren't you?"

I said, "There *is* a price."

Claudette nodded sagely, her cynicism confirmed.

"I need some large helpings of the truth," I told Hugues Bardin. "Right now I want to know more about you two. If I catch you lying to me, even once..."

I let the threat hang there, unstated. It's usually more effective that way. Extortion isn't one of my sidelines, either. But it does happen to be one of the handier, if less palatable, tools of the trade.

Claudette told me angrily, "Our relationship is none of your business."

"If I find that out," I said, "I'll have no reason to tell anybody else about it."

Dr. Bardin told her, "Be quiet, Claudette." He said it emphatically but without anger. She looked at him and choked back what she'd been preparing to say to me next. He looked at me again. "You do promise what we tell you will go no further."

I nodded and asked him, "Do you have any children?"

"My wife was never strong enough for childbearing."

"But you do have a son now, through Claudette."

He drew a deep breath and said it in a whisper: "Yes."

"And she brings the baby here for you to see and play with once in a while."

This time all Hugues Bardin could manage was a tormented nod.

"Hugues is Michel's *father*," Claudette said vehemently. "He has a right to know his own child."

And giving Bardin every opportunity to become more attached to his only child was one way to insure he wouldn't break with her. I said, "Triolet must know all this."

"Of course he knows Michel isn't *his*. I've never even been to bed with him."

"He doesn't mind?"

"Why should he?" Claudette demanded. "I assume Jean-Noel has a girlfriend or two he sees whenever he stays in Marseilles. I don't interfere with that, and he doesn't interfere with me. He's gotten what he wanted out of marrying me."

"You let him become Karl Malo's son-in-law—in exchange for his pretending to be your baby's father."

She nodded solemnly. "I wanted to have Hugues's child. And I knew my father would never stand for my having a baby without a husband, refusing to say who its father was. He'd have forced me to get an abortion."

I didn't ask how Malo could have forced it; and I didn't doubt that he would have been able to. "So you went to Triolet with your problem."

"Well, he'd been panting after me for years. And I knew it wasn't because he just couldn't resist my fabulous face and body." Claudette's laugh was spiteful. "You should have seen how *surprised* he was when I told him he could have what he wanted after all. He'd finally given up on me more than a year before."

"But he was still ready to jump at the chance."

"Jump is the right word for it. Like a starving seal." She started to laugh again and then didn't. "I'm not being fair," she said in an altered tone. "Jean-Noel did come through when I needed it—no matter what his reason. I leveled with him, and he leveled with me. And he *has* kept his end of our bargain. So far I haven't had any reason to regret it. He supplied the perfect solution—since Hugues couldn't marry me because of his wife."

"I couldn't have anyway," Hugues Bardin said uncomfortably, looking to me for understanding. "You can see how ridiculous it would be—Claudette is far too young for me."

"We *love* each other," she told him with a firmness that brooked no argument, "and that's the *only* thing between you and me that has any importance."

The look he gave her was bewitched and embarrassed at the same time. His emotional confusion around Claudette wasn't hard to understand. If a woman your own age used that tone of possessive authority on you, it might get your back up. But coming from a child, it's both amusing and flattering. And that was what Claudette was to Bardin: a child—who was at the same time the mother of his son.

She was still holding on to his hand when I left them. She hadn't let go of it once in all the time I'd been there.

* * * *

Few lights were on inside the Malo chateau, but Girard the butler was up and around. He told me Jacqueline Malo had returned from seeing her husband off at the airport but was probably asleep by now. Alexandre was back, too, but had gone out for a walk.

"He enjoys taking hikes in the cool of the night," Girard explained. "Sometimes he doesn't return for two or three hours."

"How long ago did he leave this time?" I asked.

"It's been a bit more than a half hour."

"Let me know when he gets back. If you're still awake by then."

"I will be," he assured me.

"Don't you ever sleep?"

"Frequently. In snatches. I haven't been able to sleep longer than a couple hours at a time since I was in my forties. Bad nerves, I suppose. Or a guilty conscience."

"About what?"

"Were you ever a soldier, monsieur?"

"Yes."

"In combat?"

I nodded.

"That usually," Girard said, "supplies enough memories to disturb one's sleep. Don't you find it so?"

"I try not to," I said—and I went up the stairs to my room.

When I switched on the ceiling light I saw one of the maids had been there. The windows were open, and their shutters were closed. The bed had been turned down for the night, and a terrycloth bathrobe was neatly draped over its foot. I stripped off the clothes I'd been wearing through that long, hot day, picked up the robe, and went into the bathroom for a shower.

I was toweling myself dry when I thought I heard a sound from the bedroom through the closed door. Putting on the bathrobe, I pushed the door open. The bedroom's overhead light had been switched off. A small table lamp had been turned on instead, providing a softer glow.

Jacqueline Malo sat on my bed.

She was leaning against the padded headboard with a large glass of whiskey in her hand. Her lovely legs were stretched out with one bare foot resting on the other. She wore a white nightgown that had a satiny shine in the lamplight. It was loose-fitting, but the material clung to her lovingly. The bodice was opened to the ripe swell of her breasts. She drank from her glass and smiled at me.

CHAPTER 23

"I hope you like scotch," she said, "because that's what I brought us." She nodded toward the sideboard against the far wall.

"Scotch will do fine," I said. My voice sounded steady enough to me. I walked past the end of the bed to the sideboard. In addition to the almost full bottle she'd brought along a small bucket of ice and a second large whiskey glass. Siege equipment. I poured three fingers and took a belt before adding ice. Then I turned to look at her again.

She was sitting up straighter, her marvelous eyes fixed on me like those of a lion tamer trying to gauge the mood of a tiger who might strike rather than perform. "Karl asked me to give you his number in Geneva," she said, "in case you find out anything before he gets back. I was leaving it on the writing desk over there when I heard you taking your shower. And then I decided, well…" She finished by raising her glass to me and then taking another sip.

"When do you expect him back?"

"Not for a few days at least. Perhaps a week." She paused and then asked me, "*Have* you learned anything?"

I strolled back past the end of the bed and sank into a deep leather armchair facing the other side of it. "This and that," I said, and I leaned back in the chair, making myself relax. "Getting a little background on some of you, for a start. It's too soon to expect more than that. You're a complicated family."

"If you did find out something, would you tell me about it?"

"Depends what it turned out to be." I moved my whiskey glass in small circles, listening to the tinkling of the ice cubes.

She folded her legs under her, yoga fashion, leaning toward me. "The way you looked when you came out and saw me—almost shocked."

"Surprised. Girard told me he thought you'd already gone to sleep."

"I tried, but I felt too—restless. Do you mind my being here?"

"It's a nice enough room," I said, "but you do improve it considerably." It was difficult to concentrate on what I was saying. There was too much temptation sitting there on my bed.

A slow blush surfaced in the golden tan of her cheeks. She lowered her eyes. "The way you *look* at me sometimes," she said in a very small voice. "As though you might eat me up."

"I might."

She drank again, emptying her glass. "I might not mind that," she whispered.

I tightened my grip on my own glass and stayed put. That required an effort I wasn't sure I could sustain. I wasn't sure I wanted to, either. But I waited, watching her.

She swung off the bed with her empty glass and walked to the sideboard with a fluid, sensuous grace that did nothing to lower my blood pressure. I watched her pour a generous refill.

"You once told me," I said, "that you have to be careful because it doesn't take many of those to become too many."

"Sometimes getting a *little* drunk helps," she said with her back still turned to me. "Scatters the inhibitions." She took a long swallow, put down the glass, and came around the bed to me. She sat down on the arm of my chair; desirable, vulnerable, available—and a touch frightened under the smile.

I smiled back. "Another thing you once told me about was your never going to bed with anyone but your husband."

"Did I actually say *never*? What I meant, of course, was that it isn't a habitual occurrence. In fact, it's damned rare. So much has to come together at the same moment. My mood, and the circumstances"—she ran the fingers of one hand through my hair—"and the man."

"Sure." I put my glass on the floor and slid an arm around her supple waist. The material of her nightgown was slippery beneath my hand. She wasn't wearing anything underneath but inviting, softly resilient woman. I pulled her onto my lap and kissed her.

It turned into a hell of a kiss. For a moment I felt her stiffen. Then her arms were around my neck, and her lips were moving sweetly under mine, the tip of her tongue darting to join us. The senses *have* been known to reel, and the earth to move—but not this time. I wanted her. Christ, I wanted her. But the passion she was putting into it, though genuine enough, was the wrong brand. Give Jacqueline Malo an A for passionate determination to carry through with what she'd started.

I scooped her up in my arms as I stood up. She kept her arms locked around my neck and pressed her face into my throat, her breathing quick and hot against my skin. She made a small sound that might have been stifled panic as I carried her to the bed.

I dumped her on it and picked up my drink. Taking it to the sideboard, I dropped in more ice. For no real reason except that it helped me to think of icebergs, glaciers, and deep freezes. There are acts of willpower that later give you a bit more self-respect—but at the time all you get is a dull ache.

I drank and turned around. Jacqueline Malo was crouched on the bed, staring at me uncertainly. Paradise lost. Thrown away bodily, in fact.

"Maybe I *shouldn't* have had that last drink," Jacqueline Malo said shakily. Puzzled rather than offended. There may even have been some sense of relief. "What *happened*?"

I found myself smiling at her. "Wrong mood, wrong circumstances."

Her mouth quirked briefly, almost a return to her normal humor. "Put more bluntly, you've just turned me down."

"You, never. Just the offer."

"It offends your principles."

"Call them prejudices."

She frowned, making an effort to sort it out. "You don't believe in cuckolding your clients."

"Cuckold—that's a stupid word. Implies the husband owns his wife and you're stealing his property."

"Then what *is* wrong? You do want me. I'm quite sure of that."

"With reason," I told her. "And I'm not above accepting a gift on occasion. But a sacrificial bribe—that takes the fun out of it."

Jacqueline Malo leaned back against the headboard and stretched her legs out again. She shook her head. "It wouldn't have been that much of a sacrifice, to be honest with myself. You are damned attractive. Certainly enough women have told you so."

"Some of them were softening me up—for what they were really after."

"Did they succeed?"

"Sometimes. Depended on what they wanted." I put my glass aside and walked to the bed. Taking her face between my hands, I kissed her enticing lips. She didn't flare into simulated passion this time. Neither did she pull away from me. I let go of her face and sat on the bed, looking at her.

"What is it you really want from me?" I asked quietly. "To drop this investigation? Just quit and go away?"

"No," she said. "That wouldn't help. Karl would only hire somebody else."

"Then what is it you hoped to persuade me to do?"

"Tried to seduce you into doing, you mean." Her grimace was wry. "Only that failed rather dismally, didn't it?"

"Not entirely," I told her, waiting.

She looked at me thoughtfully. "Couldn't you just go through the *motions* for a week or so? As long as you think necessary to look right.

And then tell Karl what he really wants to hear. That his son and daughter had nothing to do with kidnapping me."

"He'll want to know who *did*."

"The police haven't been able to find that out. So it won't be surprising if you can't, either. Just tell him you don't know—but that everything you've learned proves it wasn't his children. Karl will be annoyed—but not hurt by it. Not the way he'll be hurt if you really investigate and learn either Alexandre or Claudette was part of it."

"A real investigation may prove neither of them were."

"I don't want to take that chance—not with my husband's health at stake. I told you in Arles: it's over and done with, as far as I'm concerned. I don't *care* who did it. I only want it forgotten."

I looked at her in silence for a time. Then I said, "It's more than that, though, isn't it? More than protecting your husband, though I accept that's part of it. You're afraid of something else, too. Something a real investigation is likely to turn up."

She put her head back, resting it against the headboard, closing her eyes. I waited. But she stayed that way, silent.

I said, "Emil Fassler. Your dead husband."

Her eyes popped open, meeting my gaze. "So—you've already found out about Emil."

"Only that he had a little import-export firm based in Hamburg. And was killed under mysterious circumstances in Marseilles."

"But you'll keep digging at it, won't you? Until you find out more."

I nodded, keeping watch on her changing expressions. She leaned forward, raising her knees and hugging them. "That's what I came here to stop you from doing," she said tiredly. "The only way I could think of that might work."

"By giving yourself to me."

"And throwing myself on your mercy."

"I've been known to be merciful," I said dryly. "Even without being seduced into it."

Her eyes searched mine for a time. Finally she nodded to herself. "You're bound to find out anyway—if you keep on with what you're doing. Emil was—involved in some criminal activity for a time. Not for long, and not willingly—but he was."

"What kind of criminal activity?"

"I don't know. Emil said it was safer for me if I didn't. All I know is that some people were using his firm for something illegal. I didn't learn *that* until less than two months before Emil died. He was terrified of something, and I kept pressing him to tell me what was wrong. He finally told me that some extremely dangerous men had some kind of hold on him. He wouldn't tell me who they were or what it was. Just that he was afraid they'd kill him if he didn't cooperate."

"Do you think they're the ones who did kill him?"

"I suppose that's possible—but I would only be guessing."

"You didn't tell that to the Marseilles police, though."

"I never saw any police from Marseilles. An official of the Paris police came to tell me Emil had been killed, apparently by thieves. And to ask where I wanted his body sent for burial. Telling him that Emil had been mixed up with criminals—that he'd become a criminal himself—would that have brought him back to life?"

"It might have helped the cops catch his killers," I said. "But you're not one for revenge, are you?"

Jacqueline Malo shook her head. "It doesn't cure anything. It only prolongs the hurt."

"Does Malo know about your first husband's criminal involvement?"

"No. I didn't tell him. I—was ashamed, I suppose. I didn't want to say things like that about Emil. That was foolish of me, I know. If Karl finds out *now*, he'll feel I lied to him."

"People who love each other tell little lies all the time," I said. "Outright lies and lies of omission. Whatever's necessary to prevent trouble between them. It's no big deal."

"But so much of *our* relationship—Karl's and mine—is based on the complete trust he has in me. If he finds out about this, he'll begin to wonder if I haven't lied to him in other ways. It would erode that trust he feels. *Please*—you won't tell him?"

"I've no reason to," I said, "unless I learn it has some connection to what Malo's hired me for."

"It *doesn't*," Jacqueline Malo said.

I studied her carefully. "There has to be more," I said slowly. "You're too scared for it to be only about your first husband's link with criminals. You're afraid I might dig up something else."

"No, there's nothing else." But her eyes avoided mine.

"The more you tell me, the better chance I've got to protect you—from whatever it is that's worrying you."

"There's *nothing* else to tell," she swore raggedly. "I just want you to stop what you're doing and let us go on with our lives." She looked at me pleadingly. "Will you do that for me?"

"No."

"Why *not*? You'll get paid the same whether you continue to investigate or just pretend to."

"Would you sell your clients works signed by masters that you know are fakes?"

"I see—professional pride."

"Something like that."

"But *my* profession doesn't involve damaging people's lives," Jacqueline Malo said flatly. "If I learn a picture is a fake and say so, I'm only saving the client from wasting his money. But what *you* learn and reveal, in this case, can't accomplish anything except to cause considerable pain. To Karl—and to me."

"I'll have to decide if that's so when I get to it," I told her. "I can't promise more." Then I took a shot: "Do you know a man named John Duncan?"

I watched her give the name a few seconds of frowning thought. Then she shook her head. "No."

"An American," I added, "but he speaks excellent French. With a slight accent." I described Johnny in detail, including his flamboyant manner of dressing.

Something flickered very briefly in Jacqueline Malo's eyes. Then it was gone. "No," she told me carelessly, "I can't recall anyone like that." Swinging her legs off my bed, she stood up. She had to put a hand on the night table to steady herself. "I *have* had too many," she said tiredly. "Time I was in my own bed."

"You're more than welcome to stay here," I told her, "now that we understand each other better."

She gave me a wan smile. "I think not." She turned toward the bedroom door. I went past and opened it for her.

Alexandre Malo was sitting cross-legged on the floor in the corridor outside, grinning up at us.

CHAPTER 24

He looked at Jacqueline Malo in her nightgown and then at me in my bathrobe, still grinning. "Girard said you wanted to be informed when I came back. I told him not to bother, I wanted to meet you anyway. But then I listened at your door and heard you had company—so I settled down to wait."

Alexandre looked back to Jacqueline. "I must say, it was a *short* wait." He rose to his feet in one easy, athletic move. "It's what I keep explaining to you, Jacqueline. Older men get tired too soon and leave the woman still hungering. *That's* why you need an occasional fling with a young man—at the height of my virile power."

"Alexandre, you're embarrassing me and making a clown of yourself." She sounded faintly annoyed rather than truly angry. "We all know you're not a fool, so please stop acting like one."

"I'm only trying to enrich your life," he told her cockily. "And my own, I do admit. The situation's just too intriguingly classic. Doddering old father, beautiful stepmother in her prime, handsome and lustful young son. Inevitable and irresistible."

"So far, Alexandre, I've found you effortlessly resistible, as you've noticed."

He nodded amiably. "So far. But past is not present, let alone future." He took hold of her right wrist with his left hand. "I'll escort you to your bedroom while we discuss your suppressed libido."

She tried to disengage her wrist but couldn't. I said, "Let her go."

"Don't interfere," Alexandre warned me in an utterly confident and almost friendly tone. "Big as you are, you could wake up in a hospital with a number of very delicate bones smashed beyond repair."

I closed my left hand around his arm just above the elbow and dug in with my fingers. He gasped, let go of her, and in the same instant twisted in against me, driving his heel at my instep arch. I sidestepped it, but he didn't have to think out his next strike. His elbow was already driving at my heart.

I clubbed his elbow away with the side of my left fist and slapped him with my right hand, putting considerable force into it. He was spun all the way around, blundering into the corridor wall and falling down with a noisy thud.

"Please," Jacqueline Malo begged, "don't hit him again."

"It won't be necessary," I told her. "Good night." Alexandre sat on the floor, rubbing the back of his neck with both hands and staring up at me with dazed eyes. The imprint of my hand was a darkening stain across the side of his face.

Jacqueline Malo gave him a last troubled look and went off along the corridor, the fingers of one hand trailing against the wall beside her. As she vanished around the corner near the staircase Alexandre spoke again, groggily. "I thought my neck was broken. How in hell did you get past my guard to do that?"

"I've had a good deal of practice."

He dropped his hands from his neck and pressed his head against the wall, trying to blink the fog out of his vision. "So have I. My martial arts teacher keeps saying I'm the fastest student he's ever had."

"He's lying to you. Or he's had a run of unusually slow pupils. Do you like whiskey?"

"What?"

"There's a bottle in my room. And some ice. You did say you wanted to meet me."

He smiled weakly. "I think I already have."

I reached down a hand to him. He took it and didn't try any tricks with it. Just let me help him get to his feet. I gestured at the open door to my bedroom and said politely, "After you."

Alexandre laughed. "Afraid I'll get you from behind, eh?"

"Terrified."

I followed him inside and shut the door behind us.

* * * *

"Well," Alexandre asked me sardonically, "how do you like us all so far?"

"Interesting family."

"You think this is a *family*?"

"What do you think it is?"

"A gold can of worms. That's what you've stepped into here, Sawyer. Rich and messy."

I sat on the edge of the bed, and he was in the deep leather armchair. We each had a glass of iced scotch. He was using his to soothe the bruised side of his handsome young face.

"Does it bother you?" he asked me, curious. "I mean, having to deal with people like us? Or do you get used to it? I guess you've run into others like us in your job?"

"A few," I said. "Tell me, why don't you believe what I said about someone trying to get you killed in that bullring the other day?"

"Because I know what did happen. I took too many tranquilizers. And the sun was too hot—made them hit me harder than I expected. My own fault."

"Somebody spiked your water bottle."

"So you told my father," Alexandre said with a thin edge of sarcasm. "But you don't believe it."

"No. Sorry—but no, I don't."

"Why would I lie about it?"

"The obvious reason. Money. You worried my father enough to make sure he'll keep you around longer. Probably at a jacked-up fee."

"Everybody keeps telling me how intelligent you are," I said. "Maybe you are—but you're not much of a judge of character."

"There's no such thing as character where money is concerned. Money destroys character—and reshapes it. Just watch a big, tough employee tremble in front of his skinny little boss, and you'll get a notion of what I mean."

"What I get is a feeling you're testing out a theory before writing a paper on it for *Sciences Po*."

Alexandre laughed. "Not a bad idea. 'Money and Character.' Good title for a paper. I might do it."

I took a sip from my glass. "Your school is dedicated to training future leaders of the country's power structure. I doubt that your professors would appreciate that cynical an attitude."

"I'm *not* cynical—about either money or power. Merely realistic about how they function. It would be sheer hypocrisy to pretend I disapprove of them—when I know I'm going to manage one of the most important companies in France."

"You're speaking about after your father dies."

"Almost certainly well before that," Alexandre said. "I'll become part of Malo Transport's management after I finish school. Be moved around from one junior executive position to another until I acquire a firm grasp of every facet of the company. Once I have that, my father will make me his chief executive assistant."

"You expect to become second-in-command of the company."

"*That's* been his plan since I was born. And once I've reached that position he's bound to relinquish more and more of his authority to me as he gets older."

"At the moment," I said, "your brother-in-law is the assistant director of Malo Transport. Your father's second-in-command. But you expect to take over that position."

Alexandre nodded. "Oh, we'll probably let him keep the title—and create another one for me."

"You don't intend to ease him out of the company?"

He considered that. "No, I don't think so. Unless it proves necessary. Jean-Noel *is* an efficient, dedicated executive. Excellent for a secondary position—for seeing to it that company decisions are carried through properly."

"But not for making those decisions?"

"*I* don't think Jean-Noel has the kind of daring imagination that a top command position requires," Alexandre told me. "In my opinion, my father has already allowed him to take over too many of his decision-making powers. I'd strip those from him. And supervise the way he manages projects much more carefully than my father's been doing lately." Alexandre moved his shoulders in a small shrug. "If Jean-Noel could accept that without resentment, I'd keep him—even after I took full control after my father's death."

"As I understand it," I told him, "you only inherit a bit less than a *third* of the company control."

"No—I inherit that share of the company's *profits*. My father's will specifies that *I* will run the company."

I watched Alexandre take a sip from his glass—his first since I'd poured him the drink. "You're not much of a drinker, are you?"

"I prefer the diversity of pills," he told me. "They do whatever needs doing faster and better. Perk you up or calm you down. Liquor's not that efficient or predictable. That's why it's not as popular as dope these days."

"Uh-huh." I had more of my own drink. Old-fashioned unpredictability has its own allure. "How do you feel about your stepmother?"

"About her *becoming* my stepmother, I suppose you mean."

"That's part of it."

Alexandre's expression became distinctly unpleasant. "How do you *think* I feel about her suddenly appearing on the scene, trapping my father into a third marriage?"

"Is that what she did—trap him?"

"Call it what you want. But you can't expect me to be happy about a woman who causes my inheritance to get chopped down from half to one third."

Everybody seemed to ignore Triolet's five percent.

"I got the impression just now," I said, "that you liked her quite a bit."

Alexandre eyed me insolently. "I like her *body*. Who wouldn't? I'd like to find out what she's like when she lets herself go, all the way. But maybe you could tell me about that. Though it's not the same as firsthand experience."

"I *could* smack you again."

"That wouldn't be a smart idea. Once was instructive—let me know it's time to get myself a different martial arts teacher. Try it a second time and I'll have a talk with my father. I *can* get him to fire you, if I apply myself to it."

"You're terrifying me again," I told him. "And boring me, which is worse. I think I've had enough of your company—unless you have any thoughts about who kidnapped your stepmother."

I'd hurt his feelings. He shoved angrily to his feet and deliberately tossed his glass at the head of the bed. It bounced off the padded head-board, spilling its contents across the pillows.

That didn't bother me too much. I wasn't going to sleep there any-way. I stayed put, looking at him with no change of expression. "A little crude, Alexandre. But maybe that's how truly brilliant minds express themselves when they can't come up with a simple answer to a simple question. It's called throwing a tantrum, in kindergarten circles."

My lack of anger made him madder. "How the hell would I know who did it? Maybe Jacqueline kidnapped herself. I've thought about *that* possibility."

"Why would she?"

"Seven million francs is one good reason, isn't it? Money and char-acter—remember?"

"She's going to inherit a great deal more than that," I pointed out, "so you can't be talking about her future needs. You mean she's presently strapped for cash? Your father's stingy with her?"

"No," Alexandre admitted grudgingly, settling down a bit. "He's al-ways trying to give her expensive jewelry and other presents. And being miffed because she complains she already has more of everything than she needs."

"So she hasn't acted like someone that hungry for money."

"Things change—people change. Maybe Jacqueline's gotten herself a secret lover she's planning to run off with. *That* would cut her out of my father's will. The ransom would be a nice piece of change to keep her and her lover in comfort for some time."

"If you have any evidence your stepmother *has* a secret lover," I said, "I'd surely appreciate your telling me."

"No—but it stands to reason she will, sooner or later. My father is still a good-looking man, but he's *not* young. And not well. He can't be too great a lover, can he? It might bring on another heart attack."

"Your father looks healthy enough to me," I said. "He had a heart attack, sure. But the best advice doctors give people who've had one is to start relaxing and enjoying themselves more. Making love is the best relaxer God ever invented."

"Did God invent that?" Alexandre Malo jeered. "I thought it was the Devil."

CHAPTER 25

When I was rid of him I put on fresh clothes and packed my toilet kit with a change of clothing in my new suitcase. The reason I wasn't spending the night at the chateau was the plane to Paris I had to be on at nine in the morning. And there were several chores requiring me to be at the airport at least an hour earlier than that.

First I'd have to pick up and pay for my flight reservation—which usually meant a long wait behind others doing the same. *And* I'd have to check through my suitcase with my handgun inside it. I didn't intend to go anywhere without a weapon until the case was finished. But my permit to carry wouldn't allow me to wear the gun on the flight. So it would have to go through with the luggage. And I'd have to clear that with airport security before it showed on their detectors.

All that would take time. If I slept at the chateau, I'd need to be up and on my way by six-thirty at the latest. Even then, a traffic tie-up on airport approach roads could still make me miss my plane. The best way to be sure I got there in time was to drive down that night.

A call to Information got me a list of hotels close to Marignane Airport. It was the height of the season for hotels as well as flights. But the second one I tried had had a late no-show, and the room was available. I promised to be there in just over an hour.

There wasn't much traffic on the southbound highway at that time of night. While I drove it I mulled over the various things I'd learned but still didn't understand because the links between them were missing.

Someone, or several someones, had struck at three different members of the Malo family over a period of the last two months.

The kidnap of Karl Malo's wife.

An attempt to get his son killed "accidentally" in the bullring.

The shots fired at his daughter.

I also had to consider how those *might* be connected to the death of Hubert Loy, Malo's previous assistant director. And, further back, to the killing of Jacqueline Malo's first husband, Emil Fassler.

I could spin some links between some of those events, but they were tenuous. Like spider-webs: okay for tangling little flitting guesses, but hard facts barged right through them, leaving gaping holes.

I hadn't achieved much success at filling in those holes when I arrived at the hotel near Marignane.

It was a recent addition to one of the world's most successful hotel chains. The room they had waiting for me was functional and antiseptic, with furniture that would hold together as long as the hotel. Not long. Airport hotels are built for quick profit, not for repeat clientele. They don't have to supply luxury to match their prices. People who use them do so when circumstances force it and they have no other choice.

I stripped for bed and got out my little traveler's alarm clock. The hotel was only a few minutes' drive from the airport. I set the alarm to wake me at seven-thirty in the morning. That would give me a decent, if not extravagant, amount of sleep.

But I didn't get that much, as it turned out—and I didn't make my plane, either.

CHAPTER 26

The luminous dial of my little alarm clock registered a few minutes before five A.M. when the knock at my hotel room door woke me.

The surge of adrenaline got me entirely awake very fast. Eyes wide open, brain clear. My hand closed around the H & K P7 on the bedside table as I sat up and swung my feet to the floor. I didn't turn on the lamp. I stood up with the gun ready. Knuckles rapped at my door again.

It wasn't aggressive knocking. Just loud enough to wake me; not enough to wake people in other rooms.

Two and half steps across the dark room brought me to the door. I put my back to the wall beside it, raised the P7 with my finger on the trigger, and asked who was there.

The answer came with no more volume than necessary to be heard through the door: "It's me, Pete. Johnny."

"Who's with you?"

"All by myself, kid."

"I'll get upset if that's not true, Johnny. I don't want you bleeding all over this nice carpet."

"You and me both. Come on, let me in."

Keeping to the protection of the wall, I stretched out my free hand and unlocked the door. I withdrew the hand and held my gun aimed at gut level. "Step in with your hands in front of you where I can see them."

Johnny Duncan opened the door and came in, arms stretched out ahead of him, momentarily blind in the darkness of the room while I could see him plainly by the light from the corridor. He was dressed as he'd been the last time, except his shirt was bright yellow. There was nobody else in the corridor.

My gun was aimed at the small of his back. I kept it that way and used my free hand to flick on the room light and shut and relock the door. Then I moved from the wall, backing two steps away from him. "Turn and lean with both hands against the door. The usual."

"I guess I should be offended," Johnny drawled, "but what the hell." He did an about-face, spread his legs wide apart, and let himself fall forward until his weight was resting on his fingertips against the door.

I frisked him thoroughly. Including his crotch and ankles and sleeves.

No weapon.

"I only came around to *talk*," he said mildly, and he looked at me sideways. "I see you still don't wear pajamas. Ever the optimist, eh? Hoping for prettier visitors than me."

"Sit on the floor. Knees up and your hands on them." Johnny complied with my request. From that position it would require several separate moves for him to get up and reach me. I relaxed a notch and put the gun down on the bedside table. My slacks and shirt were draped over the chair next to it. I put them on. Not exactly modesty. The Naked Ape feels himself at a disadvantage uncovered in the presence of a potential opponent.

Johnny stayed on the floor with his hands on his knees, watching me blankly. "This is *not* like old times, Pete."

I sat down in the chair and rested my right arm on the bedside table, my hand near the gun. "What'd you come to talk about?"

"That appointment you've got this afternoon at the embassy in Paris. I don't want you to keep it." There was neither threat nor anxiety in his tone. It was a flat statement.

"You *do* still have those long ears," I said. "I guess one of them's in the embassy."

"Nice lady I've been friends with since a long, long way back. She called last night to tell me she'd been asked to pull the old files on me for Bob Lodish, the CIA's new station chief there. Seems Lodish also phoned Washington and got a go-ahead on talking to you and some guy from the DGSE. Subject: John Duncan. So I began calling your hotel in Arles. And you kept not being in. Finally I tried the Malo chateau. Butler said you'd been there but left."

"And since I wasn't back at the Arles hotel, and you knew I'd be flying to Paris, you checked the hotels around here."

"Right. I do remember how these things are done, when I push my old brain a bit."

"Only you weren't in Aigues-Mortes when your embassy friend called there last night," I said. "Or you'd have found me still at the chateau—or gotten here sooner than this. So your friend left a message with your girlfriend for you to call her. And you didn't until much later. When you got back from Arles."

Johnny's expression stayed blank. "What would I be doing up there?"

"Missing Malo's daughter with a couple of carefully aimed shots."

"Why would I do that?"

I didn't mind his pumping me like that, trying to find out how much I actually knew. Even his negative responses gave me indications of where I might be on the right track. Also, I *wanted* him to know I was closing in. I said, "That was just to muddy the waters, Johnny—another basic your old brain can't have forgotten. To divert me and anybody else from focusing entirely on something like your spiking Alexandre's bottle of water."

"Hell, Pete—I'm the one who jumped in there and saved that kid from being gored and trampled to death."

"That bull," I said, "had already stopped to think over what it wanted to do next. Odds were it was going to turn away and look for somebody who was still moving to chase. Playing hero like you did—that was only to show me you weren't involved in the attempt on the boy. Then all you'd have to do is wait until I gave up on the case and went away—before rigging some other accidental death for Malo's son."

"I guess you've got some kinda half-assed notions about why I'd want the kid killed."

"Incomplete—but not half-assed. It's got some connection with Jean-Noel Triolet. *He* knew what was scheduled to happen that afternoon. Rushed over to the bullring to warn you to put it off—because Malo had just hired me to do some digging. He couldn't get to you in time. But you'd already spotted me—and you knew about my working for Malo before on the snatching of his wife. You knew why I was there. Maybe you even spotted me tailing Triolet. It was too late by then for you to prevent the boy from drinking his spiked water. So you told one of your friends to stay on me—and stop me if I tried to catch your other friend removing the evidence."

I paused and smiled stiffly. "I think you told him to stop me as gently as possible—I appreciate that, Johnny."

"You do spin a crazy yarn," he said, poker-faced. "Does it include my having something to do with the kidnap, too?"

"I figure you had *everything* to do with that one," I told him flatly. "And there I don't have to grope around for motives. The ransom you gouged out of Malo is reason enough."

"You've seen the car I drive," Johnny said in an amused tone. "Do I look like a guy who's got that much loot in his pocket?"

"You're not dumb enough to start spending that kind of tainted money this soon. You'll have it buried. Not to be dug up until the last lingering questions about that snatch have been forgotten. A year or more—as long as it takes. Then go away, someplace far enough. With your girlfriend, maybe. Change of identity and a new life. No problem with that amount of cash."

For the first time since he'd entered my room Johnny gave me a flash of that old rakish grin. "Pete, I don't think you've got one damn thing. You're just farting in a windstorm."

"But the storm's blowing in your direction." I leaned toward him and said what the years between us obliged me to: "Get out *now*, Johnny. Whatever it is you're involved in, get out of it. Before you can't. Get out and go somewhere else. The further the better. Do it now and I won't put anybody on your trail."

He regarded me, seeming entirely at ease. "You know, that's the first half-friendly sound you've made since I came in here."

"Friendly or not, it's a warning you'd be smart to act on."

"Only say I already *can't*," he said carelessly. "In which case I'd want to give *you* a friendly warning. A couple of 'em, in fact. First one is, *don't* keep that appointment at the embassy this afternoon. Or ever."

"That bothers you a lot."

The pent-up force I knew to be contained inside Johnny Duncan remained invisible behind the calm facade. "I just don't want people raking up my past. Past and better forgotten."

"Unless it's tied to what's going on now."

He ignored that. "The second friendly warning is that *you'd* better get out of this. Real quick. Tell Malo your investigation isn't turning up anything at all worth pursuing any further. Which ain't far from the truth. Go away and get yourself involved in other jobs and forget this one."

"Or what? What's the sting end of the warning? If I don't quit, you'll kill me?"

"Me?" Johnny looked genuinely upset. "*I* wouldn't hurt you—you know that."

"Unless absolutely necessary."

"The thing is, Pete—I've got some nasty associates who don't like your poking around. And they've got no reason to be as fond of you as I am."

"Do they know you came here? To find out if I know too much to be left alive?"

"Right now you don't know fuck-all. All you've got is some crazy guesswork."

"You know how investigators work," I said. "Doesn't take high intellect. Just persistence. Question enough people who've never been asked those questions in combination before. You keep adding to the combination, and some of the answers begin sending you back to ask the first people new things based on them. Do that long enough and a pattern shows up, sooner or later."

"Sometimes," Johnny said. "Other times not—especially when you've got no facts backing up the guesses."

"I must be doing something right, or you and your friends wouldn't be worried."

"They're bad people," Johnny told me softly. "About as bad as any I ever got tangled up with."

"Then you'd better get untangled pretty damn fast." I added a zinger with no change of tone at all: "How do you happen to know Jacqueline Malo?"

He didn't even blink. "Don't try to tickle an old pro, kid. How would *I* know someone like her?"

I nodded. "That's another way of putting the question."

Johnny sighed. "Pete—just go away and forget it. I don't want to hurt you, and you don't want to hurt me. Your granddaddy wouldn't be happy either way."

"He liked you," I granted. "But that wouldn't have stopped him from sinking his teeth into you, if he thought you were mixed up in kidnapping, attempted murder—and maybe a couple that succeeded."

"You got no evidence at all of any of that. And you're not your granddaddy. You're more like me."

"Somewhere about halfway between the two of you, I'd say."

"Naw—your granddaddy was a bulldog. Pure, tough, dependable guard dog. You and me—we're both wolves."

"Is that what we are?" I said mildly.

Johnny nodded emphatically. "Sure. And you know that old folk saying: It's a hard winter when one wolf devours another."

"And right now it's midsummer."

"Correct. So no reason at all for us wolves to turn cannibal."

We sat there—me on the chair and Johnny on the floor—looking at each other impassively for a bit. He'd said what he'd come to say; and he knew I wasn't going to tell him more than I had. He took his hands off his raised knees. "Okay if I get up and go now?"

I stood up, taking the pistol off the table. "Okay."

He rolled over on one knee and got to his feet. "I'm not much for sitting on floors anymore," he said, arching his back and kicking his legs to restore circulation.

"Sorry about that," I said. "I get grouchy when I haven't had enough sleep."

He smiled, shrugged, and went to the door. I moved behind him, holding the gun but letting it hang down by my thigh. He *had* only come to talk.

"I hope you're gonna take my advice," he said as he unlocked and opened the door.

"I'm hoping you'll take mine."

"Aw, shit," he growled, and he started through the door.

But I'd relaxed one notch too many.

They were waiting out of sight against the corridor wall, one on either side of the door. Johnny wasn't all the way out when they swung into sight in unison, ramming into him and knocking him backward off his feet against me.

We hit the floor tangled together, a lot of Johnny's weight landing across my gun arm and pinning it to the floor. He was as startled as I was, but that didn't help. I'd been neutralized just long enough.

I started to wrench my gun out from under Johnny—and then stopped trying. They were already inside with us, the door shut again. In a room that size, four people made a crowd.

The one to my left, crouching with a .44 automatic held ready, wore dungarees and black sneakers.

The other on my right was the swarthy guy I'd tried to follow out of the bullring. He had a short-barreled shotgun aimed at my head.

CHAPTER 27

"Let go your pistol," the one with shotgun told me quietly, "or I'll blow your head off."

I kept Johnny close by tightening my free arm across his chest. "You'd blow *his* head off, too," I pointed out.

"That would be too bad," the shotgunner said indifferently. The indifference wasn't pretended.

"You'll wake up the whole hotel," I said.

"And do you imagine they'll come running out of their rooms to stop us?"

I doubted it. Gunshots would keep them locked in, screaming into their phones. By the time the cops arrived these two would have gone the way they'd come: probably via the back fire stairs and out the rear of the hotel through the parking basement.

"I won't count to ten," the guy with the shotgun warned me. The one with the automatic seemed to be the silent partner. "Drop it *now*."

"*Do* it," Johnny hissed. "I know this guy—he'll *shoot* that cannon."

I let go of my pistol. The shotgunner hooked it close to him with the pointed toe of his shiny brown shoe. He picked it up, hesitated, then tucked it in his belt and kept the shotgun on me. For some killers, the bigger the bang the better. Weapons, like wine and women, are a matter of personal taste. Beauty is in the eye of the beholder, flavor in the palate of the drinker, deadliness in whatever feels like ultimate authority in the shooter's grip.

The guy with the automatic was still crouched, having difficulty getting an unobstructed bead on me because of Johnny.

"I get a feeling," I told Johnny as I let him go, "that your friends don't care too much about you anymore."

He rolled off me, and the one with the automatic straightened—now with a clear view of me down its sights. Johnny came up on his hands and knees, glaring at the shotgunner. "You bastards. You were supposed to wait till I got back and told you what he said. He doesn't know *anything*."

"Hassan decided he wants to find that out for himself," the shotgunner said.

"He'll be real pleased to hear you gave away his name like that."

The shotgunner shrugged, giving me an unpleasant hunch that Hassan wouldn't give a damn because I wasn't scheduled to walk away after he'd questioned me. The shotgun gestured at Johnny. "Stay on the floor, face down. Don't leave this room for ten minutes after we've gone."

Johnny cursed softly and rolled over again, ending up face down against the narrow bedside table.

The next order was to me: "Stand up."

I got to my feet. I'd been listening carefully to the shotgunner's accent, but all I could be sure of was that he was from one of the countries of the Middle East. The silent one with the automatic looked as if he could be from the same general area.

"The handcuffs," the shotgunner said to his partner. And to me: "Put your hands behind your back."

I grimaced and obeyed, hearing the clink of the handcuffs as the guy with the automatic moved out of sight behind me. I listened for the clicks when he unlocked the cuffs in preparation for securing my wrists. It's almost impossible to do that with one hand and hold a gun properly with the other hand. I was watching Johnny, who was watching the guy trying to do both. When Johnny nodded I rammed myself backward, using all my strength and weight to crush the man behind me against the wall.

The automatic went off. The bullet angled past my hip and drilled a hole through the door. That told me where his gun was. I grabbed the hand holding it with my left hand and reached for his elbow with my right.

The other had started to squeeze the shotgun's trigger and then stopped himself. Shotguns have their uses; but not at close quarters when you have the man you want to hit tangled with another you don't. Luckily he cared more about his partner than he had about Johnny. He used his free hand to snatch my pistol from his belt.

Johnny seized two legs of the bedside table and swung it like a battering ram against the shotgunner's knees. The guy crashed to the floor with shotgun and pistol going off at the same time. Chunks of ceiling plaster blasted by the shotgun rained down on all of us.

I broke the other man's elbow in the same moment. He screamed, and his automatic fell to the floor. I scooped it up as the shotgunner sat up trying to bring both pistol and shotgun to bear. There was no time for me to take precise aim. I just pointed the automatic and fired it.

Part of the shotgunner's forehead disappeared. His torso flopped backward. His head struck the floor and stayed there. His arms and legs twitched as death spread toward them from his ruined brain.

The man I'd gotten the automatic from was leaning against the wall holding his broken arm, his face a mask of shock. I made sure he didn't have another weapon before looking at Johnny. He sat on the floor leaning against the side of the bed, his lips drawn back from clenched teeth. The pistol shot fired by the shotgunner had torn a hole through his suede jacket a few inches to the right of his navel. Dark wetness was spreading around the hole.

I went to him. "How bad?"

"Lousy," he grated. He put a hand on the bed and shoved to his feet. "But I can make it outta here."

"Okay," I said.

He nodded toward the man against the walls. "Got to take him, too—so he won't tell the cops about me."

I said okay again—and handed him the automatic.

He gripped it with one hand, his other pressed to his bleeding wound. "You won't tell them, either," he said raggedly.

"You saved my life just now."

"Instinctive—and stupid," he said disgustedly, "If I'd stopped to think…" He didn't bother to finish it.

I went past him and opened the door, looking both ways along the corridor. It was empty. No other door was going to open until the place was full of cops. "Go," I told him.

He went, pushing the broken-armed gunman ahead of him with the automatic. I didn't go with them. I'd registered under my own name using a credit card. No choice but to stay put and handle the flak.

They disappeared down the back fire escape stairway. I left the door wide open, sat down on the bed in plain sight with my hands empty on my knees, and waited. I didn't look at the dead man on the floor.

CHAPTER 28

I didn't shake loose from the law until shortly after one P.M.

An assortment of inspectors and commissaires from various branches of the French police system made it a full, arduous morning. Each interrogation team asked essentially the same questions and wound up feeling that my answers lacked something they couldn't define. That was understandable. What was lacking was any mention of Johnny Duncan. Keeping Johnny out of it made my account somewhat narrow.

Two men I didn't know, I told them, had knocked on my hotel room door at five in the morning, claiming to be cops. I'd been suspicious enough to pick up my pistol—for which I had a carrying permit—before opening the door to them. They had attacked me. I had no idea why. In the ensuing battle I had wounded the member of the pair who'd gotten away. (That would account for the blood Johnny had leaked along the corridor and down the fire-escape stairway.) The man on my floor had been killed by the one who'd fled with a bullet intended for me.

Getting the cops to accept that version—and to accept the fact I that couldn't discuss the case I was on—took up most of the hours until one P.M. Lieutenant Laffite's telephone confirmation that my gun permit was legit helped. What helped more was that it was endorsed by the Defense Minister. But what helped most was that I was working for Karl Malo. Government ministers come and go, but Malo Transport didn't. It had been, was, and would continue to be an integral part of the nation's power structure.

The corpse on my floor proved to be an unexpected embarrassment for the government. His papers identified him as Ahmed Kadir, an accredited member of the Libyan Trade Mission in Marseilles, with full diplomatic status. But trying to explain what he'd been doing in a gun battle was the cops' responsibility—not mine.

After they finally let me go I began dealing with my own responsibilities.

* * * *

First a call to Thierry Gallion, explaining why I wasn't able to keep the appointment he'd arranged with the CIA rep—and asking him to try setting up another.

Then trying to find Johnny Duncan, with no success. A call to his girlfriend in Aigues-Mortes—Suzanne Proslier—didn't help. She hadn't seen or heard from Johnny since the night before. She didn't know where he might be.

I asked if she knew any doctors Johnny had contacts with. The question worried her. She asked if Johnny was sick. I said he'd been having some stomach trouble when I'd last seen him. She told me she'd never known him to need a doctor, but had always assumed that if he did he'd use her family doctor in Aigues-Mortes.

That wasn't what I had in mind. What I was looking for was the kind of doctor willing to treat Johnny's gunshot wound without reporting it. So I went on a prowl of Marseilles underworld hangouts and talked to my *milieu* connections. They contacted the right kind of doctors for me—but none of those had dealt with Johnny, now or in the past.

While I was making my prowl I dropped some other questions among my *milieu* acquaintances, promising suitable rewards if they could track down the answers. I left them to that late in the evening and phoned Thierry Gallion again.

He told me his CIA contact had agreed to reschedule our appointment to just before noon the next morning. But I ran into trouble when I tried to get a flight that would get me there on time. No seat was available on any plane to Paris that night or the next morning.

I finally phoned Karl Malo in Geneva. He phoned the director of Air France, who bounced somebody off a ten A.M. flight for me.

It was times like that that almost made me like Jacqueline Malo's husband.

I checked into a different hotel that night, paying cash and using an assumed name, switched on my alarm clock, switched off my brain, and got nine solid hours of sleep.

* * * *

In Paris the next morning, at eleven-thirty, I found Thierry Gallion in the Jardin des Tuileries. He was a tall, thin man with the world's troubles in his eyes and a hearing aid in one ear. When I came upon him he was admiring the statue of Mercury riding his winged horse.

According to Thierry, Mercury was the original double agent, carrying secret messages in both directions between the Kremlin of the gods and the Pentagon of the mortals.

We strolled out of the Tuileries and across the Place de la Concorde, moving slowly because those hours inside a submarine stuck at an intolerable depth had left Thierry with a heart that made Malo's condition seem one of blooming health. He escorted me into the American Embassy, where he was received with considerably more warmth than I was.

The real purpose of our three-man get-together at the embassy—in the minds of the Washington panjandrums who'd given it the go-ahead—was to remind one and all that, in spite of recurring policy conflicts between the U.S. and France, the two nations retained a special friendship hallowed by history.

The embassy's location made it a natural place for such reminders. One side looks across narrow Rue Boissy at the building in which Ben Franklin and King Louis XVI signed the document by which France became the first country in the world to recognize the thirteen original colonies as an independent nation called the United States of America.

But the small conference room into which the CIA's Bob Lodish conducted Thierry and myself didn't face in that direction. The view from its two windows was of the corner of the Place de la Concorde where Louis XVI was guillotined when French enthusiasm for the American Revolution inspired them to stage their own.

It was a less drastic shift in national direction that dictated the CIA's willingness to discuss Johnny Duncan. Washington wanted to repair certain lines of communication that had broken down between it and Paris.

* * * *

The room selected for our meeting seemed to be furnished with items discarded by other parts of the embassy. Not that any of it was junk. But no piece blended with any of the others. Thierry lowered his skinny length into a chubby dark leather armchair. I sat down next to him in a tall ladderback with a padded brocade seat. Bob Lodish, the CIA station chief, took a roomy walnut swivel chair, swinging it around to face us across a coffee table that had straight black iron legs supporting a free-form olivewood top with interesting grain patterns.

Lodish was about forty-eight, with carroty hair that curled behind his small ears and a lean figure in a neatly tailored dark gray suit with a maroon tie punctuating a pale green button-down shirt. He had a wide, thin-lipped mouth that reminded me of Triolet, but there was a wary humor in the clever light blue eyes that made all the difference.

"Do you mind," Lodish asked Thierry, "if we conduct this in English?"

"Not at all, old boy."

The wide mouth showed small crooked teeth when Lodish smiled. "I mean American English, Thierry."

"Glad to oblige, pardner," Thierry assured him. "It's a heckuva lot better'n having to listen to your French."

"Thierry," I said, "that's got to be the worst Gary Cooper imitation I've ever heard."

"I need a few more replays of that *High Noon* videocassette you gave me."

Lodish made an apologetic gesture and said, "Afraid it's going to take me longer than that to talk the kind of French people won't sneer at. Even with Berlitz stuffing it into me three hours a night."

He took a miniature recorder from his jacket and placed it on the coffee table. "I'm going to record this conversation," he told Thierry. "The powers that be want it as evidence of how well we cooperate with you people. I can make a duplicate tape for you before you leave, if you want."

Thierry shook his head. "My powers that be like us to keep our powers of memory well exercised."

"Okay, then." Lodish switched on his recorder and spoke into it, identifying himself, me, and Thierry. "This interview is taking place at the direct request of Captain Gallion of the DGSE. It is hoped this will serve as further evidence that recent allegations about our not being completely open with representatives of our host country with regard to actions involving French interests are quite untrue."

Having delivered that required speech into the recorder, Lodish leaned back in his swivel chair and nodded at me. "Now, Mr. Sawyer, Captain Gallion has asked us to talk to you about one of our former operatives named John Duncan. What is it you want to know?"

"Start with what led up to Duncan's having to leave your service."

For a time Lodish went through some background I already knew in outline. Johnny's switch from the DEA to the CIA. The fact that he'd operated for a short period in France, and then for a longer period in Italy. Then came stuff I didn't know.

Johnny had been brought back to France to run a covert operation for the CIA. There are governments or rebel factions in various countries that are not supposed to be supplied with U.S. weaponry—according to stated Washington policy—but that the U.S. may want to supply anyway, without becoming openly involved. A covert traffic in armaments, judiciously superintended, answers that unofficial need. Johnny had been put in charge of one such operation.

The arms and ammunition had come out of Germany, from U.S. military installations whose in-and-out records were doctored so the losses wouldn't show up. The shipments were moved down through France to Marseilles and sent from there to the secret recipients that covert American policy had touched with its golden wand.

My spine stiffened on me. I shifted on the cushioned seat of the ladderback to loosen it. "How was the stuff moved?"

The answer wasn't unexpected: "Through a French firm. Malo Transport. It went through France in Malo trucks, inside sealed containers bearing misleading documentation of contents. From Marseilles it went out in Malo merchant ships, mixed in with other cargo.

"But of course," Lodish added, looking at Thierry, "Captain Gallion must already have all of this in his DGSE dossiers. Since it required an unofficial request from his own government to persuade Karl Malo to allow us to use his transportation facilities for this purpose."

I looked at Thierry. He nodded blandly. "But those dossiers are classified secret, so I am not at liberty to divulge the information in them."

Allowing a friendly rival service to divulge that same information, however, was not inconsistent. It was one way for the DGSE to check on whether CIA dossiers had any details theirs did not.

I asked, "Who was Duncan's liaison inside Malo Transport?"

"All of this is extremely confidential," Lodish said, for the record. "I'm telling it to you because Captain Gallion specifically requested that we do so. And with *his* assurance that you won't divulge it to anyone else."

"That's correct," Thierry said, also for the record.

"The man John Duncan worked through within the Malo firm," Lodish told me, "was a second-line executive at the time. He's since been moved up to assistant director."

"Jean-Noel Triolet."

"It seems you already know a good deal of this, Mr. Sawyer."

"I didn't until now. Who was Duncan's contact in Germany for getting the weaponry from the American bases?"

"An American army officer. Colonel Lyall. He died during an operation for cancer of the stomach less than two months after the work Duncan was supervising was terminated."

"What terminated it?"

"The French government. A change of policy. Dictated, one assumes, by the DGSE's becoming increasingly upset about what it felt was our infringing on its own prerogatives."

Thierry just smiled a little.

"The French government," Lodish resumed, "informed Karl Malo of its change in attitude. Malo stopped letting us use his company. And that was that—operation terminated."

"You didn't," Thierry said carelessly, "start it up again with some other firm."

"Absolutely not," Lodish said with some vehemence. Then he showed his crooked teeth again. "Not in this country."

Thierry gestured at the recorder. "You're going on record with that statement."

"That's right."

Thierry nodded. It may have been all he'd come there to get. Whether he entirely believed Lodish was another matter. It was enough that the CIA had made the statement, opening itself to difficulties if it should later prove to have been false.

I asked, "What happened with Duncan after that operation was dropped?"

"He was moved to another job. Operating out of our consulate in Marseilles. Checking on aliens in that city who might be unfriendly toward the U.S. of A.—and inclined to become activist about it. But," Lodish added with a hardening of his features, "it seems he didn't give that his full attention."

"What did he give the rest of it to?" I asked.

CHAPTER 29

"As you know," Bob Lodish said, "we supplied an enormous amount of state-of-the-art weaponry to Iran when the Shah was still in charge there. When the Ayatollah Khomeini took over all of that fell into his hands. A stinger of a combination: our arms and his violently anti-American policies. All we could do about it was clamp an embargo on any further sales to Iran."

"I do know all that," I said.

"Patience—I'm getting to it. Okay, Iran's been using up and beating up that big stockpile of military equipment very fast in its war with Iraq. They need more ammunition, replacement parts, new repair equipment—the works. And it all has to be American stuff, to fit what they've already got. And he can't get it from us."

"So Khomeini's had to buy whatever he can get from illegal arms dealers."

"Right, and pay exorbitant rates for every single bullet he gets that way. Making Iran a bonanza for any gunrunner who's got some way to get hold of U.S. material and move it to Iran."

Lodish tipped back in his swivel chair and joined his hands across his lean midsection. "Well—some of our informants inside Iran began reporting arrivals of American weapons and ammo in cases with markings indicating they'd been removed from shipments intended for our bases in West Germany. After investigation two of those informants came up with the same rumor: that those cases were reaching Iran from Marseilles—supplied by a man using his undercover connections and CIA leverage to obtain them. John Duncan."

"None of *that*," Thierry put in mildly, "is in our dossiers."

"I'm telling you now," Lodish said, trying not to sound defensive about it. "And that's purely a friendly gesture. It wasn't and isn't any business of the DGSE. Strictly an internal problem in our own house. Anyway, we kicked Duncan out, so that takes care of it."

"We might have kicked him out of France," Thierry said.

"Or recruited him for one of your own nastier DGSE outfits?" Lodish suggested cynically.

I said, "How was Duncan moving the stuff from Germany to Iran?"

"That's something we never did manage to find out," Lodish admitted.

"His old arrangement with Malo Transport?"

"No way. Karl Malo cut us off the day the French government stopped going along with our operation. If he let his firm get used for something like that again, against his government's decision, it'd be worse than illegal—close to treason. That could ruin even *him*."

"What's Duncan been doing since you dropped him?" I asked.

"We don't know. Maybe you do."

"No."

Lodish tipped forward, pointing a finger at me. "But you're investigating him. Whatever your reason, maybe you'll come up with the answer to that question. If you do, let us know. You do that, and I can guarantee there are people in Washington who'll reward it by wiping your slate clean for you." He indicated the recorder. "I'm going on record with that promise, Sawyer. Deal?"

So there was more than one reason for Bob Lodish's getting the go-ahead to talk to me about Johnny. "If I come up with something," I said, "I'll surely let you know." I said it with a nice smile and all the sincerity I could muster.

* * * *

Thierry and I walked slowly from the embassy toward the taxi rack on the Rue de Rivoli.

"You could have given me some of that background before we went in there," I said.

"I'm sorry, Pierre-Ange, but that information *is* in dossiers whose contents I'm not at liberty to divulge." We went past the corner of Rue Royale, and Thierry asked, "Was the meeting of use to you?"

"A little."

"I'd be interested in any thoughts you might have."

"I'm sorry," I said, "but I'm not at liberty to divulge them."

"That's a most unfriendly attitude. Almost unfriendly enough to make me cancel our plans to spend that August week at your place in the south."

"Almost—but not quite."

"Not quite," Thierry admitted. "I do have a tidbit for you, by the way. On another subject. Not marked secret. As yet."

"What's the subject?"

"Ahmed Kadir. The member of the Libyan Trade Mission who died in your hotel room. According to rumors that have reached our ears, he had frequent—and rather furtive—contacts with a Marseilles gangster named Hassan Salah. Purpose unknown. But Hassan Salah is *believed* to be heavily involved in smuggling. Particularly weaponry."

Thierry chose his next words carefully: "He *may* be supplying Iran, as well as Colonel Khadafy—since those rumors suggest Salah also has contacts with Ayatollah Khomeini's Islamic Jihad faction. But we have absolutely *no* evidence to verify these rumors."

Nor were they likely to get any. Thierry's government would not be pleased with anyone in its employ who came up with such evidence. France was not eager to lose oil and income by offending either Libya or Iran.

* * * *

After Thierry took a taxi back to his office at the DGSE I called Fritz Donhoff's apartment from a phone in a Rue de Rivoli *tabac*. He wasn't in. I hung up on his answering machine and phoned Air France. Neither it nor Air Inter had a place for me on any flight to Marignane until eight the next morning. I reserved that one and took a cab to Balzar, where I had a leisurely lunch of their splendid cassoulet with a *demi* of Beaujolais.

Then I took a long stroll along the Left Bank of the Seine, mulling over what I'd gotten out of the embassy meeting. Trying different ways of fitting it together with everything I'd learned up to my flight to Paris.

Some of the links between events began to feel more solid.

I gave it a rest, walking more briskly and soaking up the views along the river. At the Pont de L'Alma I crossed the Seine and walked back along the Right Bank, going fast enough to work up some circulation. I'd gone too many days without enough exercise. My blood was getting sluggish. When I reached Pont Marie I crossed over again and started climbing steep Rue Cardinal Lemoine toward the house where Fritz and I had our adjacent apartments overlooking a small courtyard shaded by a flourishing plane tree.

It was half a block from Place Contrescarpe. We'd bought the apartments before real estate prices in that homey neighborhood had begun spiraling upward. I could have sold the apartment now for a juicy profit. But it was a good base for when business or pleasure brought me to Paris. And there's the seductive French theory that, while money is great, the only permanent security is in *murs et terre*—walls and land.

I don't find the theory too convincing. In practice, Europe has seen too many homes bombed out of existence, too many families evicted from their land by wars and economic failures. And cash in hand, my American side reminds me, provides gratification now—before the goblin of the future strikes.

But I'd probably keep the apartment anyway—and try my best to hang on to my home down on the Med as well. My own theory and practice do not always dovetail. What can you expect from a man who dreams in English when he's in France and in French when he's back in the States?

* * * *

It was almost five P.M. when I went through the courtyard and up the house steps to the small landing between the doors to our apartments. I knocked at Fritz's door, but he still wasn't in. Each of us has a key to the other's apartment. I let myself into Fritz's living room and left a note for him on his desk. Then I crossed to my own place and made a number of long-distance calls.

Most were to the *milieu* connections I'd seen the day before. A few were to other contacts. What I asked of each was the same: a check into new questions raised by what Lodish and Thierry had told me that morning.

After the last call I made coffee and sat at the kitchen table with a cup of it, with sugar but no milk. The apartment was stocked with basic foodstuffs, as well as clothing, but milk doesn't keep, and I'd neglected to pick some up from the shop on the *place*. I drank a little of the coffee and tried to rearrange my thoughts along a new line. But my head was too crammed with odds and ends that wouldn't get out of the way. And I found myself having a mild case of the jitters as well. I knew that problem—and its solution. Slapping my gray cells with more caffeine wasn't part of it. If I'd been in the south, I'd have gone down to the sea for a long, hard swim.

I poured the rest of the coffee down the drain, got a pair of swimming trunks from a bedroom drawer, picked up a towel from the bathroom closet, and went out. I strode the half block to Place Contrescarpe, crossed it, and went another half block to the Piscine Jean Taris.

An enclosed public swimming pool is not the Mediterranean, but it's better than nothing. I stroked the length of it, back and forth, setting myself a fast pace and holding to it after parts of me tried to call it quits. I didn't count the laps, just kept doing them until my muscles ached and my heart was thudding and the blood pumping through my brain had washed it clean of old thoughts and made room for new.

Back at my apartment I took a hot-and-cold shower, dried myself vigorously, and put on a fresh outfit: sport shirt, jeans, and moccasins. I was returning to the living room when Fritz Donhoff unlocked my door and walked in.

Fritz had shrunk a bit in the years since I'd first met him. We'd been exactly the same height then. But he was still big and heavy and impressive, baggy-eyed and silver-haired, wearing one of his old-style velvet suits with a pearl stickpin in his tie and the black cord to his monocle poking neatly from his breast pocket. He threw his arms wide open and gave me a smile of sentimental pleasure. We bear-hugged, and he kissed me on both cheeks. That never embarrassed me with Fritz. He was more than my partner and friend. Fritz was as close to a father as I'd ever known.

"Where have you been all day?" I asked him.

"To Hamburg and back, seeking information on our Emil Fassler. A lady friend of my youth, Vanessa Meyer, lives there now. A former newspaperwoman. Unfortunately retired for more than a decade. So she had to offer a bribe to a certain police detective to obtain the information I wanted. Vanessa lives on a small pension and doesn't have enough to pay the bribe. I had to fly up with money from my own bank account. That will be on my expense sheet, along with the round-trip fare, taxis, and an excellent lunch for Vanessa and myself. I hope what it all comes to won't shock Karl Malo."

"It'll probably be less than he pays for one suit," I said. "Don't worry about it."

"Will you brew me an herb tea, my boy? I'm somewhat fatigued."

He followed me into the kitchen and sat down at the table as I took some dried vervain and mint leaves out of their screw-top jars. While I heated the water I told Fritz the things I'd learned from Bob Lodish and Thierry Gallion that morning.

Fritz looked pleased. "My trip to Hamburg may not have been the waste of time I feared. Vanessa's policeman didn't have too much to offer that was new. But one aspect of it *is* of interest, in the light of what you've just told me."

CHAPTER 30

The tea was ready. I poured Fritz a cup and put it on the table. Then I sat down and watched him take a long sip without waiting for it to cool and without wincing. His ability to drink tea scalding hot always inspired a certain amount of awe in me. If I'd tried it, I would have been screaming in pain. But they'd made men of sterner stuff in the days when Fritz was born.

"Ach, good," Fritz said, and he took another long sip. "Now, about Emil Fassler—as Jacqueline Malo already told you, two nights ago, her first husband was involved in illegal activities. She claims not to know what sort, and that may be true. But Vanessa's policeman was able to be more specific."

He drank more tea and gave me a satisfied nod. "The Hamburg police had reason to suspect that Fassler was using his import-export business as a cover for smuggling American weaponry out of Germany—and down to Marseilles."

That did tie in rather neatly with what Bob Lodish had told me about why Johnny Duncan had been bounced by the CIA. It could also be tied in to what Thierry Gallion had said about Hassan Salah's arms dealing business in Marseilles. "Did the Hamburg police come up with any connection between Fassler and Johnny Duncan?" I asked Fritz.

"No, his name doesn't show up in any of the records of their investigation of Emil Fassler. Perhaps it might have if they had dug further, but they dropped it after Fassler's death."

"How was Fassler *getting* the arms he was moving?"

"Obviously, he must have been working with some officer in the American quartermaster corps in Germany. But the Hamburg police didn't come up with his name, either. It wasn't a very thorough investigation. They didn't begin getting interested in Emil Fassler's affairs until less than two months before he was killed."

That was about the time Jacqueline Malo had told me she'd become aware that her first husband was mixed up with criminals. "What started the Hamburg police checking on him?"

"An inquiry from the police of Marseilles," Fritz told me. "I already knew about the inquiry before I went to Hamburg. Through a call this morning from my police contact in Marseilles. Lionel Clerc—the son of a good friend of mine who died a few years ago. Lionel is now an officer with the Marseilles gendarmerie. He's glad to be of help—out of respect for that old friendship between myself and his late father. Though if you cared to offer him a small gift, I don't think he would refuse it."

"Few do," I said, with more than an ounce of rue. I was thinking of Jacqueline Malo's night visit to my room. Chivalry has something to be said for it, but so does an instinct for seizing the fruit that fate drops in your path. If the romantic streak I blamed on my American upbringing was getting out of hand, it was time for me to find another line of work.

"Lionel hasn't been able to come up with further information on the circumstances of Emil Fassler's murder," Fritz went on. "But he gave me some background by phone this morning. Including what prompted that inquiry from Marseilles asking for the Hamburg check on Fassler."

He paused, and I said, "So *tell* me." Fritz raised an elegant eyebrow at me. I'd spoken with some irritation. He didn't know it was directed at myself, still dwelling on Jacqueline Malo. I made amends: "Your tea must be too cool for you by now. Shall I heat up more?"

"That would be kind of you, Pierre-Ange."

I got up to do it. Behind me Fritz said, "What prompted that inquiry was the murder of a Marseilles detective inspector of the Police Judiciare. The P.J. became suspicious of Emil Fassler because of rumors that he'd met several times with that arms dealer your Captain Gallion mentioned."

"Hassan Salah."

"Yes. This P.J. inspector—Gerard Delanoé—was given an assignment to check into what Fassler was doing during his visits to Marseilles. Less than a week later, Inspector Delanoé was found dead with a thirty-two-caliber bullet lodged in his heart. He died in a small apartment he kept over a bar on Rue Dragon, up on the hill overlooking the old port section of Marseilles near Notre-Dame-de-la-Garde. Apparently a love nest for meeting women he didn't want his wife knowing about.

"Nobody heard the shot. A little .32 doesn't make much of a bang, and the bar was very noisy at that time of night, between the customers and the jukebox. The main way up to Inspector Delanoé's apartment is through the bar, but there's a back way to the building, so his killer could have gone in and out that way. But a good-looking woman that nobody in the bar ever saw before came into the bar that night—about the time the inspector died, according to the police medical findings. She asked one of the bartenders for Delanoé's apartment. He sent her up the stairs, and that's the last he saw of her. She didn't come back down through the bar, so she must have gone out the building's rear door.

"His death wasn't discovered until more than an hour later, when one of his girlfriends went up to the apartment. And ran down screaming."

"Was Emil Fassler in Marseilles at that time?" I asked.

Fritz nodded. "He was pulled in for questioning, naturally—since the inspector had been investigating him when he was murdered. Though Delanoé failed to file any progress reports on it before he died. Which may mean he'd made no progress. Fassler held up under the questioning, swearing he didn't know he was the subject of investigation by Delanoé or anyone else, had never met him—and had never been to that apartment.

"The police had no evidence that Fassler was lying on any of those points. They didn't even have proof that his visits to Marseilles had any illegality involved. So they had to let him go. Though since his papers identified him as a resident of Hamburg, they did ask the police there to check on him."

"Which led to the same sort of results," I said. "Suspicion but no evidence."

"Exactly so."

"What about the woman who went up to Inspector Delanoé's place around the time he was killed there?"

"Fassler denied having any idea of who she could be. The bartender she talked to, and others who were in the bar at that time, gave the police descriptions of her. Rather vague descriptions, as usual. But they all said they would recognize her if they saw her again. They never did, and the police never learned who she might have been."

I drew a slow breath. "If you've got that description of her, Fritz, I'd like to hear it."

"I'm not sure you *will* like it," Fritz said.

He described her to me.

CHAPTER 31

The sightseers were crowding in and out of the Arles Amphitheater when I reached Jacqueline Malo's art gallery across from it at ten-thirty the following morning. The interior of the gallery was one medium-sized room. There was an office alcove in back, partially hidden behind a folding screen with patterned cut-silk panels that looked like eighteenth-century Chinese *kesi* textiles. The other furnishings—a curved desk, several small tables, two chairs—were modern objects of black leather and shiny metal. But the pictures on the walls were mostly landscapes in the traditional or impressionist manner. Old or new, each was worth a long look.

Jacqueline Malo stood at the curved desk, wrapping a framed pastel in thick brown paper for a customer who was making out a check. The customer was a man in his thirties. He wore an expensively casual summer denim outfit. She was wearing a white lace blouse and a peasant-style skirt that was snug around her small waist, hugging her full hips and flaring out around her elegant legs.

She looked up with an automatic smile when I opened the glass-paneled entrance door. When she recognized me she began a polite greeting—but it was stopped by something she saw in my face. For a moment she went utterly still, looking at me with her lips partly open. Then she lowered her lovely head and finished wrapping the picture.

The man carefully tore the check from his checkbook and placed it on her desk. She managed a slight smile as they shook hands and thanked each other. He took his package and turned to leave. She followed him part of the way, coming to a halt beside one of the small tables. It bore a graceful bronze sculpture of a naked couple engaged in what could have been a ballet pose or a lovers' embrace.

I held the door open for the departing customer. He nodded his thanks and went out, looking happy with his purchase. I closed the door and locked it. A card hung inside its upper panel. Printed on one side of the card was the word "Open," and the other side said "Closed." I reversed it so "Closed" faced outside.

She didn't voice any objection. When I turned from the door she was still beside the table with its sculpted nudes, staring at me woodenly.

"You'd better sit down," I told her.

But she didn't move, except to turn her head slowly with her eyes following me as I moved past her. I perched on the edge of the curved desk and returned her gaze. Without shifting her eyes from mine she reached out a hand to the sculpture beside her. A light touch, her fingertips barely resting on the smooth curve of the female figure's spine. But she seemed to derive support from it.

"You *know*, don't you," she said in a low, gritty voice. "You found out—I was sure you would."

There had been a jolt of fright when she'd first seen me and read my expression. That was gone now. Her gaze was fatalistic; not resignation—just a flat acceptance.

"I don't know it all," I told her quietly. "But some of it I figured out a while back. It wasn't hard to figure. Except I didn't know *why* you'd go along with it—until yesterday."

I'd also had to cope with the fact that—if I was right—two separate things were going on. One that had already happened, and another that was still in progress. What connected them was Jacqueline Malo—but she wouldn't find out about the second one until it touched her, later. At this point she only knew about the first.

"Let's talk about the kidnapping," I said. "Only I guess we should find another name for it. You weren't kidnapped."

She didn't move or change expression.

"First of all, there was the timing," I said. "I'm not the only one who was bothered by that. One day you decide to join your husband in Monaco, and the next morning you're snatched there. Too damn quick. Unless you planned on going to Monaco at least a couple days before you phoned your husband with that decision—and somebody else knew it."

That didn't get any response from her, so I went on with it. "That wasn't the only timing element that was wrong. You were snatched in the morning and ransomed and released that night. Too fast again. Kidnappers usually let the one paying the ransom stew in his fear longer than that. Sometimes a lot longer. To make sure he'll pay and not try to pull any tricks. But you wouldn't stand for letting Malo stay frightened any longer than that, would you?"

Jacqueline Malo didn't answer. She was concentrating on holding herself rigid, refusing to let whatever she was feeling bubble to the surface and overwhelm her.

"Another tip-off," I said, "was the amount of ransom demanded. A nice hunk of money—but people of your husband's wealth have been forced to cough up much more than that to get back their loved ones. Only that's another thing you dug in your heels about.

"And," I added, "there's that little Alfa Romeo you rented that morning. Not your kind of car at all. The ones you usually drive are conservative. You chose that one that morning because Johnny Duncan told you to. So there wouldn't be room in it for any hidden cops along with the driver and money."

She finally spoke. It was a relief to hear her voice again. I'd begun to think she'd become part of the small statue she kept her hand on. She sounded like someone trying to describe a dream she hadn't fully awakened from. "Duncan—I didn't even know his name until you told me when you described him the other night. I only met him twice."

"When the two of you planned it—and when you pulled it off."

Jacqueline Malo nodded slowly. She removed her hand from the sculpture and looked at it with a disoriented frown, as though she knew what it was but couldn't quite remember what it was for.

I said, "You told Duncan that Malo was going to Monaco. He decided that was a good place to do it because he knows the region behind there better than most. So you went to Monaco, and you rented the little Alfa the next morning and drove it to the garage in Nice. He picked you up there and drove you up to that quarry near Sospel and broke into the shed inside it. You waited there while he made the first phone call to Malo. When he made the second one you went with him, to talk to Malo and prove you were still alive.

"Then Duncan drove you back to the quarry. My guess is he let you blindfold and handcuff yourself while he went off to make the next calls, pick up the ransom, and disappear with it. Even if he got caught, he couldn't be charged with a kidnap. Because there wasn't any. The worst they could hit him with would be obtaining money from Malo by fraudulent means."

But Johnny must have been surprised as hell when *I* turned out to be the one delivering the ransom.

"As for you," I finished, "all you had to do was wait there in that shed—until I came along."

"And rescued me," she said tonelessly. She came to the desk, opened a bottom drawer, and took out a cigarette pack and lighter. Then she brought out a small ashtray and put it on the desktop.

I watched her shake out a cigarette and light it. "That's the first time I ever saw you smoke."

"I gave it up a year ago." She took a drag and made a face. "These are horribly stale," she growled, and she crushed the cigarette out with a single vicious twist.

"The thing I kept looking for," I told her, "was what Duncan could have on you to make you help him work that fraud on your husband. Then I found out about the cop who got murdered in Marseilles. Inspector Delanoé."

"I've waited such a long time for that to catch up with me, I began to think it might not. But it has, hasn't it?" Jacqueline Malo held her head up, and her voice was low but steady. "All right, then: time to pay the piper."

The lady did have class.

I watched her walk to a chair and sit down. She gripped its black arms and pressed herself back, her eyes meeting mine again.

"Which of you killed Delanoé?" I asked her. "You or Emil Fassler?"

"I did," she said.

CHAPTER 32

I didn't have to ask many questions. As she'd said, she'd been waiting a long time with it pent up inside her. There was no reason left not to get it out of her system.

It had happened while she was driving her station wagon through southern France, hunting antiques for her Paris shop. She had reached Avignon on a weekend when her first husband was making one of his business trips to Marseilles, not far away. So she'd driven down to spend a night with him.

"Emil was using the apartment of a Marseilles friend who was away," Jacqueline Malo told me. "He acted uneasy when I got there. I couldn't understand why."

It wasn't until that memorable night, she said, that she discovered Emil Fassler's business had an illicit side to it.

"He became even more uneasy when Inspector Delanoé showed up as we were preparing to go out for dinner. They apparently had some sort of relationship. Emil had to introduce us to each other, though it was obvious he didn't like it. And *I* didn't like the way the inspector looked at me. But he was polite enough when he asked me to excuse him for having to take Emil away from me for a short while. He said they needed to have a private talk. '*Another* private talk,' is the way he put it. Emil asked me to wait until he got back and went off with the man.

"I waited almost an hour. Then the inspector phoned. He told me they were at his apartment and that Emil had just gone out to buy a bottle of good wine. He said they wanted me to join them there, and we'd all go to dinner together. He told me how to find his place.

"It was an untidy apartment over a crowded, noisy bar. I didn't get a chance to see much of it before he pulled me inside and locked the door, putting the key in his pocket. Then I saw Emil. He was lying on the floor. With his arms handcuffed behind him and his ankles tied. He was gagged, with tape across his mouth."

Jacqueline Malo's hand came up to move involuntarily across her own mouth as she said it.

"Emil's shoes and socks had been taken off, and his jacket was dumped carelessly on a couch. There were burns on his feet. I started to scream, but Delanoé hit me with his fist, knocking me to the floor. Then he dragged me to my feet and threw me into a chair. He warned me that if I tried to scream again, he would kill my husband. And then he turned on Emil. He said that maybe Emil would be willing to be *more reasonable* now. That if he wasn't, he would do terrible things to me—rape me, disfigure me."

She didn't shudder at the memory. Time had wrapped insulation around it. She spoke in a dead-level monotone that was chilling.

I asked "What did Delanoé want him to be reasonable about?"

"I don't know," she told me. "I couldn't understand what he said. Something about switching to a bigger organization. Emil wouldn't explain it to me later. Wouldn't explain anything—except that he'd gotten obligated somehow to people who frightened him."

"All right," I said, "tell me the rest. Exactly as it happened."

Jacqueline Malo was silent for several moments, looking at me with an odd kind of concentration, as if she were having difficulty seeing me. Then she told me the rest. "This—inspector—he began to kick Emil. In the chest and stomach. The sound Emil made through the gag was horrible. I threw myself at Delanoé. Tried to sink my nails into his eyes. To blind him—anything to stop what he was doing."

Her mouth didn't look soft as she spoke. The lips were drawn taut, parting to show her teeth in a soundless snarl.

"But he was very strong," she went on in that even, emotionless voice. "He hurled me away from him—halfway across the room. I fell on the couch. And felt something under my hand. Then I realized what it was. Emil had begun carrying a small revolver with him sometimes, when he went on trips. He'd told me it was in case he was attacked by muggers. He'd claimed to have a license for it, but I don't think he did..."

She turned her head a little, to the left, then back to the right. Trying to relieve tension at the back of her neck. "I got the gun out of his pocket as quickly as I could. I thought I could use it to make Delanoé release Emil and let us go. But I was too slow. He saw it and leapt at me. Fell on top of me, trying to seize the gun. And—I shot him."

"You mean," I said with quiet emphasis, "the gun went off when he landed on you."

She gave me a look of sharp comprehension but then shook her head. "No. I was terrified—and I pulled the trigger. Deliberately."

It could still be called self-defense, if it went to court. But a claim like that, when the man you shot was a cop, was a hard one to get by with. And Emil Fassler hadn't wanted to be any part of the try. His own crooked operations would have come to light.

As soon as she'd gotten his gag off he'd told her where the late Inspector Delanoé had the key to the cuffs. And when he was freed Fassler had gotten them both out of there. Down a back stairway and out the building's rear door. They'd made the trek to his borrowed apartment on foot. He'd dropped the gun into a sewer a few blocks from it. He hadn't let her come in with him. Instead he'd instructed her to drive straight back to Avignon, stay the night, and leave early the next morning for Paris.

She'd left the station wagon in Paris and taken a train to Amsterdam, where she'd spent the next two weeks with a friend, letting no one else know where she was.

"Even after that," Jacqueline Malo told me, "when I did go back to Paris, I half expected to find the police waiting for me. But they weren't. And none ever came to question me about Inspector Delanoé's death."

Probably some cop had dropped around to her Paris address for a routine check while she was in Holland. Not finding her, he'd gone away. And gotten no orders to try again. There was no reason to connect her to the unknown woman seen going up to Delanoé's place. Her husband had already been questioned and released. Marseilles wouldn't have been putting any pressure on Paris to dig further. As Fritz and I had agreed the previous night, the Marseilles police hadn't pushed their own investigation into the death very hard or far.

A call to some of my *milieu* connections had gotten us the probable explanation for that. Inspector Delanoé had been on the payroll of a Marseilles gangster. Too thorough a dig into the inspector's doings would have brought that to the surface; and no police department needs that kind of public exposure. Delanoé was dead. They wanted his seamier sources of income buried with him.

* * * *

"How did John Duncan come into it?" I asked Jacqueline Malo.

"He came here a bit more than two months ago," she told me. "To the gallery—one evening when I was closing up. I'd never seen him before—and he didn't tell me his name. But," she added acidly, "he had seen *me* before. He said he knew the truth about the killing of Inspector Delanoé."

"How?"

"He—this man you call Duncan—said he used to work with the same gangster as Emil."

"Did he give the gangster a name?"

"No. What he gave me was a story about the night I shot Delanoé. He said he happened to see Emil that night in a car with Inspector Delanoé. Whom he knew to do jobs for a rival of the gangster he and Emil worked with. So he followed them. To the inspector's place above that bar. They went in the rear door. He stayed out back and waited. He didn't see *me* go in, because I went in the front, through the bar.

"But he did see me when I came out by the back door with Emil. He followed us. And saw Emil throw the gun away, into the sewer. That sent him back to Inspector Delanoé's apartment. He let himself in and found—what was there. He said he left quickly—and never told anybody else about it."

"Until he came here to see you," I said. "If Duncan wanted to blackmail you, you were ripe for a big haul from the day you married Karl Malo. A year ago. I wonder why he waited."

"I don't know." Her voice was getting irritable and draggy, as if she had to push it through an abrupt draining-away of her energy. "He just said he needed money. And he suggested a way for me to help him get it."

"In exchange for not tipping the Marseilles police to haul you down and let some of those witnesses in the bar have a look at you."

"He pointed out that two years isn't that long an interval. He said they would remember me."

"When did he come here with this? *Exactly.*"

She had to concentrate. "Six days before Karl was scheduled to be in Monaco for those meetings. This man—Duncan—said that would be as good a place as any. And I...did what he wanted me to do."

She took her hands off the arms of the chair and made a stilted, hopeless gesture. Her face had become dull. "I'm suddenly *very* tired of reliving my past. First with Duncan, and now with you." She pushed herself out of the chair and walked listlessly to the desk beside me. "And I have to tell it all over again, don't I? With the police." She picked up the phone and looked at me with empty eyes. "What do I dial to get them?"

I took the phone away from her and put it down. "Don't do that," I snapped.

She frowned at me, puzzled by something in my tone. "Don't do anything," I told her. "Or say anything. To anyone. Until you hear from me again."

She went on staring at me, not understanding what I was telling her.

"I'll see what I can do," I said.

"What do you mean?"

"I'm not the law," I reminded her. "People hire me to work for them. Right now I'm working for you."

"For my husband."

"Same thing."

"No. It's not the same."

"It is if I think it is," I told her.

CHAPTER 33

I spent much of the rest of that day prowling the lower depths of Marseilles again, asking new questions of people I knew among its denizens.

Then I made a phone call to Arlette Alfani's father at the house to which he'd retired from the *milieu* fray, in the hills above Nice.

After talking to Marcel Alfani I called a man in Marseilles named Maurice Dalmasso. By using Alfani as my reference I finally got through to Dalmasso in person.

* * * *

The business obligations of a successful gangster are as time-consuming as those of a transportation tycoon. A leisure hour is potentially loss-loaded indulgence. You have to stay on top of the details.

By nine-thirty the next morning, when I arrived at Maurice Dalmasso's house in Marseilles, he'd been tending to some of those details for over an hour with his accountant and attorney in his second-floor study. I had to wait another twenty minutes until they finished their conference. The waiting was done in Dalmasso's big kitchen, where two hefty thugs were silently nursing large cups of coffee. They had their jackets unbuttoned for quick access to the holstered revolvers clipped to their belts. Occasionally one of them would go to look out a front or back window.

That wasn't really necessary. The kitchen, like every other room in Dalmasso's house, had two TV sets, both turned on. One screen showed what was going on outside the front of the house; the other covered the courtyard out back. Those were the only possible approaches to the house. Across the street out front a couple more of Dalmasso's thugs sat on a bus stop bench. There was another pair dawdling in the rear courtyard.

Being a lord of the underworld does have its drawbacks, as Satan could have—and perhaps had—warned Dalmasso.

Wars between rival gangs was one of them. Arlette's father had been involved in them from the time of his arrival from Corsica, as a boy, until his retirement a few years back. He'd waged some of his fiercest battles against Maurice Dalmasso. That was the basis for the friendly feeling

Dalmasso now had toward Alfani. In their world a retired enemy was the closest thing to a friend you could hope for.

But gangland strife had gotten rougher after it was no longer strictly between Corsicans, the traditional rulers of crime along France's south coast. Every year they found themselves fighting an increasing number of Arab gangsters moving in to grab chunks of their territory and action. In the last year alone thirty-two hoods had died of the problem. It was also what had brought me to Dalmasso that morning.

His attorney and accountant finally left, and he came into the kitchen. He was a squat, bald man with the face of a pugnacious bullfrog. One of his thugs handed him his coffee. Dalmasso took a long swallow before shaking my hand with a surprisingly charm-laden smile.

"How's old Alfani looking these days?"

"In good spirits. Swims in his pool every day, takes walks, looks at television, gets plenty of sleep."

"And dreams of the old days, eh?"

"I guess he's got a few things to remember."

Maurice Dalmasso's laugh was too high-pitched for a bullfrog. "May he live to a hundred and enjoy every day of it. A beautiful man." Taking my arm, Dalmasso steered me toward the front entry. His first conference of the day was over, and he was on his way to his next one.

The two thugs from the kitchen went out ahead of us and looked up and down the street. The pair at the bus stop across the street were on their feet doing the same. A limo pulled to a stop in front of us. I climbed in after Dalmasso. One of his thugs got in front with the driver. The second took the jump seat facing us, looking past us out the rear window.

A smaller car with four Dalmasso men cruised past and led the way. The limo followed it. A second four-man car followed close behind the limo. All that protection should make you feel secure. But what it does is remind you that people want to kill the man beside you and won't notice if you happen to get wiped out by the same hail of bullets or exploding bomb.

Dalmasso's house was up in the Longchamp quarter of Marseilles. Heavy morning traffic slowed our three-car convoy as it turned south through the city. By the time we'd gone three blocks I was telling him about the talk I'd had by phone with Marcel Alfani the previous evening.

"He says you used to own a P.J. inspector named Delanoé who got himself killed a couple years back."

I'd also gotten it from a couple of my *milieu* contacts in Marseilles, but the reminder that someone of Alfani's prestige had complete trust in my discretion wouldn't hurt. Dalmasso shrugged his beefy shoulders. "You can't function with maximum efficiency in my business unless you've got boys like that on your payroll."

"This one was investigating something that could have hurt Hassan Salah at the time. From what I hear, you don't like Salah much."

"Not much," Dalmasso agreed. There was no venom in his voice, but I didn't need to hear it to know it was there. One of Dalmasso's more lucrative sources of income was smuggling arms and ammunition out of France. Over the last few years Hassan Salah had become an increasingly successful rival in that field, cutting into Dalmasso's profits.

There was as little chance of their working out a mutually beneficial agreement, based on a shared interest in peace and prosperity, as there was for Moscow and Washington to do the same. Among Corsican gangsters even the hottest wars eventually subsided into periods of detente. But the enmity between Arab and Corsican went too deep and wide for any detente to be even worth discussing.

Dalmasso turned his head and gave me a penetrating look. I don't penetrate too easily, so I just looked back at him and waited. "*I* talked to Alfani, too," he told me. "Last night. Alfani says *you're* investigating something that might cut Hassan Salah down to size."

"It's possible," I said. "If Salah's connected to a man named John Duncan."

Dalmasso gave that one a little frowning consideration. "I don't know if he *is*. I know he *was*, for a while. That was after Paris cancelled the CIA's right to use Malo Transport to move arms around on the sly. Duncan found some other way to move the stuff—on his own. With some help from Hassan Salah. They did pretty well at it. Until the CIA caught on to what Duncan was pulling." His knowing all about that wasn't too surprising. Dalmasso couldn't have stayed on top so long without keeping tabs on what the competition was up to.

I asked him, "What was Salah's contribution to his arrangement with Duncan?"

"He had a little company in Germany that he could use to cover subtracting arms from shipments to American military bases. All the army people Salah bribed had to do was forward some of the goods through that company and then lose the records."

"You're talking about Emil Fassler's import-export firm."

"That's right. Fassler's business was close to bankrupt when Salah saved him with a loan."

"And after that Salah would own Fassler."

"Sure, that's how these things work."

"And Duncan's contribution," I said, "was being able to move the stuff."

"That's always the hardest part of that type operation," Dalmasso said. "Getting the goods—there's lots of ways. Buy it, steal it, bribe or blackmail somebody to slip it to you. And buyers—there's never any shortage of those. But moving it over a long distance without being spotted—that's the big problem."

"How was Duncan doing it?"

"I don't know." Dalmasso sounded almost wistful. "I tried to find out but couldn't. I'd still like to know. Might be something *I* could use."

He gave me another of those penetrating stares. "I'd pay a lot for that kind of information, if you turn it up. You check with Alfani. He'll tell you—when it comes to buying something useful, I'm not stingy."

"I'll keep that in mind," I said. And added, half to myself, "No chance Duncan could have continued to operate with Salah after he got the chop from the CIA." Dalmasso shook his head. I agreed with him. The CIA would have been watching Johnny too closely over the next year or so for him to go on with it. But he *was* still connected somehow with Hassan Salah—or maybe connected *again*, after an interval.

"But," Dalmasso was saying, "Salah did get the boost he needed out of their arrangement by the time it ended. Before that he was just light-weight competition. Somebody I kept track of but didn't worry about much. But most of what Salah and Duncan shipped went to Iran. I guess you know that."

I nodded.

"That gave Salah an introduction to Khomeini's people. And them a chance to get to know him and decide they could work with him. And when they did, agents of Khomeini's friend Khadafy decided *they* could, too. Since then we've had a new kind of people moving in to beef up Salah's organization here."

"What kind?"

"I hear *you* met one of them a few nights ago," Dalmasso said with an acute, narrow-eyed glance. "When he wound up dead in your hotel room."

"Ahmed Kadir."

"What was that all about?"

"I don't know yet," I said, and since that wasn't entirely true I put considerable sincerity into the way I said it.

"Well, I can tell you one thing about Kadir. It's his kind that's making Salah heavier competition for me. Trained terrorists from Libya—and some of those Islamic Jihad fanatics from Iran."

I wondered if Kadir's silent partner whose arm I'd snapped was one of the latter. I also wondered what had happened to him—and to Johnny. "It could help my investigation," I said, "if I knew more about Emil Fassler. I know Inspector Delanoé was assigned to check into his connection with Hassan Salah. But I guess *you* gave Delanoé something different to do."

Dalmasso's response was matter-of-fact: "Delanoé knew I like to keep track of the competition—even the lightweights, which Salah still was at that time. So he told me about the assignment. That was the first I knew about Salah's connection to Fassler. I did some phone checking of my own and found out *why* they were connected." He made a small, casual gesture with one thick, stubby-fingered hand. "A man with a firm like Fassler's can always be of use. I told Inspector Delanoé to see if he could persuade Fassler to switch from Salah to me. Tell him I'd pay off his debt to Salah, give him a better deal—the usual."

"How'd it work?"

Dalmasso grimaced slightly. "Delanoé told me he tried, but Fassler was too scared of Salah."

My mouth had gotten an aching dryness that made it difficult to enunciate clearly. "So you told Delanoé to go back and scare Fassler worse than Salah did."

He didn't deny it. I don't think it occurred to him that it might be something worth denying. He just shrugged and said, "But I don't know if he got around to even making the try. Next I heard, Delanoé was dead."

"Any notion who killed him?"

"I figure it had to be one of his girlfriends. He had too damn many of those. He'd get tired of the old ones and drop them for new meat. A .32—that's a girl's gun, usually. One of them got mad enough to turn violent."

He said that with evident distaste. Personal violence *would* disturb Maurice Dalmasso. It couldn't be controlled like business violence.

"Who killed Fassler two months later?" I asked, and the dryness had spread from my mouth into my throat.

"You can draw your own conclusion. Mine is Hassan Salah. I finally decided Fassler was worth having—enough for me to give him my personal attention. Instead of leaving the persuading to errand boys. So I had him brought to see me. And had a long talk with him. He finally agreed, after I offered him much better terms than he was getting from Salah and explained how I'd make sure he was protected."

"You didn't do a good job of that."

Dalmasso sighed. "I didn't have a chance to arrange the protection. Fassler was dead three hours after he left my place. Salah must have had him followed. They questioned him the hard way—and then killed him."

A small, spiteful gesture; if Salah couldn't go on owning Emil Fassler, he *could* keep Dalmasso from getting him.

That is, if Dalmasso wasn't lying to me. It could just as easily have been Dalmasso who'd had Fassler killed, if he couldn't be persuaded to make the switch. And it didn't really matter which version was the true one. Either way, they'd *both* killed him: Salah and Dalmasso. With some help from Emil Fassler himself. His life hadn't belonged to him from the moment he'd taken that mob loan to keep his business afloat. After that he'd become merchandise, up for grabs.

I was having to work at clamping down on a creepy-crawly hatred that welled up in me whenever I was around people like Maurice Dalmasso too long. And it had abruptly gotten to be too long. I had to get out of that limo before I did or said something dangerously stupid.

"Let me out of here," I told him.

He spoke to his driver, who blinked the headlights to signal the lead car. The convoy pulled over to the curb beside the Gare du Prado. "I hope," Dalmasso said, "I've been of some help to you."

"Sure," I said, and I climbed out.

"And remember what I told you about my being generous, if you come across anything *I* can use."

I said it again: "Sure."

The cars pulled away. I went into a bistro across the street, ordered a double brandy, and drank it much too fast. Then I leaned against the bar and waited. When my heartbeat was down to normal I crossed to the train station and took a taxi back to where I'd left my Peugeot, three blocks from Dalmasso's house.

I drove it from there to the offices Malo Transport kept in Marseilles. One of the phone calls I'd made early that morning had gotten me the information that Jean-Noel Triolet would be spending the whole day there.

CHAPTER 34

The building was in the old financial district between Marseille's city hall and the chamber of commerce, two blocks in from the Vieux Port. It had been Malo Transport's headquarters until Karl Malo had shifted that to Fos. Since then the company's presence in the eight-story building had shrunk to a three-room suite on its ground floor and a convenience apartment on the second floor.

A young secretary in the front office informed me that Triolet wouldn't be back in the office until after a meeting he was scheduled to attend at the Bourse. He'd acquired a headache and had gone up to the company apartment ten minutes earlier to take a half-hour nap before the meeting. The secretary said it with a certain amount of archness—not enough to be disrespectful toward Triolet, but just enough to show she wasn't dumb enough to believe everything she said.

I went outside and called the apartment from a phone booth. The number rang nine times before I hung up. I put the franc back in the coin slot and dialed the number again. Triolet answered on the fifth ring, sounding breathless and annoyed: "Yes, who is it?"

I identified myself and said, "I've got a progress report to make. Malo's still not back from Geneva. I assume you're in charge while he's away."

"Not where this kidnap case you're investigating is concerned," he said impatiently. His lack of interest in it confirmed what I suspected. Triolet didn't know the kidnap was a fake. I was beginning to think nobody knew that, other than Johnny Duncan and Jacqueline Malo.

"It's important," I told him. "I have to discuss it, and it won't wait until Malo gets back. Look, I did you a favor. Didn't tell anybody about you going to see a girlfriend in Saintes-Maries-de-la-Mer, instead of going where your father-in-law thought you were going. You can do me a favor in return."

There was just enough blackmail in that to moderate Triolet's annoyance. "I was taking a nap. You'll have to give me time to shower and dress. Don't come here for another fifteen minutes."

"I'm all the way over by the Gare Saint Charles," I told him. "It'll take me at least that long to get there."

"Well, don't be *too* much longer. I can't spare you much time. You know the address?" I said I did, and he said, "Second floor. The apartment is marked with the initials M.T."

I hung up and went back into the building quickly. Bypassing the Malo offices, I climbed a front stairway to the second floor. I located the apartment door with M.T. on it, went into a broom closet a few doors down on the other side of the corridor, and left its door open a crack so I could peer out without being seen.

Less than five minutes later the M.T. apartment door opened. The young woman who stepped out had wiry blond hair and a hard kind of beauty. She wore a plain white shirt and faded jeans that she filled in mouth-watering fashion. She'd been putting something into a little purse as she came out. She stuck it deep inside her shoulder bag and turned to blow a grateful farewell kiss to the unseen Triolet.

He shut the door in her face. She shrugged and clattered past me on very high heels, going down a rear staircase. I gave her fifteen seconds and then followed quietly.

She let herself out through the building's service door and crossed to a brand-new white Lancia parked in front of a no parking sign. A violation ticket was stuck under its left windshield wiper. She tossed it in the gutter as I strolled past.

I stopped, turned, and gave her a tentative smile. She smiled back but shook her head. "Sorry, I've got an appointment."

"Another time, perhaps."

"With pleasure." She gave me a card with nothing on it but a phone number, got in the Lancia, and drove off.

I had to hand it to Triolet. He was even better than Karl Malo had once been about getting maximum relaxation with minimum interruption of business demands. Claudette was wrong about her husband. He didn't have girlfriends in Marseilles. He had call girls. Expensive ones who'd gotten expensive through being smart enough to understand a client's special requirements swiftly and getting down to it without wasting any part of the short session on exploratory preliminaries.

It was fifteen minutes on the dot after my call to Triolet when I knocked at the M.T. apartment door. Triolet let me in, finished knotting his tie, pointed out a chair, and vanished into a bedroom. I sat in the chair. He returned with his jacket on, buttoning it before sitting on a chair facing me. His chair looked more comfortable than mine.

He glanced at his watch and told me, "I can only give you ten minutes. What is it you have to tell me about your kidnap investigation?"

I blinked at him a couple of times. "Well, about that—nothing. No progress at all, in fact. I'm about to give up on that."

He nodded sagely. "I told you. It was done by professionals. Too professional for one independent to catch, if the police haven't been able to."

It seemed to me he believed what he was saying. "I think you were right," I said.

"And is *that* what was so urgent you had to interrupt my nap?" he demanded curtly.

I let him see that his cold stare was making me uncomfortable. "No, it's something else I think I've stumbled into. Something that affects your company."

Triolet became alert. I watched him mask the change. He said, "Monsieur Malo didn't hire you to go around stumbling into any other matters."

"No," I admitted, "but I think he'll find it worth my time. He should. It seems to be a crime in progress. Actually, several of them—but connected by a common purpose. You remember my mentioning an American named John Duncan?"

He pretended it required some thought. "The one you told me was at the bullring—yes."

"Do you happen to know a man named Hassan Salah?"

He froze a bit. "No, I don't believe so."

I gave him a slightly nervous, deferential smile, looking obviously unsure of what I was saying. "I think these people—Duncan and Salah— could be plotting to take over Malo Transport."

I didn't really believe they were running the conspiracy as a two-man team. I wasn't entirely sure yet how Johnny fitted into it, but Salah, with his power and people, had to be the one in charge. I expected to have the answer to that shortly after leaving Triolet. In the meantime what I was interested in was how Triolet reacted to whatever I said, right or wrong.

But he had his mask firmly in place. "What *are* you talking about? It's a family-owned business. How could anyone make any sort of take-over attempt?"

"With just three murders," I said, "and two people vulnerable to blackmail."

I began to hit him with it in quiet, relentless bursts. "The first murder's already accomplished. Hubert Loy's *accident*. That left his position as second-in-command of the company open. And Malo filled it with you. As they knew he would. Because by then you'd surprised everybody—including yourself—by becoming Malo's son-in-law."

"I think there is something wrong with you," Triolet said softly, sounding as if he was on the edge of being frightened. He didn't have to pretend, but the possibility that I'd suddenly gone insane wasn't the reason.

The natural thing for him to have done at that point would have been to tell me to get out. But he didn't—couldn't. He was too eager to find out how much I knew.

"The second murder victim," I said, "is supposed to be Malo's son, Alexandre. That will end the danger of his ever becoming head of the company—and easing you out or looking too closely into what you're doing.

"They'll wait a while before the third killing, so it won't start anyone putting it together with Alexandre's. A year, maybe two. But when they get to it, it'll be the easiest one. Karl Malo's already had one heart attack. It's fairly simple to kill him and make it seem the result of a second coronary.

"And that'll leave *you* completely in charge of Malo Transport."

"You're not only crazy," Triolet told me acidly, "you also don't have certain basic facts right. I would only inherit five percent of Malo Transport. That *is* quite a long way from giving me control of it."

I nodded. "With both Alexandre and Karl Malo dead, your wife and her stepmother would get a fifty-fifty split of the other ninety-five percent. And Claudette *could* decide she doesn't want you running the business—even if she doesn't divorce you. But she'll only have a forty-seven-and-a-half percent say in that. Jacqueline Malo would have the same. Add your percent and *hers* together, and you've got a fifty-two-and-a-half percent say—outvoting your wife. As I said, you'll run the company."

Triolet wasn't too bad an actor. His expression was an almost perfect meld of amusement and exasperation. Almost. "You're assuming that Jacqueline would side with me."

"They figure she'll have to," I said. "They've got a hold on her—something they can use to make her do what they want."

"What kind of hold?" His pretense of humoring me almost broke. He wanted the answer to that—I could *feel* it. He had to know that they did have something over her, but he didn't know what it was.

I said, "Let's discuss the hold they have on *you*. Because she's not their only blackmail victim. You're the other. They've got you in their fist. You could wind up running Malo Transport—on paper—but they own you. And that means they'll control the company completely. With you just a puppet on a string."

Triolet was on his feet. "I don't know *what* is wrong in your head, but I want you out of here. *Now*."

He actually stuck his arm straight out and pointed a rigid finger at the door. Overacting. I waited for him to tell me never to darken his door again, but he disappointed me.

I leaned back in my uncomfortable chair and said, "You could call the police. And I could discuss all this with *them*. The only reason I haven't so far," I lied, "is that John Duncan and I were friends for a long time. I don't want to hurt him. But if that's what it takes to put a stop to all of this, I will."

Triolet's arm fell as slowly as a snowflake. He stared at me with a kind of horrid fascination, his grim mouth open as if he were silently panting.

"It was stupid of you to tell me you didn't know Duncan," I said. "You and he worked together back when Malo Transport was helping the CIA with some covert moving of weaponry."

He didn't say anything to that. After staring at me a few seconds longer he turned away, walked across the room, and stood gazing out the window with his back to me.

I got up and shifted to his more comfortable chair. "Then Paris canceled the arrangement between Malo and the CIA," I said. "And that was that—for a while. Until Duncan met Hassan Salah—who had a little firm that could handle the receipt of American arms intended for bases in Germany. And they agreed that there was a high-profit market for stuff like that in Iran, if they only had a way to get it there from Germany. So Duncan came and had a private talk with you.

"He knew you'd finally given up any hope of marrying Malo's daughter. A little too soon, as it turned out. But you didn't know that. What you did know was that if you couldn't become Malo's son-in-law, you didn't have much hope of ever getting above second-level management in that company. You must have been considering a shift to another company where you'd have a chance to move higher. Maybe Duncan knew that, too. So he offered you a way to make a nice chunk of money to take with you." I didn't know if that was exactly how it had happened.

But it had to be close enough to keep Triolet as scared as I needed him to be.

"You went along with it," I said. "Helping them use Malo trucks and ships to get the weaponry from Germany to Iran, and doctoring the company books to cover it. The three of you splitting the profits: you, Duncan, and Salah. Until the CIA got word that Duncan was somehow involved with the stuff getting to Iran—and kicked him out. After that he couldn't go on taking part in it. They'd be watching too closely, over at least the next year. So he quit. And his being scared enough to quit made *you* quit, too.

"But a while later you did get to be Malo's son-in-law, after all. And then Duncan or Salah came to see you again. Or maybe both together.

Because suddenly you were ripe for a real power position. And ripe for blackmail at the same time. Some whispers to the law would start an investigation deep enough to prove you'd made illegal use of the company. *And* acted against your country's interests.

"But if you played ball, that wouldn't happen. Instead you could climb even higher than you expected your marriage to Claudette to take you, to become *head* of Malo Transport. A combination you couldn't resist: fear, power, and greed. So you've gone along with it."

Suddenly Triolet turned from the window. "Everything you've said is *entirely* false," he said stridently. As close to hysteria as I wanted. "I don't know where you got these ridiculous ideas, but—"

"I'll give you some advice," I interrupted coldly, and I got to my feet. "Quit your job fast. Go start your career over again someplace far away. South America or Asia, say. I might feel that was punishment enough. And Malo Transport doesn't really need this kind of scandal."

I walked to the door and then stopped and looked back at Triolet. "But if you stick around, you'll get squashed in what happens next. You won't like the inside of a French prison. Or your prospects when you finally get out. Tell Johnny Duncan the same applies to him—unless he sits down for a serious talk with me pretty damned soon."

I left then, deliberately slamming the door behind me. Hoping it sounded like the crack of doom to Jean-Noel Triolet.

In the corridor I took several deep, slow breaths to help my guts unknot. Then I hurried out of the building to see if what I'd really been trying to accomplish with Triolet was going to work.

CHAPTER 35

I had left my Peugeot a block away in the parking garage of the Centre-Bourse shopping and museum complex. I sat in it and waited.

Fourteen minutes later Henry Varin climbed into the front seat beside me, carrying a cassette recorder and a small plastic case of cassettes. "Got it," he told me.

Varin was an electronics engineer who was into his eighteenth year of working for the French telephone system. A large family and a small mistress made it necessary for him to earn extra money by moonlighting.

He put the cassette case on my car floor. "Those are the taps on the office phones. But he made the call from the apartment phone." Varin handed me the recorder, with a cassette in it. "Here you are."

"Only *one* call?"

"Just the one. Then I saw him leave the building. He didn't look too good."

"You got the number he dialed?"

Varin looked at me reprovingly. "Naturally. And the address it belongs to." He gave me a slip of paper. On it he'd written a company name that went with the number and address: Duvier Salvage & Scrap Metal.

That was one of the quasi-legitimate firms owned by Hassan Salah.

I breathed a little easier. Just a little. I'd scared Triolet enough to make sure he'd dump his fears on whoever was in command of the takeover conspiracy. He'd yelled for Salah.

It confirmed what I'd figured—but had to *know*. Triolet—and the conspiracy—was under Salah's control. Not Johnny's. I didn't know if that was going to help. But it might.

I pressed the "play" switch and listened. My voice came through first, phoning Triolet and saying I had to see him. After that there was a slight crackling of static. Then the dialing of the apartment phone, followed by a click as the phone at the other end of the line was picked up. A man's voice said, "Who is it?"

Triolet's voice, with the hysteria in it barely repressed: "I have to talk to Hassan. Immediately. Tell him this is Jean-Noel."

"He's busy. Give me a message and I'll give it to him. And what's your last name?"

"Just tell him Jean-Noel. He'll know. Tell him we've got *trouble*! Bad trouble."

"Hold on."

A couple of minutes passed. Then another man's voice came through—heavy, assured, calming: "What's the matter, Triolet?"

"This whole thing is about to *explode* on us, Hassan! That detective—Sawyer—came to see me. He just left. Hassan, he knows everything! *Everything* we're doing! He said the only reason he hasn't taken it to the police yet is his friendship for John Duncan. My God—I hope he's still alive."

"He is," Hassan told him, the voice remaining calm. "I'm keeping him safe."

"Maybe we can still use him—to keep Sawyer from doing—"

"That's why I've got Duncan in safekeeping," Hassan interrupted sharply. "Insurance. Just in case. Now you cool down and tell me just what it is Sawyer knows."

Triolet: "I *told* you, he knows all of it. Almost every detail. From how it started, back when I helped you and Duncan, all the way to what our ultimate goal is and how you plan to get us there. Everything, everything. We have to call it off, Hassan! Before—"

"Shut up, Triolet! Just shut up and calm down and go about your business and forget it."

"*Forget* it?"

"I mean don't worry. I'll take care of the problem."

"How?"

"Leave that to me. You don't need to know. You got work to do, go do it. No reason to panic. I'll let you know when the problem's over with."

There was a click, and the line went dead.

I stopped the machine and gave it and the slip of paper back to Henri Varin. "I want a fast tap on *this* phone, Henri. But not close to it. These people are too dangerous for that. How long would it take you to tap it from a central exchange?"

"Give me an hour."

I nodded. "I'll phone your apartment an hour after that, to see what you've picked up by then."

Varin climbed out of the car and then looked back at me. "By the way, my friend's still got that tap on the phone of your Johnny Duncan's girlfriend in Aigues-Mortes. But she *still* hasn't gotten any call from him—or about him."

"Keep your friend on it."

"You know, all this is going to cost you a fortune."

"Not me—my client."

"In cash."

"Naturally."

Getting paid with checks means having the tax people looking up your nose. Moonlighting income is no good if you have to declare it.

* * * *

He went off to put the tap on the phone line at Salah's scrap metal company. I made a call from the garage phone. Then I went to a brasserie on the Quai du Port and had lunch. While I ate I considered the phone conversation between Triolet and Salah.

It meant Johnny Duncan had been relegated by Salah to hired help in the plot to take over Malo Transport. And that made me more sure than ever that Johnny had pulled the kidnap fraud on his own, without the others knowing. And if Salah didn't know about that, it wasn't what had soured their relationship and made Johnny expendable.

What had caused that had to be *me*—and what Johnny had done when Hassan's gunmen came into my hotel room to get me.

Which created some obligations I didn't want but couldn't shake off.

The man I phoned from the garage came into the brasserie. I had a look at my watch while he took a fast pastis at the bar. Then we left together, and I went to pay a visit to Hassan Salah.

CHAPTER 36

The Duvier Salvage & Scrap Metal Company was located northwest of the city. It was on the eastern shore of the Etang de Berre—sixty square miles of shallow lagoon surrounded by the raw industries that spread between Marseilles and Fos. The scrapyard was dominated by hills of wrecked automobiles and piles of dismantled parts from old locomotives and freight cars. You had to shout to be heard through the noise of the machines ripping and crushing the scrap into compact blocks.

The management office was atop a two-story shed alongside the conveyor belt that carried the results to the firm's barge pier. Two men were inside going through one of the company ledgers. The Venetian blinds were closed to keep out the main force of the afternoon sun. But enough light came through to make turning on the office lamps unnecessary.

One of the men fitted the description I'd gotten of Hassan Salah. He was a sandy-haired guy in his mid-thirties, with a wide, hard-boned face. Above prominent cheekbones there was a pair of deep-sunk pale gray eyes that betrayed no vestige of human feeling.

Salah was built like one of the compressed blocks going past on the conveyor belt. No excess flesh. A compact concentration of bone and muscle. His short neck was as broad as his head, joining it firmly to his thick torso. But his solidity didn't have a look of heaviness. There was the potential of a tightly-wound spring in him, even sitting perfectly still behind the desk.

When I opened the door and stepped in he looked at me with no change of expression. Which meant no expression at all. His hands slid off the ledger and dropped out of sight.

"Go outside, Duvier," he told the other man.

The story around the *milieu* was that Jacques Duvier had refused to sell his business to Salah but had reconsidered during the six weeks in a hospital while getting extensive breakage repaired. He also hadn't wanted to come back and manage his former company for Salah. But there he was.

His eyes had a cowed blankness in a face that still looked like it had been through one of the scrap crushers outside. He didn't look at me when he stood up and limped past out of the office, shutting the door quietly behind him.

"You're Sawyer," Hassan Salah said.

"My fame has spread."

"You were described to me." Salah's tone was neither angry nor menacing. It wasn't anything at all. "How'd you get up here?"

"The characters you've got on guard duty outside didn't try to stop me," I said. "The one at the top of the stairs thought he might, but then he went to sleep instead."

"*I* won't go to sleep," Salah told me. He brought his hands up holding a Beretta and rested them on top of the desk with the pistol aimed at my stomach. That was something else I'd picked up from the *milieu*: unlike older mob bosses of Dalmasso's generation, Salah didn't mind doing his own dirty work.

From my vantage point the Beretta's dark muzzle looked very small. But so is a viper's fang. "Look out the window," I advised Salah. "You'll see why your three watchdogs down there were so hospitable."

Salah got out of his chair and took a couple of sidesteps to the window. He used one hand to part two slats in the Venetian blinds. The pistol in his other fist stayed lined up with my midsection as he flicked a glance down through the opening.

The car that had brought me was parked outside. Lionel Clerc sat behind the steering wheel smoking a thin black cigar. The son of Fritz Donhoff's old friend was off duty, but that didn't diminish the impact of certain basics: Clerc was wearing his gendarme uniform and waiting in a blue police Renault, with a radio-telephone close at hand that would bring a lot more cops very fast if there was trouble.

Salah lowered the Beretta and went back behind the desk. He sat down and put the gun away in a drawer. "Have a seat," he said. "Might as well be comfortable while we discuss this."

I shook my head and remained standing. "I don't have that much to talk about—at this point. I just want to make sure you understand something. I know every detail of how you plan to take control of Malo Transport. What you've already done, and what you intend to do. I've kept my mouth shut because I know Johnny Duncan's part of it, and I don't want to be the cause of his winding up in prison. We've known each other a long time, and I owe him."

My voice got hard and cold as I finished. "But if Johnny's dead, what I owe him is revenge."

"He's not dead," Salah said.

"He had one of your employee's bullets in his guts when I saw him last."

"An accident," Salah said. "And a mistake. He's being taken care of.

By my own doctor. He'll be all right."

"I have to make *sure* of that," I told Salah flatly. "Sure that Johnny's alive—and that he's going to stay that way. If both those conditions are met, you and I can sit down and have a longer discussion."

"Of how much you want to go on keeping your mouth shut."

I looked pleased with how quickly he'd understood me. "But if Johnny's not all right—or if he's going to stop being all right because you're sore at him—we're not going to have that discussion. I'll give everything I've got to the authorities."

"I can take you to him, if you want." Salah gestured at the window. "But without any cops along. You can see for yourself he's in no danger."

"I've got a better idea." I took a slip of paper from my pocket and put it on the desk. "Have Johnny phone this number at eight o'clock tonight. It's his girlfriend's place."

Salah didn't look at the paper. "I know the number. You'll be there to take the call?"

"Maybe not," I said. "So don't bother setting any traps for me there. I might just call her and check whether Johnny phoned and sounded right. After that I'll talk to you again. About taking him away from wherever you've got him. To someplace safe."

Salah gave me a little smile. It wasn't an expression of anything he felt. Just something he manufactured to assure me he understood and approved. "You're a careful man. And smart. I think we can come to an agreement. Maybe even a better one than you've got in mind."

"Only if Johnny makes that phone call," I told him. "At eight o'clock. Exactly."

I turned on my heel and walked out.

An hour later I was with Henri Varin, listening to his recording of a phone call Hassan Salah had made immediately after I'd left him.

* * * *

The man who picked up at the number Salah called said, "Who is it?"

"Hassan. How is Duncan holding up?"

"I *guess* he'll pull through. But he doesn't look or feel too good. I have to keep giving him those painkillers."

"Can he talk all right?"

"Sure, when he's awake. Most of the time he's knocked out by the pills. Maybe that doctor ought to have a look at him again."

"I'll decide that after I get there tonight. Don't give him any more pills after six. I want him in shape to handle a phone call."

"Right."

"And make sure there are always two of you out there covering that approach road, just in case."

"We're doing it just like you told us to."

"I'll be there around seven," Salah said, and he hung up.

Varin gave me a page from his little notebook. "Here it is."

On it he'd written the location of the phone Salah had called.

CHAPTER 37

The flat-bottomed fishing boat chugged south of the Etang de Vaccarès, threading through the Camargue marshes in the direction of the Vieux Rhône, one of the ancient tributaries of the main river. This one had been cut off from its source ages ago by a combination of river silt and sand pushed up by the sea. It now formed an aimless, partially stagnant bend inside the delta. My target was near its open end.

I sat in the bow until we passed the Canal du Japon, with the target area coming up. After that I lay stretched out in the boat, in case one of the enemy happened to be near enough to see it. I raised my head to squint over the portside gunwale at what we were passing. But at five-thirty that evening there was as little chance of spotting any of the enemy at that distance as there was of their seeing me.

A mistral was blowing down from the mountains through the Rhône Valley to the Mediterranean. Inside the Camargue a thick mist rose off the warm marsh waters into the wind-cooled air. The mistral hadn't built to its usual force yet. The movement of the mist was still a relatively sluggish drift.

I watched part of that shifting gray curtain shred apart with dramatic slowness. Through the opening there was a crystal-clear view—across lagoons separated by sand dunes and spreads of high marsh vegetation—of a dazzling white flat-topped hill in the distance. A storage mound of sea salt, more than twenty feet high, from the reservoirs of a Camargue saltworks.

Then the curtain closed again, just as languidly, and visibility was confined once more to a blurred fifty or sixty yards.

That would help me make the reconnoitering approach unobserved. At the same time it was going to make for greater difficulty in locating the positions of the guards stationed around the place. One large problem: I didn't know how *many* of them I had to locate. According to Salah's tapped phone conversation there had to be at least three. But there could be more.

The noise of the boat's outboard motor carried much further than the limits of visibility. It startled a stork into flying off its perch in a patch of scrubby Tamarisk. But it wasn't the kind of noise that would alert the enemy. Commercial fishermen moved through the Camargue all the time, prowling the lagoon for carp, perch, and eels or heading out toward the sea after mackerel and bass.

The wizened old man at the boat's tiller had been one of those fishermen most of his life. His name was Augustin Bouix. For the last few years he'd been scraping by on his old-age pension. It provided a subsistence-level income he didn't mind improving with some undeclared cash.

He steered the boat between the swampy shore off the port side and a small island overgrown with mixed scrub brush. There was a similar island coming up, about the width of a one-bedroom house. Augustin Bouix angled the boat to starboard so that when we reached the second island it would be between us and the swampy shoreline.

He nudged my leg with the heel of his yellow rubber boot.

I picked up a black waterproof sack and hung it around my neck. It contained a few items I'd purchased from a *milieu* connection—along with my holstered H & K pistol. I slung the strap of another recent purchase from my left shoulder across my torso to my right side: a canteen of fresh drinking water. The air of the lower Camargue is almost as loaded with salt as its shallow waters. It dries you out fast. Dehydration saps your energy. I was going to need all the horsepower I could generate over the next hour or so.

Other than the canteen and the sack all I had on was dungaree shorts. I waited until the little overgrown island hid us from the shore. Then I swung out of the boat and waded to the island, thigh-deep in water, with my bare feet sinking into silky-soft bottom mud.

The boat chugged on past. The eyes of any watcher ashore would automatically follow it for a while. He'd see nothing different about it. Its direction would lead him to assume it was heading for a break in the line of dunes forming the last barrier between the lagoons and the sea.

I'd instructed Augustin Bouix to circle back to the point where he'd dropped me off in forty-five minutes. If I wasn't waiting there to be picked up, he was to make another big circle and try again after half an hour. If I *still* wasn't there, he would steer for the nearest fishing port and make an anonymous phone call to the cops.

But I was hoping to keep the police out of it for a while longer, if I could. Once they came down on Salah's organization they could turn up things that implicated Johnny. I owed him his chance to get away before that happened.

And that wasn't the only reason for wanting Johnny out from under. It reduced the risk of anyone's learning the truth about Jacqueline Malo's "kidnapping."

Thick reed beds grew out of the water all around the little island. The reeds were taller than me. I didn't have to crouch much to stay hidden as I moved through them, circling the island.

I stopped when I could see across some thirty yards of clear channel to the shoreline of the area where Johnny was being kept. Calling it a shoreline was something of an exaggeration. It was a line of bogs covered by tangles of wild bushes, interspersed with low sand spits and more watery reed beds. The mist hid the higher and drier land behind that. It also hid the land end of a dilapidated little pier poking out through the reeds.

A watcher *could* be at the hidden end of the pier, looking in my direction. Not likely, but possible. And my nerves were dealing with as much risk-taking as they could handle. So I didn't wade across the intervening channel. I submerged and swam it underwater.

The sack around my neck made it awkward. But its weight helped keep me down, with my cupped hands pulling as much mud as water. I didn't surface until I was snared inside a tangle of reed roots. When I raised my head into the air I found the reeds providing sufficient cover on all sides. Peering through them, I saw the pier a few yards to my left.

There was no watcher on it, nor anywhere else within my restricted field of vision. Well, as Babette used to tell me when she was having one of her motherly moods, better a dozen unnecessary precautions than one misstep into danger. I spread my feet in the bottom mud and rose waist-high out of the water. Unscrewing the cap from the canteen, I used a double handful of its fresh water to wash the salt from my eyes, nostrils, and lips. Then I took a long swallow to clear my throat.

As I recapped the canteen a snow-white egret raised its long neck out of the water off to my right. There was a wriggling eel trapped in its beak. The egret swallowed it and waded a few steps closer on its stilt-like legs to fish for more. A pintail duck swam out from under the pier and cruised past me in search of its own goodies, as undisturbed by my presence as the egret. The birds come to the Camargue because they know they're safe there.

That was more than could be said for me. I felt closer to the eel at that moment, separated from its fate only by vigilance and a few of mankind's less peaceful tools. Opening the waterproof sack, I took out my H & K pistol. With the P7's comforting hard weight in hand I moved inland.

The wind was rising. I wanted to get to Johnny before it whipped all of the concealing mists away.

Staying low, I made my way between a couple of sand spits and across a spongy bog, stopping every few yards to scan the terrain ahead and on both sides. I crossed a weed-choked drainage canal. On the other side the ground inclined upward a few feet before leveling off again.

In the Camargue a few feet above sea level constitutes a hill. This one had been formed by a number of dunes that had merged centuries ago and then gotten one end attached to the mainland. The result was a narrow peninsula jutting out into the marshes and covered by a solid layer of mainland earth. Thickets of creeping juniper, Tamarisk shrubs, and low parasol pines grew across it. I moved through the blowing mists, entered the westernmost thicket, and angled north inside its cover.

* * * *

Six minutes later I was squatting under a short-trunked parasol pine whose lower branches almost swept the ground. I peered through a clump of weeds at the dwelling that contained the telephone Salah had called.

It was a whitewashed, thatch-roofed *cabane*: a large one-room house of the type built for the herdsmen of the Camargue ranches. Salah had bought the little peninsula it was on from one of the ranches almost four years earlier.

Its isolation made it a good terminal point for small-scale smuggling using a fishing boat to move the goods to and from ships waiting off the nearby seacoast. When Salah had bought it he'd still been relatively small-scale. One proof he'd risen above that category was the telephone line strung on thin poles following the dirt road from the mainland.

In France it takes years of fighting red tape to get a new phone installed in even the most populated area. Getting a line strung to a place this remote was almost impossible. But "impossible," as Napoleon liked to say, is not a French word. Especially not when you've got a high-bracket gangster's leverage.

The north end of the *cabane* was typically rounded, to streamline it against the mistral. In midwinter the force of that wind can become awesome. What was building now was the mild summer variety. For additional protection the *cabane*, like all sensible buildings in that region, had no door or windows in its north end and east side. That was why I'd made my approach from that direction.

There was a newer structure some fifty feet south of the *cabane*: a wide shed with a peaked metal roof. The two sides I could see had no openings. There was nobody in sight around either of the buildings. I scanned the wooded areas around them and along the road but didn't see or hear anyone.

My mouth and throat were getting parched from the salinity of the wind. I took another long drink from my canteen and continued to study the area.

A thickset man wearing a T-shirt and dungarees appeared around the south corner of the shed and walked to the *cabane*. He had a compact MAC-10 submachine gun slung over one shoulder and a pistol in a belt holster. I waited until he disappeared into the *cabane*. Then I backed deeper inside the thicket and worked my way south through it.

When I'd gone far enough I angled to the thicket's edge and crawled under some bushes that provided deep shadow. From that vantage point I could see the south ends of both the shed and the *cabane*. That end of the shed was wide open. A tall, skinny man sat in the shade just inside the opening, on a wooden bench where he had a view down the dirt road toward the mainland. He had a revolver in a shoulder holster and a rifle across his thighs.

There was a four-door Renault sedan parked inside the shed behind him. It was too dark behind that to see if there were more men.

The door of the *cabane* was open, too, but I couldn't see the interior through it. I scanned the woods flanking the road again from my new vantage point. Still nothing to indicate more men out there. I switched my attention back to the *cabane*.

The thickset guy with the MAC-10 came out carrying two coffee mugs. Leaving the door open, he walked back to the front of the shed. He settled on the bench next to the skinny one and handed him one of the mugs. The two of them sipped their coffee in silence and gazed stolidly up the dirt road. One of the skills hoods have in common with cops is an ability to sit and wait endlessly, with neither expectation nor restlessness, when required.

Only two coffees and one car, I was beginning to think there were no others around beside the pair of watchers in the shed and whoever was inside the *cabane*. That was still more than I wanted to deal with. But there was one factor in my favor: the blind side of the shed was toward the *cabane*.

I crawled backward inside the thicket and worked my way back to my original vantage point northeast of the *cabane*. There I tucked the P7 into the waistband of my shorts and took a last couple swallows from the canteen. I put the canteen behind a bush, unslung the waterproof sack, and emptied it.

The first item I got from it was a weighted blackjack. I slipped that in my back pocket. The next two items were hand grenades. The last was a pump-action shotgun with a short barrel and a pistol grip, carrying a four-shell load. I placed the grenades neatly on the flattened sack next to the canteen and left them there. But not the shotgun.

I couldn't predict which way I'd be going when I made my getaway. I wanted something useful waiting for me in at least two directions.

Drawing my pistol from my waistband and balancing the shotgun in my other hand, I moved on through the thicket. My route circled around the blind north end of the *cabane*—which also kept me to the blind end of the garage shed. When I was west of the *cabane* I did the last ten yards on my knees, behind covering brush all the way. I came to a halt at the thicket's edge and peered out.

Most Camargue *cabanes* have a smallish window in their west wall. This one didn't disappoint me. The window was set low under the thatched roof. And it was open, to let the cooling air circulate through the interior after the day's midsummer heat. The window's lower half was concealed by the unkempt hedge of closely planted bushes that surrounds every *cabane* as an extra windbreak. But its lower sill would be about hip-high.

I stowed the shotgun in the brush that screened me and waited. The mistral was tearing the mist apart. It no longer formed curtains—only scattered, fast-moving patches. When one of the patches came into the open stretch between me and the window I scooted through it, crouching, and slid under the hedge.

For ten seconds I lay there, holding my gun up and ready with both hands, listening hard. There was no sound to indicate anyone had spotted my run.

I snaked deeper under the hedge until I was against the wall. Then, very slowly and carefully, I lifted my head until I could look in over the windowsill.

CHAPTER 38

There was only one guard inside: a stocky character with a livid knife scar across the side of his face that I could see. The scar added to the brutal look of a face that didn't need extra help in that direction. There was a revolver holstered on his hip. It looked like a Colt .357 Python.

He was filling a mug with coffee at the rudimentary kitchen end of the large room, next to the fireplace. Carrying the mug, he went past a rustic table and its flanking benches to one of the four metal-framed cots placed side by side at the left of the low window.

Johnny Duncan lay on the cot nearer the window, wearing only his undershorts, and he appeared to be asleep. There was thick bandaging across his midsection, part of it dark with dried blood. The stocky guard turned away from me and bent to poke Johnny's shoulder with his free hand. "Hey, I got some nice strong coffee for you."

Johnny turned his head slowly and squinted up at the man with no expression but total exhaustion. I raised myself higher to get a better look at him. He looked about as bad as a man could, short of being entirely dead. His breathing was slow, weak, and labored. His skin had a ghastly pallor and was as dried out as old parchment. His lips were cracked and bloodless, and his eyes had sunk deep in their sockets, with black smudges under them. He shut his eyes and turned his head away without any response.

His guard poked him again, harder. "Come on! Time for you to start waking up."

I stuck the pistol in my waistband, tugged the blackjack from my hip pocket, and went in through the window. The stocky guard half turned at the sound of my bare feet landing on the floor inside. He didn't get more than halfway around because I slammed the blackjack across his skull just above the ear, as hard as I could.

He thudded to the floor and didn't make another sound or movement. The mug rolled out of his limp hand, spilling coffee under the cot. I bent and slugged him with the blackjack again. I didn't know if he was dead, and at that point I didn't care. Just so long as he was one enemy I didn't have to worry about.

Johnny's eyes had snapped wide open, staring at me. He tried to raise his head, but it fell back on the mattress. I slipped the blackjack into my pocket and got the P7 back in my fist as I looked at the open doorway. There was nobody in sight outside, nothing but the back of the garage shed.

"How many are there besides this one?" I demanded softly.

It took Johnny a few seconds to get his voice working, and then it came out as a weak, slurred whisper: "Two more."

That was some relief, but not enough to make me stop watching the area outside the doorway. "Get up, Johnny," I growled. "We're low on time. Salah's due in about forty minutes. Probably with more of his hoods."

Johnny made a croaking sound that was supposed to be a laugh. "Hell—I can't even stand up, let alone walk out."

I spared him a glance. He hadn't moved. "The slug still in you?"

"It's out...but I've been leaking blood ever since. Can't be more'n a couple spoonfuls left in me."

That accounted for the way he looked. A fast blood transfusion would pull him through, but I guessed Salah wasn't interested in Johnny's future. Just in keeping him going long enough to serve as insurance against me—and maybe as bait.

I looked out the door again, then through the window. So far so good. I took the revolver from the inert hood's holster and anchored it under my shorts at the small of my back, tucking my own gun under the waistband in front. "This is gonna hurt you worse than me," I warned Johnny, "but save the screams for later."

Seizing his ankles, I swung his legs off the bed and let his feet thump to the floor. A hissing noise came through his clenched teeth, and his eyes squeezed shut. I took hold of his shoulders and hauled him to a sitting position. His torso started to slump forward, but I grabbed his wrist, bent at the knees, and dragged his arm across my shoulders. Then I straightened, lifting him up off the bed and hooking my left hand under his armpit.

"Sweet Jesus," he whispered raggedly. His legs hung limp with me bearing all his weight.

"You can pray when I get you to a church," I growled. "Right now concentrate on walking. You know the routine: left foot, right foot."

He did his best. It wasn't much, but it had him gasping for air by the time we reached the doorway. Fresh blood was soaking through his bandages. I hoped he had more than those two spoonfuls left, or I was going to all that trouble for nothing.

The other two hoods were still out of sight in the other end of the shed. The thicket east of the *cabane* was closer than any other cover. I turned Johnny toward it. "Left foot, right foot," I reminded him, and I started out. He stumbled along with me, but I was still carrying more of him than his legs could support.

We were halfway across the open ground when I heard a sound that almost froze me to a halt. A car was approaching along the dirt road from the mainland.

I flicked a glance in that direction. The car was a gray turbo diesel Lincoln Continental. You don't see many of that make in France. The last one I'd seen had been parked inside the Duvier scrapyard, near the management office. It was Salah's car. He'd decided to come early.

* * * *

The Continental increased speed suddenly. If I could see it, the men inside could see us. It raced toward the end of the narrow peninsula, churning up dust that was instantly torn away by the wind, along with the last shreds of mist.

I moved Johnny along faster. He helped as much as he could but grunted with pain as he managed each stumbling step. His eyes were squeezed shut again. Drops of blood fell from his bandages and ran down his legs.

The Continental came swinging around the front of the shed as we entered the woods. I dragged Johnny in deeper, went to my knees, and lowered him into a slight hollow between clusters of wild brush. He pressed both hands against his bandaged midsection and forced his eyes open a little. His breathing was too quick and shallow.

"Stay put," I told him. "I'll be back when I can." I pulled his bloodied right hand from the wound and stuck the hood's revolver in it. The hand and gun fell to his chest, and his eyes shut again.

Out there beside the shed the Continental had squealed to a stop. There were two men in it, both in front. The driver jumped out his side, Salah out the other as the two hoods from the shed came running to them. The driver drew a heavy-caliber automatic from under his jacket. Salah was at the back of the Continental, opening its trunk.

Johnny seemed to be passing out again when I left him. Staying just inside the edge of the thicket, I worked my way quickly toward the spot where I'd left the grenades. I'd have preferred the shotgun in the situation. But I hadn't been able to predict *what* situation I'd find myself in, and it was too far now.

Halfway to my goal I paused to peer out through the high weeds and check the enemy. They were still around the Continental. Salah had taken a rapid-fire AK-47 from the trunk and was getting it ready for action. He did it with the swift ease of a man who hadn't forgotten the tools that had helped him reach the heights.

They were too far for accurate shooting with a pistol. I ran on, trampling underbrush noisily and shoving high bushes out of my way. They couldn't fail to spot my progress. I wanted them to—to draw them away from where Johnny lay.

It worked. At my next pause to check on them I saw the skinny hood bringing his rifle to his shoulder. For a rifle the distance between us was no problem at all.

I dove to the ground in the instant that the rifle shot sounded, followed quickly by another. The bullets ripped through the bushes over me at waist height. Tom leaves and broken twigs fell on my face.

I slithered the rest of the way. The grenades were there waiting on the emptied sack next to my canteen. One I stowed carefully in the front pocket of my shorts. The other I held ready in my left hand when I rose enough to sneak another peek at the opposition.

They had split up, running fast and keeping outside pistol range—let alone throwing distance. The rifleman and the one with the MAC-10 submachine gun circled to enter the woods off to my right. Salah and his driver with the big automatic were circling off to my left.

It was the pair to my right I had to worry about first. Their route was going to bring them into the thicket close to Johnny. He was probably unconscious by now. Even if he wasn't, he was in no shape to manage any kind of active defense.

They might miss seeing him there. Then again, they might not. And now that they were closing the trap on me they didn't need him alive any longer.

I headed back toward the point where they would reach the thicket, staying just inside its edge again, but this time going quietly and not moving anything in my path. But swiftly—and in a relatively straight line, while they were still circling. I reached their entry point just before they did. Pulling the grenade's firing pin with my teeth, I lobbed it out at them.

They reacted in opposite ways when they saw it coming. The thickset one with the MAC-10 shifted direction but kept coming, sprinting into the bushes off to my left. The rifleman blundered to a stop, staring wild-eyed at the live grenade bouncing on the ground near his legs. Then he unfroze, spun around, and started to run away. But he'd taken one second too many. The grenade exploded before he'd gotten far enough. The blast shredded his back and hurled him forward off his feet. He sprawled in the dirt, lay still for a moment, and then began dragging himself away like a half-killed spider, weapon and motivation forgotten behind him.

I'd dropped to my hands and knees just in time. A long burst from the hidden MAC-10 lashed the area where I'd been standing. I crawled deeper into the woods, keeping a wild hedge of interlaced thornbrush and juniper between me and the machine gunner. Then I angled to my right for six yards, crawling under low trees and high bushes. Finally I cut back toward the position he'd fired from. After three more yards I went flat under a spread of gnarled Tamarisk and stayed that way, the remaining grenade in one hand and my pistol in the other.

I waited, watched, and listened. The waiting dragged on. My nerves didn't like it. Salah and the man with him would have heard the explosion and gunfire. They'd be coming in this direction. They had a long way to go, but it wouldn't take them forever. I put a clamp on my nerves and continued to wait.

Fifteen feet to my left there was a stagnant pool choked with tall marsh grass. About the eighth time I looked in that direction some of the grass moved. I didn't think it was the wind howling around the outside of the thicket that did it. Very little wind was getting inside this far.

I pressed flatter, digging my chin into the dirt. Placing the grenade on the ground, I gripped a dead branch of the Tamarisk with my left hand and twisted. It broke with a sharp crack.

The submachine gun hammered at me from inside the marsh grass. Flat as I was, the burst whipping past my back didn't miss by more than ten inches. But the barrage also mowed down a lot of the grass, unveiling the thickset man with the MAC-10.

My first bullet got him in the stomach. He lurched forward in the stagnant pool, his weapon lowering but not spilling from his hands. I fired again. The bullet broke through his teeth and penetrated upward into his brain. His knees folded, and his torso toppled backward. His head sank under the stagnant water and didn't come up again.

That left two. I didn't know where they were, but I did know they'd be getting close. I snatched up the grenade and bolted out from under the Tamarisk, scuttling crablike seven yards to the right and dropping behind a clump of weeds. Then I angled to the left, snaking forward silently until I was under another tangle of brush.

Again I went flat on the ground, holding my pistol and grenade ready, looking and listening. More than four minutes went by with no sound or movement anywhere around me. Then I heard something very faint, like a light splash.

It seemed to come from the other side of the stagnant pool where the body of the dead machine gunner lay half-submerged. I concentrated on that area, alert for any further sound, any sign of movement. There was none.

Finally I got my feet under me and moved out behind cover in a low crouch, starting to circle to where I'd be able to see the other side of the pool.

The shot didn't come from there. It came from behind.

My right leg was kicked out from under me. The force of it dropped me heavily on my right side and rolled me all the way over onto my left. I started to bring the gun in my right hand up to fire back—and then realized both my hands were empty. I'd lost both grenade and gun when I'd fallen.

Cursing, I used the empty hands to shove myself to an awkward sitting position. My right leg lay on the ground as if it weren't part of me. I could see it but not feel it. The bullet had drilled clear through the calf. I didn't know if it had broken bone, but the whole leg had gone dead from toes to hip.

Salah stepped out into the open above me with his AK-47. He thumbed its change lever to full automatic, preparing to put a full burst into my chest. I spotted where my pistol lay: not far, but not within quick reach, either. There was no way I could get and use it before that burst shattered the life from me. On the other hand, it just wasn't in me to tamely sit there waiting for oblivion.

"Wait a minute," I told Salah, "there's one thing you don't know."

It made him pause. But it didn't alter the aim of his assault rifle. I couldn't think of anything clever to say next, so I tensed myself to do a fast roll and grab for the pistol. I knew I couldn't make it, but at least I wouldn't go gentle…

The part of Salah's face that had contained his left eye disintegrated in the same instant that I heard the two gunshots from behind me.

Salah's head was jerked back by the impact. He turned away from me very slowly, started to take an even slower step, and then fell. His entire body shuddered as though high-voltage electric shocks were passing through it. When that stopped he was just part of the ground.

I turned my head and saw Johnny Duncan step through the marsh grass in the stagnant pool. Just one step. Then he stopped, his feet braced apart in the water beside the body of Salah's machine gunner. His mouth hung open, and he looked worse than when I'd left him. I couldn't understand how he'd made it from there—and still can't.

He was holding the revolver I'd given him in both hands as if it weighed a ton. It sank as I watched, dragging his arms down with it, and all of him tipped forward. He fell on his face, half in and half out of the stagnant water.

I did the roll I'd prepared and snatched up my pistol when I heard movement in the bushes to my left. I was up on one elbow with the pistol aimed at Salah's driver when he emerged. He had the big automatic, but it was pointed in the wrong direction. When he saw the muzzle of my gun looking up at him he froze in position, considering how long it would take him to shift aim and fire.

"No chance," I told him. "None at all. And why try it?"

He looked beyond me at what was left of Salah. Several moments passed. Then he shrugged and nodded. A dead boss can't repay life-risking loyalty. He tossed the automatic on the ground, turned, and walked back into the bushes.

When he was gone I crawled to Johnny. Using two elbows and one knee, with the useless leg trailing behind. I sat and turned him over on his back. He was out but still breathing. I hoped that just lying there quietly would stop the bleeding before those last couple of spoonfuls were really gone.

After a time I heard the Continental start up and drive away.

And after that there was nothing I could do but sit there with Johnny and wait for Augustin Rouix's phone call to bring the police.

CHAPTER 39

My leg wasn't broken, they told me after the x-rays. There *was* a crack in the tibia, but it wasn't serious enough to require a cast if I would promise not to put any weight on that leg for a while. A while meant a couple of weeks with crutches and a wheelchair until the next X-ray session determined how the cracked bone was repairing itself.

The healing of muscle and nerve damage caused by the bullet was given a head start with thirty minutes in an operating room of the hospital in Arles, using a local anesthetic. After the local wore off the heavily bandaged wound began to hurt like hell. They offered me a choice: a mild painkiller or something that would knock me out. I took the mild one. I had an urgent reason for staying wide awake a few hours longer.

I was assigned one of two beds in a room with a pleasant view of the trees in the hospital's large courtyard. The other bed was still empty, waiting. I sat with the back of my bed cranked up and waited along with the empty bed.

There was a telephone on the stand between the two beds. I used it to call Arlette Alfani in Nice. Then I resumed my waiting.

The only other call I'd made had been via a police telephone—to Karl Malo.

I'd told him my investigation was complete. I was calling him, I'd explained, because I might need his help to avoid any unpleasantness with the law—resulting from the fact that I'd been forced to use some unorthodox methods to solve the case.

I kept the story I gave Malo—and the police—simple, but effective for my purposes.

Malo's wife had been kidnapped, I said, by a notorious gangster named Hassan Salah. No one in Malo's family had been involved. *That* had been determined by an old acquaintance of mine, John Duncan, whom I'd hired to infiltrate Salah's organization in order to help me learn the truth. Unfortunately, Salah had finally gotten suspicious of Duncan. I'd had to use violence to rescue Duncan from Salah's vengeance.

And that—minus some decorative details—was all of it.

Malo liked my story. The police didn't exactly buy it, but they did accept it. There seemed to be no end to the wonders one could perform with the timely use of Karl Malo's magic name.

Johnny Duncan was still unconscious when they brought him from the operating room and placed him gently on the waiting bed. The usual life-sustaining tubes were inserted into the veins of both his arms. The young doctor supervising that told me they'd pumped a lot of blood into Johnny before patching up his insides. Another transfusion had been necessary after they'd finished the stitching and bandaging. But Johnny should be just fine in a couple of weeks, the doctor said, with sufficient rest and proper care. He had a strong constitution that would help.

After the doctor and his team left, a nurse on floor duty came in to look at Johnny and check his chart. My right leg was throbbing badly, sending shooting pains through the rest of me. I asked her for another mild painkiller.

She looked at me uncertainly. "Are you sure you wouldn't prefer a stronger sedative, to make you get a sound night of sleep?"

"Not yet," I told her.

Shortly after she fed me the pill and left, Johnny began making tentative sounds and movements.

That was what I'd been waiting for. I swung my legs off my bed. The right one sent me an agonized protest. Keeping that foot off the floor, I hopped across on the other one and sat down on the edge of Johnny's bed. I patted his cheek and began to speak to him, quietly but urgently.

He murmured something, but his eyes stayed shut. I pinched his cheek, hard. His eyes opened a little. His gaze was dopey, without recognition or understanding. That was perfect. The stuff they administer to keep you oblivious through an operation is fabulous. In very small doses, or when large doses are wearing off—but haven't worn off completely—it acts like the best truth serum you can find.

I began questioning Johnny, alternately patting and pinching to prevent him from sinking all the way under. His first mumbled responses didn't make any sense at all. I kept at it. My questions were actually all the same one, just phrased differently in my effort to get through to him. It took time. Not that he was resisting; there was no resistance in his drugged state, but no comprehension either. That was the problem. He kept swimming in and out of semi-consciousness, and I had to keep fishing in it.

When he finally told me what I wanted to know it didn't mean any more to him than all the senseless things he'd said. I was quite sure he wouldn't remember it later. Letting him sink back into the drugged sleep, I hopped back to my own bed.

Waiting until I could be certain Johnny was all the way out of it, I used the phone between our beds to call Crow. That was Frank Crowley, my best American friend in France. His house was in La Turbie, a couple miles above my own. I told Crow what Johnny had just given me and explained what I wanted done.

Crow said he would take care of it. I hung up sure of that. We'd found out we could count on each other long ago, while we were soldiering together in Vietnam.

* * * *

By the next morning Johnny was well enough to be propped up on his bed for the hospital's early breakfast. He downed all of it with a keen appetite. His voice was raspy, but his eyes and skin had most of their normal color back. His major problem had been the loss of blood. You can bounce back fast from that, if you survive it.

As I'd expected, he didn't remember anything about my questioning him the previous night. After the breakfast, when we were alone in the room, I told him the story I'd given the police about him.

"I guess I should thank you," Johnny said. "On the other hand, I think you owed me."

"When it comes to what's owed and what's paid off," I told him, "I'd say we're about even."

"You're probably right," he agreed. "And now we *stay* even. I keep quiet about that little killing in Mrs. Malo's past—and you keep quiet about everything I've done that could land me in jail."

"How'd you get mixed up in all that, Johnny?"

He didn't mind telling me some of it. But he took his time. He still wasn't entirely recovered, and he had to give what he said consideration to make sure he wasn't telling me anything he didn't want me to know.

Most of the basics I already knew or had guessed. When he'd heard about Triolet marrying Malo's daughter he'd had a talk with Salah. Johnny figured the CIA had stopped keeping its close watch on him by then. And as Malo's son-in-law, Triolet no longer had to be afraid of somebody in the company digging into what he was doing. His position in Malo Transport was bound to become so secure that even Hubert Loy—then second-in-command to Malo—would have to treat him with kid gloves.

Salah agreed with Johnny: the situation was ripe for a renewal of their old three-part arms smuggling operation. If Triolet didn't like it, he could be blackmailed into going along with it with a threat to expose the fact that he'd done it before. So Johnny had arranged for a meeting with Triolet in Arles, and Triolet was too scared of what Duncan and Salah knew about him to say no.

Johnny and Salah had been waiting outside a bistro for Triolet when they'd seen Karl Malo get out of his chauffeured car and enter a restaurant with a woman. The woman was a surprise. The last time Johnny had seen her she'd been Emil Fassler's wife.

"Did Salah know she was the one who killed Dalmasso's crooked cop?" I asked Johnny.

"Sure, I'd told him back when it happened."

"You told *her* you never said it to anybody else."

"So I lie sometimes. Like you. But Salah was the *only* one I told."

When Triolet had joined them they'd asked about the woman Karl Malo was with. And he'd handed them the important surprise: she was now Malo's wife.

"That's when Salah started thinking along much bigger lines," Johnny said bitterly. "Bigger than just using our hold on Triolet to run another arms smuggling setup for a while. The way he figured it, combining our hold on Triolet with the one on Malo's wife could lead to getting complete control of all Malo Transport's worldwide operations."

Johnny was quiet for a few moments, seeming to go into himself. Then he looked at me again and said, "I never liked it from the start. Salah's idea was *too* big, involving too many risks, with the payoff too far in the future. He said the size of the payoff made the waiting worthwhile. But…I didn't like the killings involved, either."

I wasn't so sure that part had troubled him that much. "But you went along with it," I said.

"I was broke. And Salah began advancing me dough. Yeah, I went along—for a time. But I got to like it a *lot* less when I finally got it through my thick skull that *I* wasn't going to get much of that big payoff in the future. Salah wasn't treating me like a partner. He was using me like an errand boy, paying me off with small change."

"So you decided to use that hold on Malo's wife to work a quick one on your own, without Salah knowing. Grab a little fortune and get out."

"I'm a simple guy, Pete. Controlling a big company, even if Salah would've let me have a part in it—that's too complicated for me. All I want is a good quiet life with no money worries bugging me. Seven million francs, that's a fortune to me—but nothing at all to a guy like Malo. I'd say my demands were modest, considering that."

"*I'd* say you'd have liked more—but she wouldn't let you go for more."

Johnny smiled a little. "Yeah, that little lady *really* dug her heels in. That's when I was sure Salah's long-range plans weren't gonna work. She'd've never gone along with what he'd ask of her after killing her husband. Even scared as she was of having the cop killing pinned on her. She'd have taken her punishment rather than give in on that. So Salah wasn't as smart as he thought he was."

"I guess not," I said. "That's why he's dead."

"Yeah…" Johnny fell silent, looking at me and waiting for me to try hitting him with the big question.

When I didn't he looked puzzled. Not worried—just puzzled. At that point he didn't know he had anything to worry about.

* * * *

After lunch—the kind of lunch with which all hospitals seem to feel obliged to torture their patients—a nurse brought in a wheelchair with its right leg up to support mine. "The doctor says you'll be able to leave us tomorrow," she said. "He wants to make sure you know how to handle one of these before you go. We'll try you out on crutches later."

"I'm really looking forward to those," I told her.

She helped me into the wheelchair. It wasn't difficult to handle. I practiced racing up and down the corridor outside the room for a while. Then I wheeled myself out into the open air and did some Grand Prix circuits around the big courtyard.

My wheelchair and I were taking a break under a shady tree when Jacqueline Malo came through the courtyard. She stood before me, holding a handbag in both hands like a shield between us, her expression a bit awkward.

"They told me you were out here," she said slowly. "I was very sorry to learn you'd been injured."

"Me, too," I told her. "But I'm getting used to it." I indicated the stone bench beside my wheelchair. "Have a seat, Madame Malo."

But she continued to stand. "Is it *really* all over?" she asked softly.

"Really. Only two people knew about you and that inspector in Marseilles. One of them is dead now. And Johnny Duncan will never tell anyone else. Because it could lead to the law nailing him for the fraudulent kidnap scheme."

"What you mean, I imagine, is that he knows you'd make sure it led to that."

"Something like that," I conceded.

Jacqueline Malo opened her handbag. "Karl gave me a check to give you. He would have come to see you himself, but hospitals depress him. And he has more work to tend to at the moment than usual. For one thing, he has to find himself a new assistant director for the firm."

"What happened to Triolet?"

"I don't really understand that. But he stunned all of us this morning with a sudden announcement that he was quitting the company. *And* leaving Claudette. No notice and no explanation. Except that a shipping firm in Hong Kong offered him a job he likes better, managing their Pacific operations."

She glanced at her watch. "I think he's on his way there by now. Apparently the Hong Kong offer was an immediate-or-never one."

What was apparent to me was that Triolet had decided it would be wise to take my advice. With Salah dead there was no one present to protect him against me. He might also be feeling a certain amount of relief at being no longer under Salah's thumb.

"I always enjoy getting checks," I told her, "but this one's a little premature. I haven't sent your husband my expense sheet yet. It'll be high. Including medical bills."

"Karl is aware of that," she assured me, and she took out the folded check. "But we want you to have this in the meantime. It covers your basic fees—plus a small bonus."

I opened the check. "As small bonuses go, I'd call this one generous."

"You deserve it. Karl is very grateful. You relieved him of a great deal of worry when you told him neither of his children was responsible—for what happened to me."

She looked embarrassed when she said that last bit, but she didn't avert her eyes. "And *I'm* very grateful, too," she said quietly. "I want you to know that. I do appreciate what you've done for me."

She smiled at me suddenly. The smile that had hooked me when I had first looked at her picture. "You did turn out to be my knight in shining armor after all, didn't you?"

She leaned down and kissed me softly on the mouth. Then she straightened and turned and left me. My gaze followed her. It was a pleasure to watch her walk—even away.

I was sticking the check in the pocket of my hospital bathrobe less than twenty seconds later when Arlette appeared. She sauntered across the courtyard to me. "I hope you appreciate my timing," she said. "I *waited*. Didn't want to break up your farewell scene with your enchanting, unavailable princess."

She bent and kissed me. I pulled her down on the knee of my good leg and kissed her back. By the time we broke that up I'd decided there was a lot more going on when Arlette and I kissed than when it happened with Jacqueline Malo.

"I didn't expect you until tomorrow," I said.

"I was anxious to check the extent of your injuries," Arlette told me. "At the moment I have the definite impression you haven't lost anything vital. Which is a comfort."

"I'm still all here," I assured her.

"In that case, I suggest we use the station wagon I'm renting tomorrow to take you to my apartment. More convenient than your house, while you have to ride around in one of these chairs. You can take the elevator down and wheel yourself around Nice all day. And nights you'll have *me* coming home to you."

"I thought this was a heavy month at your office."

"I'll make the time," Arlette said, and she settled more comfortably on my knee. "A nice doctor inside there just told me it would be good for you to start getting some exercise in a couple of days. As long as it doesn't involve putting your weight on the bad leg." She gave me one of her wickeder grins. "So all you and I have to do is figure out something we can do without your being on your feet."

"We'll work it out," I promised.

"Oh, yes," Arlette said, "I'm quite sure we will."

* * * *

When I wheeled myself back into our room, Johnny was putting down the phone between our beds.

"That was Suzanne I was calling in Aigues-Mortes," he told me. "Just reassuring her I'll be okay."

"I did some checking on your girlfriend a few days back," I said. "Through a guy with a lot of contacts in Aigues-Mortes. Consensus there seems to be that she's a fine and sensible person. Except for this strange aberration she's got about wanting to marry an old bum like you."

He laughed. "I just might do it. Serve her right."

"Might not be a bad thing for you. I hear her restaurant does a nice steady business."

"Steady," Johnny agreed dryly, "but small."

"Maybe if you marry her and help with it full-time, you can make it grow."

"I'll think on it," he said, with a complete lack of sincerity.

"I'd advise it," I said. "Because if you're counting on that ransom money, forget it. When you get around to going where you stashed it, it won't be there."

His expression became pure Johnny Duncan: the hard eyes in the blank face.

"I always thought you must have hidden it somewhere near where you picked it up," I said. "Why risk taking it out with you? You could have run into a police block on any road. Without the ransom you wouldn't have a problem. Then all you had to do was wait until a lot later before going back to get it.

"What I didn't know," I went on, "was exactly *where* it was. So I pumped you last night while you were still in a stupor after the operation.

That bunker near Sospel. Back room. Under a corner where the cement's fresher than the rest, even if it doesn't look it."

"You bastard," Johnny said softly, without any change of expression.

"Then I called a friend," I told him, "and he went up there and got it. In a few days he'll turn it over to Malo's insurance company for the reward. Not a fortune, but a tidy sum. I'm gonna split that with him. His photography business isn't going as well as he'd hoped."

"And what's *my* share?" Johnny demanded.

I gave him my most affable smile: "Not one bloody penny. I earned it, doing my job. An extra little bonus for the work and its risks. What did you work at to earn any of it?"

"Bastard," he repeated—and then he sighed and said, "Hell, I should've worried about this happening soon's I knew *you* were involved. Like I told you once, I know you're a wolf, just like me."

"Like I told you, not quite the same."

"Maybe not quite," Johnny Duncan said, "but close. Very close."

www.ingramcontent.com/pod-product-compliance
Lightning Source LLC
Chambersburg PA
CBHW031428250626
47155CB00004B/1668